DATE DUE			
AP 26 '04	JUL 10 2012		
MY 20 '04	JAN 2 2 2013		
OCT 1 8 2004			
OCT 3 0 2004	JUN 4 2013		
DEC 1 1 2004			
3/24/10			
APR 17 2010			
AP 19 11			
MAY 9 2011			
OCT 1 7 2011			
JAN 2 6 2012			
JUL 3 1 2012			

LP   D.G.   02-909
F
VOG
    Vogt, Esther Loewen.
     The enchanted prairie   25.95

The Enchanted Prairie

*Also by Esther Loewen Vogt
in Large Print:*

The Flame and the Fury
The Splendid Vista
Edge of Dawn

The Enchanted Prairie

Esther Loewen Vogt

Thorndike Press • Waterville, Maine

Published in 2002 by arrangement with Christian Publications.

Thorndike Press Large Print Christian Romance Series.

The tree indicium is a trademark of Thorndike Press.

The text of this Large Print edition is unabridged.
Other aspects of the book may vary from the original edition.

Set in 16 pt. Plantin by Al Chase.

Printed in the United States on permanent paper.

Library of Congress Cataloging-in-Publication Data
Vogt, Esther Loewen.
    The enchanted prairie / Esther Loewen Vogt.
      p. cm.
    ISBN 0-7862-4604-9 (lg. print : hc : alk. paper)
    1. Kansas — History — Civil War, 1861–1865 — Fiction.
2. Women pioneers — Fiction.   3. Young women — Fiction.
4. Large type books.   I. Title.
PS3572.O3 E54 2002
    813′.54—dc21
                                   2002072797

DEDICATION

To my daughter Naomi Eitzen whose love and encouragement and tender faith in Jesus Christ have supported me throughout the writing of this story.

AUTHOR'S NOTE

For readers like me who like to have the fact and fiction sorted out, I offer the following:

Marion (Centre) really exists. It is a small, thriving city of over 2,000 persons, situated in South Central Kansas, sprawled along the confluence of the Cottonwood River and Luta (once called Mud) Creek, and up the bluff to the east from the valley below.

The first settlers — William and Keziah Billings and their family, and the George Griffith and William Shreve families — actually arrived in 1861 from Indiana. William Billings opened a store and post office on the lower level of the large log cabin nestled in a grove of trees. The Shreve cabin was surrounded by an enclosure which served as a fort in case of Indian attacks.

The Kaws (or Kanzas from which the state derives its name) from the reservation at Council Grove along the Santa Fe Trail were permitted to roam through the area to hunt and fish along the rivers. Hence they frequently visited the settlement. They were peace-loving and never attacked the settlers. The Indian squaws' "social call" to Keziah Billings actually occurred; so did Kit

Carson and his army officers' breakfasting with widow Strawhacker.

Silas Locklin who married Hannah Butterfield, really was an Indian scout. Abraham Atlantic ("Lank") Moore actually owned a cattle ranch at Cottonwood Crossing (now Durham) some 15-20 miles northwest of the settlement. Indians occasionally attacked the ranch and drove off his cattle. Once Grandma Griffith was ready for them with her axe during the time when Hannah's baby was born. The Indians whom the settlers feared most were the roving bands of Osages, Cheyennes, Kiowas and Comanches. Hence Indian scares were fairly common.

Later arrivals at Marion Centre included Evin and Molly Hoops and their daughters (Molly was Grandma Griffith's daughter) as well as Roddy (R.C.) Coble, Reuben Riggs, Alex Case and others. Quaker Elder Buck of Emporia was a circuit preacher who actually visited the Shreves from time to time, and preached in the homes about once every three months before the church was built. The diphtheria epidemic really happened during which time Beecher Billings and others died. The events of the Civil War are, of course, factual. Quantrill's raid is a black blot of horror on Kansas history.

Historic Council Grove, once the last civilized outpost along the Santa Fe Trail, is still an active little city, steeped in Kansas history. The Kaw Indian mission building is there; also Hays House with much of the original structure as it appeared in 1863 when Barbara spent one night under its roof. Seth M. Hays actually was the dark-bearded proprieter.

The Daniel Moore family and Barbara Temple are fictitious as well as Charlie and Willie Warren, the Fosters and Barry Keaton.

I have tried to portray this segment of Marion history through Barbara's eyes. Hence, if it has deviated from fact, it is no less stranger than the facts themselves which were sometimes vague and unclear in my research of Marion's history.

The area of Marion and the town itself were flooded following heavy rains on occasion and once water stood nearly three feet deep on Main Street. Small wonder one Indian chief's prediction of floods came true when he told the first settlers: "Heapie much water some day." After the engineering of the Marion Dam and Reservoir, plus some rechanneled waterways in the 1950s, the problem of Marion's flooding was solved.

Esther Loewen Vogt
Hillsboro, Kansas

CHAPTER 1

The Kansas rains had been copious in late June of 1863, and the valley was a lush green. Grassy stretches of open prairie bordered the Wakarusa River winding to meet the Kaw, and a warm summer wind swept steadily, incessantly, as vast waves of verdure kept time to the rhythm of the wind. Away to the north the bluffs cowered like gray shadows against the blurry skyline, and to the southwest a wooded height marked the bold beginning of the swell that melted into the Flint Hills and undulated toward the eastern horizon.

The Santa Fe Trail zigzagged among sharp stone ledges, overhung by dusty tree branches. From the foot of this rocky road the path of the Trail sloped away evenly to a deep ravine, cutting an irregular line across the plains. Beyond this ravine it crossed a rough, billowing belt of ground and gave way again to a soft, gentle prairie.

For over two days the stagecoach had rattled along this wide, rutted highway that wound like a narrow brown ribbon between low-lying hills. The sweet aroma of dry prairie hay lifted in the wind and blew through the open coach windows.

Snorting and flinging foam-flecked manes, the three teams pulling the stage sprang over the Trail, whinnying and snuffling as Doyle, the driver, called out, "Haw! Haw! Move, you dad-gummed critters!"

Barbara Temple, seated in the rear of the coach, drew her breath sharply. On either side of the Trail she noticed the prairie now stretched like a vast sea, dipping and swelling in long waves of dark green foam on the light green ocean of grass. To the southwest a thin fringe of timber clung to a deep draw, then merged with the distant Neosho River. She drew back her head quickly. The scene reminded her of an unfinished painting that had been smudged by the imprint of a huge hand.

Leaning back in the coach, she frowned at the drab country that seemed to flash forever past the open windows of the jolting stage. With a grimace she adjusted the blue satin bows of the tan straw bonnet under her soft white chin. Her blue traveling suit felt gritty and grimy from the long, dusty stage ride.

Letting out a long, weary sigh, she glanced at Martha Cox, the prim, spinsterish woman of 28 who sat beside her.

"Will this day ever end?" she pouted, her lips parting over even white teeth.

"Are you anxious to reach Council Grove?" the Cox woman asked.

"Oh, I don't know." Barbara pressed her lips tightly. "At least, it's the end of my journey."

"You've come a long ways?"

"From Atlanta. I had no idea Kansas was so far away. First, the railroad, then the steamboat up the Missouri, and the stage for two days now."

The Winston Condors, seated across from Barbara and her companion, smiled unitedly. They had been silent on the long ride from Westport, some 130 miles to the northeast. Barbara knew only that the middle-aged couple planned to go on to New Mexico to visit their married daughter.

"It's even farther from Tennessee to our destination," Mrs. Condor volunteered. "But gettin' away from the war's worth it."

Not for me, Barbara thought with a lump in her throat. If only her mother hadn't died. But 16-year-old girls weren't trusted to live alone, especially when there was no money, and vicious war was being fought between the North and the South.

"Who'd you say was meeting you at Hays Tavern?" Miss Cox asked in her gentle, well-bred voice.

Barbara drummed her fingers on her

13

knees and frowned. "I didn't say! But it's my Uncle Daniel Moore. He and Aunt Prudy have invited me to live with them."

"How nice. At least you have a place —"

"But it's only until the war is over," Barbara cut in, "and I can go back and marry Matthew Potter."

"You look mighty young to think of marryin'," Judge Welch, beside Miss Cox, put in.

Barbara jutted out her jaw. "I'm 16! Matthew and I have been betrothed for over two years now. If Papa hadn't been killed in battle right after the war began, we'd have been married before Matthew was called up to fight." She squinted at the sky against the hot sunlight, remembering. "But Mother needed me . . . and then the . . . the Northern sympathizers came and the field darkies fled." Anger shook her as she recalled the time, and she clenched her fists. Life was so unfair. The war had turned her whole safe world topsy-turvy.

Miss Cox placed a gentle arm on Barbara's shaking shoulders. "I'm so sorry, Miss Temple. This awful war —"

"This rotten war has torn up so many lives! That Abraham Lincoln, he ought to be tarred and feathered. If the Yankees hadn't started the whole mess —" She

14

jerked away from Miss Cox' consoling grip.

"I believe it was the Confederates that seceded from the Union," the judge said testily. "The question of slavery, the disunity. If the Confederates hadn't fired on Fort Sumter in the first place —"

"But President Lincoln had no right to free —"

"States' rights!" the judge cut in. "All men are created equal and it's every country's right to protect itself from division, from corruption."

Barbara shut her ears to the judge's vitriolic pronouncements. What did he know? He hadn't lived in the South, so how could he pass judgment on plantations that needed slaves to produce cotton and tobacco?

The coach grew silent. There was only the rumble of wheels and the pounding of hooves over the hard-packed Trail which took Barbara farther and farther away from her home in the South and Matthew.

She winced. Matthew was all she had left. When her father was killed after he left to serve with General Hill, the plantation was deserted and later burned to the ground. With no money for taxes, she and her mother had moved into a modest cottage on the outskirts of Atlanta with the last bit of crop money. Their darkies — those who hadn't run off — were sold for a paltry sum.

Her frail mother, Candace Moore Temple, became ill with fever and soon died, leaving Barbara alone. Two years before, her only brother, 10-year-old Whatley, had succumbed to the fever.

When her mother's brother Daniel Moore of Marion Centre in Kansas invited Barbara to live with him and his family, she had accepted reluctantly as the only way to survive. She'd all but forgotten the five lively Moore cousins. Perhaps she should be grateful to her uncle for giving her a home, but why did Kansas have to be so far away?

With the last money left from selling family heirlooms, Barbara had bought her tickets west — railway, steamboat and stagecoach. All were necessary steps to bring her to her new home. It was a tiring, bone-wearying journey. Sometimes she thought it would never end.

Now she almost looked forward to reaching Council Grove, the last civilized outpost along the Trail before Santa Fe in New Mexico. A quiet ride in Uncle Daniel's carriage to Marion Centre would bring her to her new home at last. To crawl between fresh, clean sheets, draw the bed curtains and sleep all day would be pure heaven after this hot, uncomfortable trip.

The horses slowed to a trot now and seemed to sense that the journey was nearing its end for the day. Barbara pulled off her straw bonnet and shook out the long, dark curls that swept across her shoulders. How she longed for a good hot bath! Her hair needed washing and some curling, but that must wait. When she arrived at Uncle Daniel's, she could take out her wrinkled gowns from the horse-hair trunk and have them pressed and hung in a closet with clean cedar shavings.

"Prairie Homestead" had a nice ring to it. "Sturdy and well built," he had said. It wouldn't be as roomy as the large plantation home near Atlanta, but he had promised it would be home.

The long afternoon had drawn to a close, and the incessant wind had died down. The air was very sweet, and the prairie above the draw still and dewy. As the last gleam of sunset gold swept over the Trail, a ripple of bird song in the draw melted into the stillness.

Beyond the bend of the Trail, the stage rolled slowly around the bluff. Nestled among the gentle rolling hills where the glassy waters of Elm Creek mingled with the Neosho, dusty shacks of the town crouched on either side of the river.

Martha Cox picked up a small reticule and dusted it with a fine linen handkerchief, and Barbara pushed back her hair and jammed the straw bonnet on her head. She tied the ribbons loosely under her chin. I must look my best, she told herself, for they were coming into town.

As the stage creaked down the town's wide main avenue from the east, her heart hammered. A row of makeshift houses and shops straggled on either side of the street, and the horses pulled up before a modest, two-story hotel tavern on the north side. Its shaded porch overhung the front with a dangling, crooked sign:

HAYS HOUSE
Seth M. Hays, Prop.

Barbara noticed horses tied to the hitching posts, and here and there stood a team with its buckboard. The town didn't look impressive. In fact, it seemed quite backwoodsy and primitive, compared to Atlanta. Perhaps it wasn't quite the "civilized outpost" it was touted to be. She'd been warned that Kansas was a raw, new state, but how new and how raw she hadn't realized.

Uncle Daniel had said it was a good place to live. Only 18 months before, on January 29, 1861, Kansas had become a state, he wrote proudly. So far all she'd seen were vast, open spaces, gently rolling hills, and high, windy prairies. Like a smudged painting. Was this the land where she was to make her home?

"Whoa!" Doyle cried in his gruff voice, and the horses jerked to a stop. Barbara waited until he had tied up the teams and helped her to the ground. She turned toward him uncertainly.

"Better go inside," he told her. "Somebody'll prob'ly be around to pick you up. I'll bring in your trunk after I help the other passengers."

She glanced around anxiously. No carriage was in sight, and she moved slowly toward the wide, board porch. Dirt sifted between the planks with each step, and she lifted her dainty, black-slippered feet as she crossed the threshold into the large room beyond the wide open door and looked around the dim interior.

The lamps had not yet been lit, and in the trailing twilight Barbara could make out a bar across one end and several small scattered tables. A few persons were seated at the tables, sipping coffee from thick white mugs or drinking whiskey from bottles.

Seth M. Hays, the tall, bearded proprietor, came toward her. "You Miss Barbara Temple?" His voice was brusque.

"Yes, I'm Barbara. Where's Uncle Daniel Moore? He said —"

"He sent word he'll be around in the mornin' to pick you up. He wasn't sure on which stage you'd be, so he said to stay here until he comes. It's a 40-mile drive out to Marion Centre, you know."

Barbara pressed her lips together again. No, she hadn't known. She should've realized everything here was vast and crude. "I . . . I guess that's all I can do," she stammered. "But the cost of the room —"

"It's 50 cents if you share it," he said. "They's a lady who needs a partner. Have a seat while I carry up your bags. Better have a bite to eat, then get a good night's rest. It's a long drive by wagon in the mornin'."

"I'm not hungry. Besides, I'm waiting on a carriage to come for me," she said.

Seth Hays cocked his head. "Don't get your hopes up, Miss. Folks here don't drive fancy carriages. We have enough to keep one step ahead of the Indians."

He lit a lamp and beckoned to a helper who hoisted her small trunk on heavy shoulders and headed for the stairs.

Barbara shivered a little at his words as she followed him up the crude wooden stairs to the tiny bedroom off the hall and opened a creaking door. In it stood an iron bedstead and a washstand with a bowl and pitcher and a few nails on the wall for her clothes. She felt dirty with the grit of the road imbedded in her fair skin and traveling garments.

Her roommate, to her relief, was Miss Martha Cox. At least they weren't total strangers. Barbara undressed quickly, shook out the traveling suit and crawled into the bed with its lumpy straw mattress and small pillow which must have been stuffed with prickly goose quills instead of down.

Outside, the night was filled with commotion. A woman sobbed, horses whinnied and across the prairie came the plaintive howl of a coyote.

Tears slid down Barbara's cheeks and she wiped them away with the long sleeve of her dainty white muslin nightdress.

What had she let herself in for, coming to this raw, forsaken prairie country?

CHAPTER 2

Barbara awoke the next morning and sat up with a jerk. The bed squeaked under the sudden movement. Martha Cox was already up and washing herself at the porcelain bowl on the gray-painted wooden stand.

"You must've been tired," her companion said, sudsing her arms with a square of homemade lye soap. "I don't think you stirred all night."

Barbara swung her feet onto the bare floor. The room was pale in the morning sun, and a cool breeze blew in through the open south window. She glanced at the rough board walls and uncurtained windows. *What this room needs,* she thought, *is some pretty blue-sprigged wallpaper and dainty dotted Swiss curtains.* Why did frontier people insist on being so crude?

She stretched her slender arms and yawned. "I thought I'd never sleep again after that rattly stage ride." She paused briefly and frowned. "What do we do next?"

"When you're washed and dressed, you'd better go down for breakfast. I'm due to hop the stage again in a few minutes for my destination. You're lucky you've almost reached yours."

Barbara slipped into a fresh pink dress embroidered with tiny red rosebuds on the skirt and puffed sleeves. "Where are you headed, Miss Cox?" she asked politely. They had hardly spoken on the entire trip.

"Didn't I tell you? I'll be teaching school in the Pawnee Rock Settlement when the fall term begins. My sister and her husband begged me to come out. It's another three days' journey or so. The stage is to leave shortly."

Picking up her reticule, the woman hurried down the stairs with a wave of her hand.

Outside, horses and wagons clattered down the street, and somewhere a rooster crowed. Barbara washed herself, combed her rich brown curls and pinned them up into a neat bun. Peering into the cracked mirror, she studied her reflection. Lustrous deep blue eyes, like her mother's — her best feature. A nose that was unimportant, and a mouth that was definitely too thin. The chin belonged to her great-grandmother Moore — the chin of a girl who possessed more spirit than was sometimes good for her.

She slid into her dainty black slippers and started down the rough stairs, swinging her fashionable straw bonnet by its blue satin ribbons.

Stepping into the dining room, she glanced around. Several men were seated at a table eating their breakfast, but none looked vaguely familiar, and she paused awkwardly and waited by the stairway.

"May I help you, Miss?" A brisk young woman wearing a dark blue pinafore over her gray skirt and black striped blouse spoke at her elbow. Barbara spun around.

"Oh, I was looking for my Uncle Daniel Moore. He was to pick me up." She hesitated.

"You'd best have a bite of breakfast before he gets here," the woman said. "Why not sit over there?" She motioned to an empty table. "I'll fix you up a plateful of fried mush."

"But —"

"We always cook plenty on the day the stage leaves. No charge. Folks need a hearty breakfast before they go out on the Trail. I'd hate to have to throw it out."

Barbara glanced around wildly for Miss Cox. The stage had probably already left. With a shake of her head, she walked toward the table with a few battered unpainted chairs. The table, covered by dingy yellow oilcloth, wobbled as she sat down.

Just then she heard a commotion by the door. To her horror three black-haired, black-eyed Indians shuffled in, stolid and silent in their faded red tunics and buckskin trousers. Frantically Barbara's hands flew to her hair. Then with presence of mind, she jammed her bonnet on her head. They weren't going to scalp her without a struggle.

The young cook, obviously sensing Barbara's dismay, scurried from the outside kitchen toward her with a plate of the fragrant fried mush and sausages.

"Never mind them, Miss," she said, motioning toward the Indians. "They're Kaws who live on the reservation just outside of town. They're perfectly harmless."

"They . . . won't attack?" Barbara stammered.

"They haven't tried for the past three or four years. The last time was in '59, but that's long forgotten. In fact, the Quakers have opened up an Indian school and mission just last month with Mahlon Stubbs. He's doing a good job too. The Indians' response is amazing."

Barbara let out her breath slowly. She removed her bonnet and laid it on the table, then picked up her fork and began to push tiny bits of the fried mush between her shaking lips. She had almost forgotten how hungry she was.

The three Kaws lounged in the doorway and moved only when a tall, rugged man pushed his way in. He looked around curiously, then approached Barbara's table and doffed his straw hat.

"You must be Barbara Temple, my sister Candace's child, if I don't miss my guess," he said, reaching out his hand. He was middle-aged, shaggy-browed and sunburned, wearing a blue shirt and dun-colored trousers held up by brown suspenders. His deep blue eyes, she noticed, looked as though they were focused on distance horizons.

Barbara thrust out her hand. "Oh, Uncle Daniel, I thought you'd never come!"

He pulled out a chair and sat down. "Welcome to Kansas, Barbara. After you've finished breakfast, I'll drive you out to the homestead. My, you're even prettier than I remembered. I'm so sorry you lost both folks in such a short time, but please keep in mind that our home is yours for as long as you wish."

"Yes," she said, nodding, "and I'm grateful that you've offered to take me in. But it will be only until the war's over and I can go back and marry Matthew Potter."

His pleasant face grew solemn. "God

grant that the war will end soon and this senseless killing can stop!"

He grew silent, and Barbara finished her breakfast. With a quick flip of her wrist, she replaced the straw bonnet on her head and got to her feet.

Her uncle rose and looked around. "Where are your bags? It's time we load up and head for home. It's a good day's ride."

Just then Seth Hays came from the rear, carrying Barbara's little trunk. "Here. I'll take it to the door for ye."

"And I'll bring the team around so we can get started," Uncle Daniel called as he walked out the door.

Barbara waited awkwardly, her heart beating with trepidation as she fingered the blue ribbons under her chin. Soon she would reach her new home. She didn't know whether to be relieved or sorry.

Several minutes later her uncle returned, picked up the trunk and motioned to her. She followed him out into the bright June morning. The sky was blue, and an occasional white cauliflower cloud drifted overhead. She spied the lumber wagon and team of horses tied to the rail. Was Uncle Daniel putting her trunk into the back?

"Ready, Barbara?" he called out. "We'd better get going if we're to reach Marion

Centre by nightfall."

"You mean —" she stopped and stared at the crude wooden seat behind the horses, "you mean I have to ride in . . . in *that!*"

Uncle Daniel walked toward her slowly "My dear niece, how else did you expect to get to our place? The stage doesn't go that way."

"I thought . . . I thought you'd have a . . . a carriage. In Georgia we Temples always rode in carriages!"

What had Seth Hays said last night? *Don't get your hopes up. Folks in these parts don't drive carriages.* But to ride in a wagon like a common wench! Her blue eyes smoldered.

"I'm sorry, Barbara," Uncle Daniel said. "I thought you knew. We're new settlers. Some day this country will be great. But we're just beginning. All beginnings are slow."

With a resigned sigh she allowed herself to be hoisted up to the high wagon seat.

I should've known, she thought bitterly. *I should've realized that this wild prairie country would be crude and backwoodsy.*

"I've already stopped at the overland mail office to pick up the post. It'll be a week or two before the next mail comes in. We pick it up here whenever we have a chance," Uncle Daniel told her, "and take it to Marion Centre."

At least there's mail, she thought.

As the wagon lumbered out of town, Barbara stared straight ahead. With groaning and creaking wheels, the wagon rumbled southwest along the Trail, the same road the stagecoach had taken half an hour or so earlier.

The lush, green prairie grass, tall enough to bend before the stiff breeze, stretched as far as the eye could see. It was embroidered with blue lupines, pink wild asters and delicate mauve windflowers, like a tapestry. The Trail looked indistinct. Far ahead it appeared to end abruptly, but never came to a point, for the ruts made by wagon and stage wheels were always visible for a little way.

The silence in the wagon grew ominous, and Barbara's fear of being alone and betrayed began to overwhelm her. It wasn't Uncle Daniel's fault, she reminded herself, that his transportation was a team and wagon. Beginnings were hard he'd said. *I must seem awfully ungrateful,* she thought.

She saw his eyes were deep blue, so much like her own. His dark hair curled faintly like her mother's, and the intense look on his sunburned face was kind. She reached out her left hand impulsively and touched his sleeve.

"Lonely?" he asked, looking at her with a

lopsided grin. "I'm sure you must be. This wild, new country would scare anyone. It scared us, too, when we came — except we knew this was where we belonged."

Barbara nodded, tears blinding her eyes. She *wanted* to like Uncle Daniel's land, but it was too awesome, the prairie too desolate and wide.

"Uncle Daniel," she began, "please believe me. I'm grateful. But it's . . . it's all so vast and so terribly —"

"I know. Still, it's a rich country. Some day it'll thrive with farms and cities. When the war is over and more settlers come —"

"When the war is over I'll go back to Georgia," she cut in. "But until then —"

"Until then we want you to be a part of us as we eke out a living on this wide prairie land." He clucked at the team which had slowed to a trot. Already the sun crept higher into the sky, and the breeze that fanned the wagon grew hot and sultry.

Barbara pulled her straw bonnet snugly over her head to keep the blazing rays from beating down on her neck. As the wagon jolted and bumped down the Trail, she felt bruised and sore.

"Your Aunt Prudy had hoped to come along and meet you," Uncle Daniel said, probably to make conversation. "But it's a long drive. I started out yesterday morning and reached Council Grove just before dark."

"Where did you sleep?" Barbara asked more out of politeness than concern.

"See that blanket in the back of the wagon? No settler ever travels without one. Rolled out, it makes a good bed. But at the cabin you'll sleep on fresh straw ticking and goosedown pillows."

"You have geese?"

"A few. Cows and chickens, too. We're breaking sod for wheat and corn these days, and the girls are always busy in the garden."

"Aggie? Evangeline and Elizabeth? And the oldest?" Barbara asked. "I've almost forgotten my cousins."

"Well, that's Rosie. She's the oldest, married to John Frazer. They live on the claim north of us. Aggie's second, and Josh follows. He's 20. Then Vange and Bitsy — that's what we call Elizabeth. You're more their age. They're all looking forward to having you."

Barbara vaguely remembered her cousins as being full of giggles and fun, the two youngest always in some scrape. *I hope they've grown up now,* she thought. *After all, I'm an engaged woman and above such childish whims.*

31

"Uncle Daniel," she began hesitantly. "Why did you leave Indiana and come to Kansas?"

His blue eyes took on the faraway look as he gazed over the prairie, now shimmering with silver mist.

"We sold our place because we didn't have room to expand. Farmland was carved into small plots and we needed more land. As we prayed and sought God's will, my eyes fell on the book of Genesis in the Bible where God told Abraham: 'Leave your country, your people and your father's household and go to the land I will show you.' This land for us was the Cottonwood Valley of Kansas."

"But . . . but that promise was for the Bible Abraham, wasn't it?"

"Oh, but God's Word is always for today! He also showed me a verse in Deuteronomy 30 that said, 'I command you today to love the Lord your God, and walk in his ways, and to keep his commands. Then you will live and increase, and the Lord your God will bless you in the land you are entering to possess.' Barbara, for us, this is it — God's land of promise."

Barbara was silent. To her, God seemed very far away, and she wondered if He cared what happened to her. Sometimes it didn't seem that way.

Some miles ahead she noticed a cluster of log cabins. Surely this wasn't Marion Centre? Uncle Daniel pointed with his hands. "Diamond Springs. We'll stop and water the team. It will give you a chance to get down and stretch your legs."

"Are there . . . an Indians?"

"Oh, perhaps you may see a few. The Kaw or Kanza Indians that ride this way are peaceful. That's where Kansas gets its name, you know. The Indians we fear most are the Cheyennes and Kiowas or Osages. But they rarely come this way — especially the Kiowas and Comanches. The Kaws have their own trail just a short way south of here, which they use on their annual buffalo hunt."

"Buffalo!" Barbara echoed. "Do those wild creatures still roam across Kansas?"

"Maybe a few. There used to be thousands, but not any more. Every now and then some come near enough so we can shoot them from our windows, but not often. Roast buffalo is delicious though. We're always glad to shoot one of the critters. It really helps our food supply."

Uncle Daniel pulled the team to a stop near the creek where a fresh spring bubbled from a triangle of rocks just off to one side and helped Barbara down from the wagon. She walked around on the trampled grass to ease the kinks from her stiff legs. Then she sat down in the cool shade of a cottonwood tree and took off her bonnet. Fanning her hot face, she noticed her arms. *A lady would never allow herself to become sunburned,* Mammy Crissy had always said.

"Oh, Mammy," she sobbed softly. "What's going to become of me?"

A moment later Uncle Daniel brought her a paper parcel. "Here," he said, tossing it into her lap, "some food for our dinner. Better eat now. There's cornbread and some fried sausage. The ride to Marion Centre is long."

While she opened the sack, he went to the spring with a pail and came back with water to drink. They ate in silence.

Barbara was already sore and tired. How long until they reached the claim? she wondered. A few minutes later they were back on the wagon, and the team moved ahead with a jingle of harness.

Now the Trail dipped southwesterly where the prairie lay flattened by the wind as though some heavy hand had pushed it down.

On the horizon she caught sight of several dark moving specks. Uncle Daniel must have seen them too. Suddenly he began to urge the horses on faster.

"Haw! Haw!" he yelled hoarsely. "Prince, Dolly. Go! Go!"

As the wagon bounced and jolted over the rough trail, Barbara felt the wind roar in her ears. She held on tightly to her straw bonnet, for the sudden speed seemed to unleash the prairie wind in fury. Faster, faster the team flew, galloping along the ruts with force that threatened to tear the sturdy wagon box apart.

She glanced wild-eyed at Uncle Daniel. "Why are we hurrying?" she screamed into the teeth of the howling wind.

He merely kept flogging the horses, the wildly-swaying wagon jerking with each furious pull of the team. She feared her bonnet would be wrenched from her head in the force of the wind.

Just when she was sure it would fly away, Uncle Daniel slowed the team to a trot. He touched her shoulder. "Sorry, Barbara, for that wild chase down the trail. But I couldn't be sure . . ." He paused, and the deep blue eyes took on their far away look again.

"Couldn't be sure of what, Uncle Daniel?"

"That what I saw was a band of friendly

Kaws — or Osages. It pays to be careful."

A shiver crept down Barbara's back. "But you said they rarely come this way. That the Indians —"

"I said the Kaws were friendly, but we never know about the wandering tribes when they decide to attack us. We've lived here a year now, and have seen no hostile bands. But I couldn't take a chance."

The wagon left the Trail and turned south now, onto a less traveled road. A few miles down the jutted tracks, Barbara caught sight of a log cabin sprawled along the road-side. It was no more than a crude, one-room dwelling with a barn tacked on behind.

"Look! That house is so tiny!" she cried. "Our plantation —"

"You won't see any plantations around here, Barbara, although our cabin's about as nice and snug as any. Some folks live in dugouts or build homes of adobe bricks where there are few trees, but we were lucky to build a cabin of logs on our claim along the Cottonwood," he told her. "Logs are sturdier, you know."

Barbara grew silent. The trail wandered southwest and meandered south again. The prairies took on a hue of tans and browns and grays. Ahead she could make out a fringe of thick woods, and wondered if they were nearing the settlement.

Uncle Daniel clucked to his team. "Come, Prince, come, Dolly. That's Clear Creek over there. We're coming into the Marion Centre area now. Get moving!" The team jogged faster.

Several minutes later the wagon rumbled down a well-marked road that angled straight toward the grove of trees.

"That's Marion Centre," he said. "Our home lies about a mile northwest of here. The houses here are still rather scattered, but some day this will be a real town. See? That's the George Griffith place, and the next cabin belongs to William Billings, in that horseshoe bend of the creek. We'll stop there and leave the mail. See where the river swings into that circular bend? Billings is putting in a store and post office. That will be handy."

Uncle Daniel stopped before the two-story log cabin and carried in a pouch of mail. Barbara waited until he came back to the wagon.

"*This* is a town, Uncle Daniel?" she burst out. "Why, it's nothing more than a couple of cabins squatting along a muddy river-bank!"

"This is prairie country," he said in a hushed voice that reminded Barbara of being in church. "It's God's country, Barbara."

Barbara tried to swallow a lump in her throat, but it wouldn't go away. The long afternoon was drawing to a close, and once again she witnessed a prairie sunset. The sun had slipped below the horizon in a glow of red and pink. The wildly blowing wind had stopped. A shimmer of purple covered the landscape, like a glow of enchantment over the prairie, hiding its wildness. The wagon bounced over the hill and around the bend, then clattered toward the north.

"There it is, Barbara. Our homestead."

The two-room Moore cabin sat quietly among the grove of native trees like a big speckled brown bird in its green nest of oaks, maples and elms that touched the roof at the rear and sides.

As the wagon creaked up the dim lane, the cabin door stood open, without a soul in sight. Barbara felt a shiver of uneasiness as though this wild prairie country was about to change her life.

CHAPTER 3

As Uncle Daniel helped her from the wagon, Barbara looked around. From the rear of the cabin came a high, clear singing voice proclaiming that it was standing on Jordan's banks, followed by peals of laughter. In the background she heard a dog's shrill bark and a voice, "Down, Woodson. Behave like a mutt, not like a coyote."

The tiny figure of a woman stepped out of the cabin doorway, her round face brown as a berry. Perched on her head like a bump on a log was a topknot of sparse gray hair held together with grotesque brown tortoise shell pins. She wore a dress of dark blue percale, partly covered by a commodious gray apron. Her blue-gray eyes behind wire-rimmed spectacles crinkled into a smile as she hurried up to Barbara, then hugged her and stood back.

"Welcome home, child. We're so glad you've come. Wait! Let me call the girls."

She scudded around the corner of the house and called out, "Vange! Bitsy! Aggie! Barbara's here!"

Turning back to Barbara, she grabbed her arm and pulled her toward the front door on the south side of the cabin. "Come on in. Your uncle will bring your trunk later." Scurrying ahead, she lit a kerosene lamp and set it on the table.

Barbara crossed the log stoop made from a tree trunk and stepped inside the two-room cabin. In the pale, dim light she saw the huge stone fireplace on the west wall that held a swinging crane with an iron cooking pot and a shovel and tongs leaning against the wall. The mantel shelf was topped by a gun, a Seth Thomas clock which ticked away beside a sheaf of ripe wheat and a pair of tallow candles in pewter holders. A walnut cupboard with white porcelain knobs stood on the south wall to the left of the door, and a square, black cookstove squatted to the right of the front door. Built-in shelves draped with green calico curtains graced one wall where the corner hugged a huge woodbox next to the cookstove.

In the center stood a large, wooden table covered by a yellow checkered oilcloth. Several homemade chairs with red calico covers were placed around the table. A barrel-stand near the back door held neatly folded pieces of sewing and a Bible. On the clay-plastered, white-washed wall hung a cal-endar with a poster picture of President

Lincoln and a framed Bible verse embroidered in cross-stitching:

TRUST IN THE LORD.

A bench across the room held an array of milk pans and butter crocks, scalded and shining. Iron utensils hung from the walls above it, and a bright, braided rug covered the center of the wide board floor.

On the east wall a door opened off into Uncle Daniel and Aunt Prudy's bedroom. The door was closed. Barbara wondered where the other bedrooms were.

A small lean-to tacked onto the back door contained a flour barrel, wooden water pail and dipper and pegs for hanging wraps. A brace of harness hung on a nail, probably always in a state of being oiled.

Barbara took the whole scene in one glance and thought, *How will I ever fit into such a place?*

Suddenly the rear door banged and three laughing, barefooted girls bounded into the kitchen. *The skinny brown one in a simple dun-colored percale with merry hazel eyes and mousy hair caught up in a braided bun, must be Aggie,* Barbara thought. The plump girl with the glorious crown of auburn curls that caught fire in the lamplight and wearing gray poplin was Evangeline. The willowy blond wearing a skimpy blue and white checked pinafore and hair hanging down her back in two fat pigtails was Elizabeth.

Amid a wild tangle of arms and rash of bare legs, punctuated with shrieks of laughter, they greeted Barbara with warm hugs and damp kisses.

"Welcome to the Castle on the Cottonwood!" Vange burst out exuberantly.

"In the heart of the Divided States of America," quipped Bitsy.

"Where the grass grows so tall you can't see Indians a-tall!" giggled Aggie. Then all three dissolved into peals of laughter.

Barbara blinked at their dry humor, their droll greetings. How could they feign happiness in this uncivilized land where nothing grew but wild grass, and Indians popped up unexpectedly behind every door!

"Remember us?" Vange chattered on. "That's Aggie over there, the one with freckles thick as speckles on a turkey's egg. She can fix a fancy meal out of water and cornstalks and make a charming ball gown out of half a flour sack."

Aggie pretended to pick off her freckles, scattering them like seeds. "Me and my stirring spoon and needle . . . we're never far apart."

Bitsy swept on. "And that's Evangeline with the hole in her chin. She calls it a dimple and pokes it in with her fingers."

"Oh, yes, and that's Bitsy," Aggie added, her eyes gleaming with mischief. "She thinks her hair is gold, but it's really egg yolk."

Barbara shook her head, bewildered. What should she say? Low laughter swept around her like a prairie wind of which there was no stopping.

"You must be hungry," Aunt Prudy said, coming to her rescue. "Here, sit down in that barrel chair. Girls, get the table set and we'll eat in a minute. Aggie, flour these prairie chickens and pop them into the skillet. Where's Josh?"

"He's helping Pa tease Prince and Dolly into tasting that perfectly pungent wild onion hay," piped up Vange, slamming black-handled flatware onto the table while Bitsy slid crockery plates and cups at each place setting. Then she set a cracked blue vase of yellow buttercups in the center of the table.

"Which they'll eat if they know what's good for them, after smelling Indians all day," Bitsy mumbled.

"Barb, did you know that horses can smell an Indian a mile away?" Vange said, her blue eyes dancing. "Of course, I wouldn't be above meeting a handsome Kaw brave myself."

"Oh, come now, Vange," Aggie said, stirring something in a pot on the stove.

"You haven't given up on Charlie, have you?"

"Not as long as Bits wants him!"

"To Charlie Warren, girls are a necessary evil," Bitsy scoffed. "Trouble is, he's forever got sheep on his mind. Barbie, wait till you meet Charlie, the catch of the Cottonwood. He'll steal your heart away like he has ours."

Barbara drew back in her chair and clamped her lips together. Obviously this constant girlish chatter was about as hard to stop as vinegar from a keg's bunghole. "Never!" she snapped. "I'm marrying Matthew Potter when this war is over!"

"Now you've scared her off with your guff about Charlie and sheep and Kaw braves," Aggie scolded her younger sisters as she heaped freshly fried pieces of prairie chicken onto a platter. "You'd better get used to our nonsensical chatter, Barbara. It's as much a part of this claim as night follows day. Now put the cornbread on, Bits."

Soon there was a bustle as Uncle Daniel and Cousin Joshua came in from the lean-to. Josh grabbed Barbara and hugged her soundly.

"Welcome home, Cousin Barbara," he said with a peck on her cheek. "I hope you'll have the stamina to put up with my three silly sisters. Just don't mind their vicious barbs and gusty conversation. Here, come sit beside me," he added, pulling her down next to him at the table.

As soon as the platter heaped with fried chicken, the bowl of fresh creamed peas swimming with tiny new onions and plates of cornbread oozing with butter were on the table, Uncle Daniel bowed his head.

"Father-God," he prayed, "thank You for bringing Barbara safely to us. Grant that her stay with us will be one of joy for us all . . ."

Barbara pressed her lips together again. *Not much chance of that,* she thought. *How can I ever adjust to a life so different from what I've been used to?*

The chatter and laughter resumed like a burst dam when the prayer was over.

"Here, Barb," Vange handed her the platter of meat, "try this prairie manna. You haven't lived until you've eaten Aggie's heavenly hummingbirds' wings."

"Don't forget who shot the critters," Josh put in. "Joshua Moore! Bang-bang!"

"Yeah. Better watch out for B-B's when

you eat. That's Josh's trademark." Bitsy grimaced, and everyone laughed again.

Barbara forked bits of prairie chicken between her lips for a taste, then picked the bones clean. It tasted better than she had thought it would. After the meal ended, the girls cleared the table and Josh gathered up the plate full of bones. "One thing about those birds," he told Barbara as he walked toward the door. "Woodson, our collie, always thanks us for the bones."

As one girl scraped plates and put away the food, the other two washed the chipped crockery plates and cups in hot sudsy water and dried them. Barbara sat on a barrel chair and watched. There was never a moment of silence.

Barbara thought back to life in Georgia when the black mammies took care of kitchen chores, and the memory of those carefree days stabbed her. "Darkies were created for work," her father always said, so she had never offered to help. When Matthew visited her on Sunday afternoons, they went riding in his phaeton as he held her dainty blue silk parasol over her. She'd had no worries about frying prairie chickens and podding garden peas. Would things ever change for her again?

After the dishes were cleared away, Vange

hung the wet tea towel over the back of a chair and turned to Barbara.

"It's time to escort you up the spacious stairway to the chambers above," she announced pertly, picking up a candle. "I think Pa has already carried up your trunk. Come with me."

Barbara glanced around quickly. "Stairway? I don't see —"

"Up there." Vange pointed to a strong ladder that went up into a loft from the east wall of the kitchen. "Did you ever climb a tree? Well, this isn't much different. Watch!" She scrambled nimbly up the ladder and disappeared into the darkness above, waving the candlestick. "Come on up, Barb!" she called. "You're to sleep with me. Aggie and Bits will fight over who gets the biggest feather pillow in the other bed."

Slowly Barbara approached the ladder, a strange feeling prickling her neck. *She* was to climb up that ladder into an obscure darkness and sleep on a straw tick mattress with only bare rafters above and a goose-feather pillow under her head? Barbara Temple, who'd had her own large pink-and-white bedroom with a four-poster bed and soft, downy quilts and draw curtains to make her comfortable? Why did everything have to be so hard now?

With an angry shake of her brown head, she set her right foot on the first rung, then pulled herself hand-over-hand up the rungs until she reached the floor above. Vange had lit the candle. It glimmered with a feeble light on a wooden box that stood between the two beds on either side of the small east window.

"Come over here," Vange called, her plump figure outlined against the window. "Take a look at our prairie moon before we tumble into bed."

The slanting roof overhead made standing up difficult unless one was in the center, and she stumbled toward Vange across the loft bedroom in the semi-darkness. As she looked out, the moon came up, yellow as a prairie cowslip. The faint aroma of dew settling on coarse grass and crushed moist vegetation filtered to her nostrils. The dark world looked unbelievably peaceful.

She was startled by Bitsy and Aggie's squeals as they scrambled up the loft, and Josh's chuckles on the other side of the heavy gray curtain that separated the loft into two sleeping rooms.

As the straw tick scratched her back, Barbara was sure she would lie awake for hours, but she fell asleep as soon as her head touched the pillow.

When she awoke, the morning sun streamed through the tiny east window and needled its way through pin-point holes in the bark shingles. She rubbed her eyes and looked around. Her three cousins were gone, their nightgowns hung neatly on nails tacked to the rafters. No wonder the loft was so quiet.

She pulled on her blue-and-white checkered lawn. Then she brushed her hair and wound it into a bun on the back of her head before the small unframed mirror that hung above the apple-crate dressing table. She admired Vange's glorious auburn curls and Bitsy's gold braids. But Aggie's straight, mouse-colored hair fairly irked her.

What Aggie needs, Barbara decided, is someone to coil her hair low in the nape of her neck, and soak her brown face in a cucumber poultice. The way these girls ran around with bare arms and legs would ruin anyone's complexion. Mammy Crissy would've had a fit if she'd caught Barbara scrambling around outdoors with her limbs bare.

I'd better go downstairs, she told herself with a deep sigh, knowing the day would be hard to face.

Letting herself down carefully, she looked

around the silent kitchen. No one was around, and she wondered where everyone had gone. She glanced at the Seth Thomas clock on the mantel. Nine o'clock.

Just then she heard a clatter of milk pails and the door to the lean-to slam as Aunt Prudy poked her head through the door.

"Good morning, Barbara," she called out cheerfully. "Sleep well?"

Barbara nodded. "I guess so. I was tired from the long trip, I guess."

"Isn't anything to beat the fresh, clean prairie air to clear one's lungs and close tired eyelids. I'm glad you're rested. The girls are in the garden attacking the weeds, and I've just washed the milk pails. Now what will you have for breakfast?"

"I . . . I'm not very hungry, Aunt Prudy," she said. "At home Mammy always fixed fried country ham, but please don't bother."

"Sorry, we have no ham, Barbara. Our sausages are usually of smoked venison, but we seldom have them. How about cornmeal mush with molasses?"

Cornmeal seemed to be a popular staple here in the West, she thought. With a wry smile Barbara nodded.

"That will be fine. I'm much obliged to you for taking me in, Aunt Prudy."

"That's what families are for, child. We couldn't have done anything else, could we?"

Aunt Prudy fired up the stove and slammed a heavy iron skillet onto the front burner. In minutes the aroma of fried mush filled the room. She was hungrier than she'd thought.

The morning dragged for Barbara. She watched her aunt set a pan of salt-rising dough for bread, scour the top of the black stove and cart out ashes from the fireplace. It seemed Aunt Prudy never stopped for breath but bobbed from stove to table to cupboard to lean-to.

Out of sheer boredom, Barbara walked to the front log stoop and looked out. To the east the lane met the Trail that led toward the scrubby little town. To the west the Trail stretched away endlessly. She left the front door and crossed to the lean-to out back and stepped outdoors. Sturdy young maples and oaks dripped morning shade in the grassy backyard. On a post by the back door Aunt Prudy had turned over her milkpails to dry.

Farther north she saw the girls wielding their hoes in the garden. From their shouts and laughter it was apparent that they were attacking more than weeds. Northeast of the cabin Uncle Daniel was turning sod with Prince and Dolly hitched before the walking plow, while Joshua appeared to be setting fence posts into the ground next to the barn. Beyond the farm to the northwest, the land dipped into a draw. Barbara could see the fringe of trees along the river they called the Cottonwood.

She sighed. Everyone was busy, but for her there was nothing to do. How would she pass the long weary months ahead? As she sat down on the back stoop and looked at the prairie, sweet and bright in the morning sun, Woodson, the tan and white collie, came toward her and licked her out-stretched hand. She patted his tawny head.

"I'm about as useful as a second button on a collar," she muttered aloud. "I wish I'd stayed in Georgia, war or no war."

"Oh, you must be Barbara!" Someone spoke beside her, and Barbara looked up.

A tall, bright-eyed young woman with cheeks pink as wild roses stood beside her. She wore a gray chambray dress that ballooned out from the waist and showed her pantalets. A faded blue bonnet fell back from her neatly combed brown hair.

"I'm Rosie Frazer, your oldest cousin," she went on. "John and I live on the next claim and Ma said for us to come on over and eat dinner with the family so we could meet."

"W-what?" Barbara stammered. "I . . . I really appreciate everyone being so nice to me, but it's all so . . . so . . ." She paused awkwardly.

"So different?" Rosie offered gently. "I know. But this country will grow on you, please believe me."

"Never!" Barbara spat out. "This will never be like Georgia."

"Oh, I didn't mean that. But our prairie has its own personality. It's like Pa says. Land and God are all that matter. If you have land you are somebody in this world, and if you have God you're somebody in the next."

Rosie reached out her hand and pulled Barbara to her feet. "Come. Let's help Ma get dinner on the table. She said she was fixing a roast with the last of the antelope John shot earlier this week. I think there are tiny new potatoes, too."

Barbara followed her cousin back into the house. The aroma of meat roasting in the big iron pot hanging from the fireplace filled the room.

"Rosie, give me a hand with these loaves of bread, will you?" Aunt Prudy called. Rosie helped her mother lift four fragrant, golden brown crusty loaves from the oven onto a wooden rack on the table.

Bustling around with chatter and dishes, the two women soon prepared dinner while Barbara stood in the doorway and watched. She absently picked up a fly swatter and slapped at the flies that swooped down on the food.

Aunt Prudy ambled to the back door. "Dinner's on!" she hollered. "Better come and eat before it gets cold." Then she lifted the venison roast onto a platter with a heavy two-tined fork and carried it to the table.

Seconds later the three girls rushed in from the garden, their sunbonnets dangling from ties onto sweaty backs.

"I told you Ma'd throw it out if we didn't get here in five shakes of a snake's rattle," Vange cried. "Look, she's already dumped it out of the pot."

"Anyway, I picked off more potato bugs than you did," Aggie grumbled and the other two argued hotly.

"Two to one we'll have wild strawberries from Charlie's patch by the creek," Bitsy said changing the subject. "I told you I saw Ma hike out over the footlog across the river as soon as she shooed us into the potato patch!"

"With cream, I bet!" Vange said,

smacking her lips. John Frazer, Rosie's young husband, came in with Uncle Daniel and Josh just then. John was tall and fair, and Barbara caught her breath sharply. He reminded her of Matthew, except that Matthew's hair was close-cropped and he was younger.

"Welcome, Cousin Barbara," John greeted her, his voice low and throaty. "May you live long to sing Kansas' praises!"

Barbara didn't answer. How did one respond to all this exuberance?

The venison was tasty and the new potatoes in brown gravy, succulent and sweet. Bitsy was right. The dinner was rounded off with huge bowls of fresh strawberries swimming in cream.

During the meal there was much talk about the war. Governor Robinson, John said, had already ordered 13 regiments and some batteries of light artillery from Kansas to the battle front.

"I heard in Council Grove yesterday that while Lee's Grays camped at Fredericksburg, General Hooker's army launched a drive on Richmond by trying to surround both flanks of Lee's army," Uncle Daniel added. "Lee sent Stonewall Jackson to flank one wing of Hooker's army while he held the other in check. Jackson's assault lasted three days, and the Union's lost over 17,000 men. That's tragic."

Barbara pinched her mouth into a thin line. "Why should it be tragic? I don't have much use for that Abraham Lincoln," she muttered sullenly.

The lively chatter died and John looked up, his face grim. "I think the South is wrong in trying to break up the Union. Mr. Lincoln is doing what's right for the whole country. But if this keeps up, the North may have to yield to the South's demands."

"That's what I'm afraid of," Uncle Daniel added soberly. "If President Lincoln calls for more men from Kansas, I wonder how many of us will have to enlist."

Barbara stared at her uncle's words in dismay. "*You* . . . you're for the Union army?" she hissed.

Uncle Daniel laid down his fork and patted her shoulder, "Barbara, I'm for the country, not for divided states. But if President Lincoln can pull our nation back together, then I'm for the Union," he said quietly.

"No!" she flung off his hand. "My family — the only ones I have left — are against me! You . . . you've killed my father . . . and now you want to kill Matthew!"

With that, she jumped from the table and

rushed out of the house, tears strangling her throat.

"My only family. . . . Dear God," she cried, "how much more must I be called upon to bear?"

CHAPTER 4

Barbara grew moody and withdrawn in the days that followed. She felt trapped and life for her dragged from day to day. The family whose hospitalities she had accepted had turned out to be her political enemy. Oh, they would never shove her out; they were much too kind for that. But their sympathies were obviously with the North and hers were with the South. How could the gap ever be bridged? Yet, there was nothing to do but make the best of a bad situation. She couldn't leave because her money was all spent, and she tried not to show her antipathy; still, there were times when it rankled.

On Sundays the whole Moore family gathered in the large kitchen for a church service since there was no church or school in the settlement. Rosie and John joined them, and occasionally some of the Billings and Shreve or Griffith families showed up. So far there had been neither time nor money to build a church and call a preacher. Having been a church deacon at their former church in Indiana, Uncle Daniel strongly believed in gathering for worship.

Usually they sang hymns, and Uncle

Daniel read Scriptures; and there was a prayer session. The gathering or "assembling" was what counted, he said.

"We wear our Sunday-go-to-meetin' dresses, in case Charlie and Willie show up," Vange told Barbara when the two girls walked down the dewy lane to gather sheep sorrel, which Bitsy called "sheep showers." Barbara was bored and she accepted Vange's invitation to join her.

"Who's this Charlie you always drool over?" Barbara asked, kneeling beside Vange who had spotted a bed of the four-leafed herb on the east side of the wagon-rutted lane.

"Charlie? Oh, he lives just across the Cottonwood on that luscious piece of bottom land with his brother Willie. You cross the branch creek to get to their cabin in the glen. They moved onto their claim shortly before we came." Vange looked up and grimaced. "But believe me, if Charlie won't come to the Fourth of July picnic tomorrow, we'll have to put the fear of God into that boy!"

"I take it, he doesn't mingle much?"

"Mingle, my foot!" Vange snorted, heaping a pile of the sheep sorrel into the wicker basket. "He bought a flock of fancy sheep and now he's scared the Indians will make off with them so he never leaves the premises longer than necessary. If it wasn't for Bo —" she paused, popping a handful of sorrel into her mouth.

"Bo?"

"Beauregard. That's the head sheep. We call him 'Bo, the Boss Sheep' because he has the run of the flock."

"Named for General Beauregard, I s'pose?" Barbara's lips curled in scorn. "How could he be so thoughtless?"

Vange scrambled to her feet and grabbed the basket that now overflowed with greens. "Maybe. He has white whiskers, doesn't he — like a sheep? Even if he defended Fort Sumter."

"They're black!" Barbara flared. "Why, I've seen pictures —"

"Rumor has it they're white. The Union blockade has prevented the black dye from reaching him." Vange continued. "But like I said, Bo could mind the sheep as well as any collie, like Woodson. Of course Charlie won't believe that. And he won't leave Willie home alone, so they both stay on their claim. We've got enough sorrel now."

When the girls returned to the cabin, Bitsy stood at the table, pressing her best blue cotton. The fire in the stove sent waves of shimmering heat through the kitchen as the sadirons grew piping hot.

"Heavens, Bits, are you trying to burn down the cabin?" Vange yelled, slamming the wicker basket on the table.

A slow smile played over Bitsy's small mouth. "Anything for the Fourth of July picnic, my dear sister. I figure I'd better press my dress now so it's perfect. By the way, there's plenty of starch left for your sunbonnet."

"You didn't wash mine? Well, never mind. You always starch the brim so stiff that it takes an axe to chop the ties apart."

Bitsy glided the iron carefully over the ruffle around the big roomy pocket. Then she set down the iron and hung the dress over the back of a chair.

Barbara drew a deep breath and fingered the puffed sleeve of the blue dress. "How'd you learn to do that?"

"Do what?"

"Make those sleeves stand out like that?"

Vange burst into laughter. "Oh, you should've seen her when she first learned to iron clothes. Let's see, she's 15 now, so she must've been 10 when she tried out the iron on Ma's big gray apron. Scorched a hole clean through the very first time."

Bitsy glared at Vange, then winked at

Barbara and grinned. "I was young then, re-member?"

"Why do you call her Bitsy?" Barbara burst out with sudden curiosity.

"When she began to talk that's what she called herself. What'll you wear, Barb?"

"Wear? To the picnic?" Barbara paused. "Do I have to go? I don't know a soul —"

"Of course you'll go. A year ago we didn't know anyone either. We're all going. If you need a fresh bonnet —"

Barbara drew her chin up sharply. "I have my straw bonnet. Slat bonnets are for country folks." *I have some pride,* she thought stubbornly.

Bitsy and Vange stared at each other. Then with a sparkle in her eyes, Vange clapped her hands.

"That's great! Then you'll *love* Charity Shreve. She's so graceful — plump, mind you, but graceful — and so high-class looking that we call her 'Queen Victoria' behind her back. You've got to meet her. And you'd never guess she has seven chil-dren, although she reminds me of a doughy pancake. She makes absolutely the best coffee by roasting sweet potatoes."

"You mean . . . she's a *somebody?*"

"Oh, I'll say she is," Bitsy cut in airily. "The Shreves are Quakers, and she hardly ever forgets her *thee's* and *thou's*. Sometimes she calls us poor country bumpkins *you*."

Barbara colored. She knew they were putting her on. With a helpless gesture she threw out her hands.

"Well, all right, I'll go. But my green-sprigged delaine is all crushed from lying in the bottom of my trunk all these weeks, and I don't know how to . . . to iron."

"Never fear. Aggie will just love to do it. Won't you, Aggie?" Vange said, as Aggie came into the kitchen carrying a panful of defeathered prairie chickens.

"Won't I love to do what?" Aggie said, setting the pan on the table.

"Press Barb's delicate, gorgeous, delightfully dreamy delaine. Nobody can do it like you can."

Aggie glared at Vange, then looked at Barbara. "Of course, I'll do it. But not because Vange asked me to. You girls better wash your hair so your heads are dry by morning."

Barbara threw Aggie a grateful glance. *If only I could fix her hair . . . that mousy brown . . .* she thought, then shook her head. *No, I could never do that.* Of the three girls, Aggie seemed the most calm and sensible — most of the time.

While Bitsy and Vange washed their hair,

63

Aggie rolled out pie crusts and filled three tin pans with dried apples topped with wild honey and dotted with fresh butter.

An air of excitement stirred the cabin that night, with Vange, her auburn hair wrapped tightly in rag curls inspecting the stiffness of her freshly-ironed slat bonnet, and Bitsy fingering the crispness of her blue cotton. Aggie seemed more intent on food than finery.

At bedtime Barbara thought she would never fall asleep, for the three girls giggled and chattered about the picnic until long past midnight.

"I heard Edward Griffith — drat that mosquito — will be there," Aggie said as she swatted at a buzzing sound near her ear.

Bitsy giggled, "If Edward knew you called him a mosquit—"

"I didn't mean Edward. I meant —"

"Sure, we know." Vange and Bitsy burst into laughter. "Wait 'til tomorrow. Between Silas and the Griffith boys, Aggie shouldn't lack for beaus. It's about time she caught a man."

Aggie cuffed Bitsy until she howled.

In the morning the family was up early, for this was to be the first Fourth of July celebration in the new settlement. The air was fresh and clear, and white cloud pillows scudded across the blue summer sky. Not a breath of wind stirred the maples in front of the cabin.

Aggie had been up since dawn frying prairie chickens. The two younger girls packed crockery plates and tin cups in a big woven basket, while Aunt Prudy took out a clean, mended tablecloth from the cupboard drawer.

"I know Kizzie Billings won't have near enough cloths for all the tables," she said, folding it into a small square and laying it on top of the dishes.

Barbara watched silently, her hoops bulging under the green-sprigged delaine. There was chatter and laughter as always.

"The Billings-Butterfield household will have scrambled around since daybreak, setting up tables in their grove," Aggie said. "William Billings really took on something when he married Keziah Butterfield and her brood."

"Three of them, and lively and pert as you please," Bitsy said. "Hattie — although she's married now — and Hannah and Chub. And since then there's been Beecher and Edith. They're Billings. Isn't that Hannah a beauty? Wish I had her eyes. They look like prairie violets."

"Silas Locklin's been making sheep's eyes

at her ever since he came here," Vange put in. "Well, we're about packed. Did you put in that jug of fresh dills, Ma?"

"You know I wouldn't forget, Vange," Aunt Purdy snorted. "Better get your bonnet, Barbara. Pa's got the wagon and team out front."

"And for heaven's sake, Barb, take off those hoops! A picnic's no place for them!" Vange snorted.

Minutes later the family had scrambled onto the wagon and stashed away the picnic basket between Uncle Daniel's and Aunt Prudy's legs. With a shriek of wheels flying down the dusty lane, they were off. Barbara sat sedately on the straw-filled floor of the wagon, her skirts spread out carefully. She hated to go without her hoops, but maybe no one here cared what she wore. The three cousins squatted flat, curling their bare legs under piles of straw, their laughter spilling over the sides of the wagon. Josh had ridden his horse Petunia on ahead.

Wagons jolted and jounced down the river road, sending up skiffs of dust along the well-worn trail that curved along the Cottonwood to the secluded glen, between a horseshoe bend, to the Billings' cabin.

Shortly a grove of trees burst into view and soon Uncle Daniel slowed the team.

The two-story cabin appeared just beyond the trees. It was about 24 by 12 feet and faced west. Cottonwoods and walnut trees spread welcome morning shade to the south.

As soon as the wagon stopped, Bitsy and Vange jumped out. Together they grabbed the basket and lunged toward the tables set up under the shade trees. Barbara waited until Uncle Daniel had helped her down. Then she smoothed her rumpled skirt and paused near the wagon.

"Come on, Barbara," Aggie yelled, grabbing her arm. "Join the crowd."

The hustle and bustle continued as the grove swarmed with people carrying food and stopping to greet one another. It reminded Barbara of a country fair in Georgia. All that was missing were the wares and produce and the music.

Minutes later Vange and Bitsy were back. "You should see all that food!" Vange bubbled. "Roast venison, baked sweet potatoes in molasses, chicken dumplings, ears and ears of sweet corn, rabbit stew, corn meal mush, Aggie's dried apple pies, Mindy Reeves' squirrel casserole —"

"Squirrel!" Barbara shrieked. "Never, never, never!"

Bitsy laughed. "Oh, you'd never guess.

Josh caught her skinning a squirrel yesterday. She probably brought what she had. Oh, well. It won't hurt Vange to eat it. They say Mindy's soap is better than her food. I'd rather eat it any day than her cakes and pies."

Barbara grimaced. Was Bitsy serious? Trouble with her cousins was, you never knew.

"Who cares?" Vange shrugged, pushing her way through the crowd. "Better squirrel than dog. That's an Indian favorite."

Nausea stirred Barbara's stomach at the thought as she followed her cousins toward the tables.

Uncle Daniel beckoned her from the fringe of the crowd, and she made her way through clusters of chattering women and clean, chin-stroking men.

"Over here, Barbara," Uncle Daniel called. Then he shoved a tall, thin, black-bearded man toward her. "Barbara, I want you to meet Abraham Atlantic Moore. Lank is our cousin — your mother's and mine. Lank, meet Candace's child."

Lank picked up Barbara's white hand and lifted it gently to his lips. "So you're Barbara. You're as pretty as your mother. I'm so sorry to hear you've been orphaned."

Tears cut shiny paths down her cheeks,

and she wiped them away with a lace-trimmed handkerchief. "Oh, if only Mother hadn't left me! My life's all topsy-turvy, and sometimes I think it will never turn right-side-up again."

"It will. You must come out to my ranch at Cottonwood Crossing some time," he said in a consoling voice. "We'll help you forget some of your sorrows. Wait 'til you see our large herds of cattle and horses."

"The ranch is only some 15 or 20 miles to the northwest," Uncle Daniel added. "I believe everyone within miles is here today. You've brought your cowboys, too?"

"All I could spare. Some had to stay to keep an eye for Indians. Yes, Barbara, we must get together again."

At that moment Vange broke through the crowd and waved at her. "Over here, Barb. Come with us. It's practically time to stuff ourselves with our famous prairie grub." With a hasty backward glance at Lank and Uncle Daniel, Barbara followed her cousin toward the well-ladened tables.

A tall, broad-shouldered bosomy woman wearing a long, full white apron over her gray percale rushed around, giving orders.

"That's Aunt Kizzie," Bitsy pointed out, "Making sure everyone knows what to do."

"Aunt Kizzie?"

"Keziah Billings. Everyone calls her Kizzie. She used to be Keziah Butterfield, remember? She's the one who married William Billings after her husband died. They live on the floor above the store and post office."

Bitsy steered her toward a plump, regal-looking woman dressed in a blue-and-red skirted print with a tight-fitted basque. She wore her bright hair coiled like a crown on her shapely head. "Mrs. Shreve," Bitsy called out, "our cousin Barbara Temple is eager to meet you!"

Barbara hesitated. Meeting the Quaker woman Charity Shreve wasn't her idea. But her cousins seemed to think she would appreciate someone with class, and Charity was known as "Queen Victoria," wasn't she?

Charity curtsied lightly and beamed as she clasped Barbara's hand in her cool one. "Welcome to Marion Centre. It's good thee came, Barbara," she said in a low voice. "We need more young folks. The more the merrier, as the saying goes. We hope thee will like us well enough to stay for a long, long while."

"Only until the war . . . is over," Barbara gulped, "and I can go back to Georgia to get married."

"Of course," Charity Shreve said graciously. "Meanwhile, do feel at home." She paused, looking toward the tables. "Oh, my, I do believe we're ready to eat. William is ready to ask the blessing."

As the murmur of voices died, brawny, broad-shouldered William Billings bowed his shaggy head and implored the Almighty to bless the nation on this great day of celebrating its freedom and to guide the settlers from this day forward, especially as they joined to spend the day.

Barbara made her way back to Vange and Bitsy as soon as his "Amen" sounded and the stir and bustle began again. The girls took their turn with a group of young people waiting to heap their plates with foods from the long tables. A comely young woman stood beside the food with a willow switch, swishing at flies that buzzed over the sweet potato pots and Aggie's dried apple pies.

"There's Hannah Butterfield," Vange whispered. "Isn't she gorgeous? Silas Locklin's been mooning over her ever since he got here. I think they may be fixin' to get married. You'll like Hannah."

Barbara looked at the pretty girl with the dimpled chin and round, pink cheeks. Her long golden blond hair was tied back with a bit of red ribbon. Vange was right. Her eyes were lovely violet-blue with fringed black lashes.

"Who's Silas?" Barbara wondered out loud.

"Silas? Don't you know? He's an Indian scout. Swashbuckling and dashing. You can't miss him He's got reddish sandy hair *and a mustache.* Do you like a mustache on a man? Well, I'd rather see Charlie here," Bitsy added with a wry grin. "Charlie and his dark curly hair!"

The line had thinned, and the girls began to pile their plates with food. Barbara had to admit the dishes looked tasty. She avoided what looked like squirrel.

After filling their plates, Vange and Bitsy made their way to a group of young people who were seated on blankets spread out in the shade and motioned Barbara to follow. Vange, who sat down on a log beside several young folks, clapped her hands for attention.

"Look, everybody!" she sang out between bites of buffalo and cornbread. "Meet our cousin, Barbara Temple. Barbara, meet Mollie Griffith, Rebecca Shreve, Hannah — and that's Silas next to Hannah — Ed Griffith, Jack Griffith, Elisha Shreve, . . . Oh, and I see Charlie made it. Hello, Charlie. It's time you left Bo to the ewes to fend for themselves."

A young man with deep blue eyes and dark curls that tumbled over his broad forehead, jumped to his feet and reached for Barbara's hand.

"Pleased to meet you, Ma'am," he said, his face crinkling into a broad smile. "I live on the other side of the Cottonwood along the branch creek. And if you'll 'low me to, I'll be happy to escort you for a good look at our prairie moon some night."

Barbara jerked her hand away, her face burning. "I don't need anyone to show me a prairie moon or a prairie anything," she flared.

She pulled herself away and half-hid behind Bitsy. As she ate she paid no attention to the lively chatter and laughter around her. How dared he? How dared this crude Charlie-person suggest anything so brash? If this was the kind of settlers Marion Centre boasted of, it was the last place she should've come. Except there was no other place to go.

Couples sauntered back to the tables for seconds, but Barbara stuck at Bitsy's side like a burr on Woodson.

When the conversation turned to the first arriving settlers, Barbara found herself listening with interest.

"Five covered wagons left Indiana in May

of '60," Molly was telling a young man who had come late. "When we arrived here, the wagons pulled to a stop at the crest of the bluff up there. We looked down and saw the Cottonwood River winding slightly to the south and east, and below was the valley. Here's where we would stay. My father was the first to file for a homestead."

"Five wagons!" Edward Miller burst out. "How many folks were you?"

"Twenty-three. We camped in this grove until we built cabins."

"Wasn't it awfully lonely?" Josh asked.

Hannah Butterfield laughed, and her voice sounded like bells. "Lonely! We were much too busy those first months chopping down trees and building our cabins. Unless you count window-peeking Indians and buffalo and deer."

"There was always something. And the prairie fire that fall almost drove us back east," Silas put in, slipping an arm around Hannah's slender waist.

"The snows were deep and the winds fierce that first winter," Molly Griffith added. "And the food. All we had to eat was boiled wheat, hominy and cornmeal. And look all the food we have today!"

Rebecca Shreve shuddered. "Yes, remember when we ran out of food and Tom

Wise and his father from Lost Springs drove all the way to Atchison to buy something to eat? What he brought back wasn't fit for a dog. Tough, leathery bacon, wormy beans and musty cornmeal full of moldy lumps. Ugh!"

"But, we've come a long way. Buffalos thundered across the prairie by the thousands," Silas Locklin chuckled, and his sandy mustache wiggled. "We shot 'em from our windows. The Kaws followed them critters clear across to Western Kansas just to get food."

Barbara listened quietly. Come a long way? It was unbelievable. How could people live like this? And to think she had come to this land which would probably never be civilized. If there were only some way she could get away quietly. But there wasn't. She was trapped until the war was over and she knew it.

Already afternoon shadows lengthened across the grove and sunlight needled through the hissing leaves in golden patches.

The sudden rattle of an empty pie tin from the cabin area attracted the attention of the young people.

"Come on! Let's sing," Aunt Kizzie shouted in her strident soprano. "Let's gather 'round and cheer up. We've hashed through enough of our past troubles."

"Yes, we've got better things to do than live through that awful first year again," George Griffith mumbled. He jumped up and began to wave his arms. "What shall we sing first?"

" 'Shall We Gather at the River'," someone yelled.

After a low pitch, George led out. Soon hymn after hymn rang through the quiet, shade-drenched grove. When no one could think of another hymn, folksongs and ballads brought young people to their feet. Someone had swept the ground free of twigs and they joined in swaying to the lively folk dances. There were no instruments. Clapping and singing and whistling were the only accompaniment, except for an occasional creaky cricket somewhere in the brush. Barbara began to clap her hands and sing along.

"Come on," Elisha Shreve shouted, "How about 'The Miller Boy'? All you young folks form two circles — boys outside and girls inside."

Vange jumped up and pulled Barbara to her feet. "Here, Barb. Let's move. You're going to be stiff if you squat all day."

"But I —"

"No argument. Here, join hands!" She jerked Barbara into the inner circle. Already the young men were moving rhythmically around the outer rim, facing the girls. The singing began again.

> "Jolly is the miller's boy who lives by
> the mill;
> The wheels go 'round with a right good
> will.
> One hand in the hopper and the other
> in the sack . . ."

The circle swung in opposite directions.

> ". . . ladies step forward and gents step
> back."

Barbara fumbled forward, then back, her heart pounding and her head reeling. To her dismay she was paired off with Charlie Warren. He grinned at her and swung her around gently, his dark curls tumbling over his forehead and his deep blue eyes twinkling. She stiffened and backed away. I hate him, she told herself fiercely. I don't know why, but I can't stand this brash young sheep man.

She whirled around and rushed from the circle, running wildly among the trees. If only she could escape. She heard footsteps behind her. How dare he follow her!

"What's wrong, Barb?" Vange spoke softly beside her. "I thought you were having a good time. Back there you actually seemed to have fun."

"I was . . . I did," Barbara stumbled. "Until that . . . that *sheepman* spoiled it!"

Vange's blue eyes widened in surprise. "So that's it! Well, you're the first girl he's paid any attention to since he came. All I can say is, Matthew Potter had better watch out!"

"Oh . . . you!" Barbara sputtered as she spun around and struck Vange's face sharply. Then she hurriedly fled from the grove.

CHAPTER 5

Barbara was silent on the ride home from the picnic. The sun had already dipped below the horizon and the red glow faded from deep orange to pink. A deep quiet seemed to pervade the evening and the prairie became pregnant with the sound of crickets chirping, owls hooting and sheep blatting from the draw. As the wagon creaked with a tired rumble down the lane, the three usually lively cousins were strangely still.

Vange gazed dreamily across the prairie, her arms hugging her knees over her ballooning skirt, and Barbara felt a guilty twinge. She leaned toward her cousin and whispered,

"I . . . I'm sorry, Vange. I shouldn't have slapped you."

"And I shouldn't have said what I did," Vange responded quickly. "God forgive me. It was just what Charlie did was so out of character . . . for Charlie."

When the team pulled up in front of the cabin everyone scrambled out. Josh had already gone ahead and stabled the two cows for milking. Bitsy and Vange changed into everyday chambray, grabbed milk pails and went toward the barn while Aggie took the tin bucket and headed for the henhouse. Barbara followed Aunt Prudy into the kitchen. Aimlessly she helped her aunt unpack the picnic basket.

"We'll wash up the dishes in the morning," Aunt Prudy said, lighting the lamp against the growing dusk.

"Maybe I can help," Barbara offered lamely.

"Don't feel you have to, although you might give a hand now and then. How did you enjoy the day?"

For a moment Barbara didn't answer. Then she sighed. "Oh, it was all right, I guess. But I'm not used to this kind of thing. Why, everyone mingled. In Georgia there would've been . . . cliques."

"I suppose so. Here we're all in the same situation. All of us try to wrest our living from this raw, new country." Aunt Prudy pattered to the lean-to and soon Barbara heard her slamming around with milk pails.

Barbara slipped up the loft and undressed for bed. She was tired, for it had been a long, wearying day. The settlers had accepted her as though she belonged, as though she was a part of the settler crowd. Still, their aims were different, as well as their politics, and she could never quite belong. Yet for Uncle Daniel's sake she must accept this as a part of her life for as long as she remained in Kansas. He'd obviously been happy to introduce her to this tall rancher-cousin with the black beard.

As she lay down on the crackling straw mattress she closed her eyes. In the distance she heard the howl of a coyote and an answering yelp from the draw. Would she ever learn to accept wild animal sounds as a part of this new land? Yawning, she turned over on her side. Drowsiness soon overtook her and she was hardly aware of the three girls laughing and chattering on their way to bed.

Sunlight streamed through the tiny east window in squares of yellow light on the bare floor when she awoke the next morning. The beds were empty, Aggie's and Bitsy's neatly made, with the gay patchwork quilt tucked pertly around the edges of the mattress.

Barbara yawned, pulled on her blue-and-white gingham and scrambled down the ladder. The family had already eaten breakfast and Bitsy was clearing the table. Aggie was lugging water from the spring to fill the huge iron kettle that squatted under a cottonwood tree, a brisk fire snapping under its three solid legs.

"It's wash day," Vange told Barbara as

she sorted soiled laundry on the kitchen floor. "Got anything that needs scrubbing? Bring it now or forever hold your peace!"

Barbara nodded. Her green-sprigged delaine was dirty from yesterday's picnic, and an array of dresses and pantaloons she had worn on the long trip needed washing. She brought down her pile of dirty clothes from the loft and watched as Vange and Aggie set wooden tubs and washboards on sawed-off tree trunks under the trees. Gulping down a piece of bread and butter, Barbara shooed Bitsy away from the dishpan.

"Let me wash these," she said. "Maybe you have other jobs."

"Oh, Barbie, you're such a dear," Bitsy said, giving her a gentle hug. "It's my job to hang up the clothes to dry. I'd drape the bushes clear across the Cottonwood — if I thought Charlie would notice."

"Don't you dare let him see my pantaloons!" Barbara shrieked, and Bitsy hooted with laughter.

"Never fear. Ma would never allow us to parade our undergarments for anyone to see. Well, happy dishwashing," Bitsy sang and flounced out of the house.

After Barbara had finished, she hung up the damp tea towels over the backs of the barrel chairs as she had seen her cousins do. Then she grabbed her straw bonnet and slammed out the back door.

The strong, clean smell of suds and lye soap seemed to fill the outdoors. Vange and Aggie bent over the washboards, rubbing sheets and underwear and Uncle Daniel's white shirts, while Aunt Prudy wrung out the clean clothes from the rinse tub and plunged them into the starch basin. Then she dropped them into a wicker basket. It seemed strange to see the cousins handle the back-breaking laundry that Louisy and Pansy had always managed at the plantation.

I wonder where our darkies have gone, Barbara thought. True, Louisy had stayed with them in the small house in Atlanta for as long as Barbara's mother was alive, but in order to pay for her mother's burial Barbara had been forced to sell the scrappy black woman. It had been painful, and her heart lurched, remembering Louisy's wail as she rumbled away in the slave trader's buckboard. If only Uncle Daniel's family understood. *We took care of all those people,* she thought. *We cared for their children and their grandchildren. We were responsible for them.*

The morning was bright and calm, and Barbara followed the footpath that led

83

toward the river. She had never walked this far alone before, but she needed a quiet place to sort her thoughts. Ahead lay the magnificent stretch of sky and earth with only a few white clouds overhead, deepening to a dull gray in the southwest.

The water formed a quiet little pool where the river backed up around a triangle of logs and several large, moss shouldered rocks. Barbara sat down on a log under a tall wide-branched cottonwood and smoothed her checkered skirt over her knees. She watched as water striders skated back and forth over the water and raced away in jerky panic. Sunlight made warm freckles of light everywhere, slanting down through the trees.

The peace of the quiet, lapping river seeped into her troubled spirit as she let her thoughts roam. When the war was over, Matthew would come back to Atlanta and work for his uncle. He would send money for her to come back and they would get married.

"I won't be able to afford a plantation house," he had written her before she left, "but my mother's house will be our home. It's comfortable and roomy. Maybe we'll have at least one darky to take care of the work."

She recalled Widow Potter's modest clap-board house behind the white picket fence under the elms. She would sit in the summer house and crochet doilies for the highly polished parlor tables. Perhaps she and Matthew would join other young couples on walks through the parks on Sunday afternoon, or listen to violin concerts — if the opera house wasn't too badly shelled.

Her brow furrowed. War was hell, and the merciless Yankees would have no qualms about setting fire to Atlanta's finest homes — if they came. Still, going back to a city blackened by smoke and gray with ashes would outweigh living on this lonely, end-less windy prairie. At least so far Atlanta was safe.

A faint rustle behind her startled her and her hand flew to her throat. Cousin Josh had warned her that Indians crept along the streams to fish. Perhaps if she were very still, she wouldn't be discovered.

The sound of approaching footsteps along the brush by the river was unmistak-able, and just as Barbara was ready to slip behind a nearby blackberry bramble, she heard a young voice sing out shrilly:

"Here we go looby-loo, here we go
    looby-lee,

Here we go looby-loo, all on a Saturday
    ni—

"Hey, what're you doin' here, pretty lady?
Sorry I startled you."

A boy of about 10 or 11 stepped in front
of her. His tousled, fawn-colored hair tumbled over a pair of blue eyes and freckle-
spattered cheeks. *Whatley!* Barbara's eyes
widened. Of course, it wasn't her brother,
but he reminded her so very much of him.

Jerking at his dun-colored trousers he
grinned at her. "Dont'cha know it's dangerous sittin' out here like that?"

"You mean . . . Indians?" she faltered.

He laughed, his voice musical. "Well, I
wasn't thinkin' of Kaws exactly, although
they wouldn't be past snoopin' around
these parts, ya know. I was thinkin' more
about rattlesnakes."

"Rattlesnakes?" Barbara sputtered. "No
one's mentioned —"

"Prairie rattlers. They'll warn ya before
they strike. You can't miss their whirrin'
noise," he said, rolling his r's. "But when
they do, well, . . . the poison can kill you
quicker'n' you can blink your eyes. Just be
careful you don't step on any big clods. You
never know when you'll disturb a rattler
sunnin' hisself."

Barbara sucked in her breath sharply. "What else," she began icily, "have these implacable settlers forgotten to warn me about?"

"Ya mean . . . like prairie fires? Of course, we're all most careful."

"Well, what about prairie fires?"

The boy squatted on his haunches and picked up a blade of grass and chewed for a long minute before answering.

"When a prairie fire starts, it stops for nothin'. It sweeps over the grass and gobbles up everythin' in its path. It won't stop for no cabin. Everythin' goes. When you see great black clouds rollin' across the prairie, look out."

"But . . . but . . ."

"Oh, we fight 'em, if we see them comin'. First we fill tubs with water and toss in all the gunny sacks we can find, soak 'em and start the backfires by settin' fire to the ground by us and plow a coupla rows of furrows around a cabin. Prairie hens and rabbits and snakes all rush out of the way, and we beat at the flames with the wet sacks to keep the fire away from our cabins. The fire can't cross the furrows and the little backfires crawl real slow to meet the racin' big fire. Then the big fire roars past and the cabin's safe. We're all most careful and it's happened only once since we came."

Barbara moistened her lips. "What . . . what happens to the prairie after it's all burnt? Do you pack up and go back to civilization?"

He laughed. "Oh, my no. The fire don't hurt the grass roots. When it rains, the grass soon grows again. We'll always have our prairie until all the sod is turned and crops come up."

Barbara was silent for a few seconds. She tried to wipe out the memory of the fire that gutted the plantation only a year earlier — the fire believed to have been set by Northern sympathizers. Then she asked, "How long have you lived here?" Her interest in the keen-eyed boy was growing. He reminded her so much of her brother who died when he was almost 10. Perhaps that's what had drawn her to him.

"We came about a year and a half ago."

"We?"

"My brother Charlie and me. We —"

"Charlie!" Barbara spat out the name. "You . . . you're that sheepman's . . . that Charlie's brother?"

"Sure. My name's Willie. What's yours?"

She frowned and hesitated. "Barbara Temple." Pointing toward the cluster of log buildings to the east, she went on, "I . . . I'm staying with my Uncle Daniel Moore's family until the war is over. Then I'm going back to Georgia." Her brow furrowed. Let Charlie know she wasn't going to be around long.

"Oh." The merry face clouded. "Well, I'll sure hate to see ya leave then, Barbara Temple. I thought maybe you'd like our prairie country and stay."

"No!" She shook her head staunchly. "If I had any other place to go. . . . But when the war's over I'll go back and marry Matthew Potter."

Again he nodded his tousled head. "I see. Maybe goin' back is all right for you, but not for us."

"Why'd you and your brother come here? Why didn't you stay wherever you came from? You'd have been better off —"

Willie laughed again. "What else could we do? My folks, my sister Nellie May and Charlie and me, . . . we sold our land in Illinois and started for Kansas in our covered wagon. When we reached the Missouri, Indians attacked and killed Pa and Ma and Nellie May. There was nothin' else left for Charlie and me to do. We couldn't go back, so we decided to settle on Pa's claim. We live right across the branch crick in that cabin you can see through the trees in that little glen."

"I'm not sure I want to look."

"Well," he paused awkwardly, "I take it you don't like my brother Charlie much?" His gaze was direct and serious.

She gave her brown head a toss. "Let's say we didn't hit it off when we met yesterday. But you . . . you're not like him, Whatley . . . Willie."

He stared at her with his deep blue eyes, and Barbara looked away. Puffs of cloud shadows made patterns of light and shade on the prairie field to the east, and she sighed. He squirmed and got to his feet.

"Oh, Charlie's all right. But you'll talk to me?" he asked eagerly, breaking into her bleak mood. "Even if ya don't like my big brother for some dumb reason?"

This time it was Barbara's turn to laugh. She jammed her bonnet back on her dark head and scrambled to her feet.

"There's nothing I'd like better, Willie," she said, shaking out her full skirt. "I think you're the one friend I've found in Kansas. You know, you remind me of my brother Whatley. And thanks for the education. At least, someone's not afraid to tell me about prairie fires and rattlesnakes!"

She whirled around and fled from the shade-dappled river and up the path that led toward the log cabin. Willie Warren was like one ray of sunshine on the bleak, lonely prairie. It was as though part of her family had come too.

CHAPTER 6

One August morning as Barbara climbed from the loft, she sniffed the air. A peculiar odor drifted through the open windows and she looked out.

Aunt Prudy, her slight form bent over the big iron cauldron under the trees, was stirring something with a heavy wooden paddle. Her huge gray apron covered her drab, dark blue percale, and her grayish hair blew in tangled strands from the loosened bun in the ever-present wind.

Vange and Bitsy swung up from the river path, carrying armloads of dried wood. They were laughing and chattering as usual.

"You could just see that smoke curl up from his cabin," Vange chirked, laying down her arm load beside the large kettle.

"And smell biscuits scorching," Bitsy sniffed. "I tell you, that Charlie Warren needs a wife so bad." She paused and shoved a few pieces of firewood under the kettle into the brisk, snapping fire.

"Not so much wood, Bitsy," Aunt Prudy warned. "We don't want it to boil over."

Barbara hurried outdoors. What in the world were they cooking now? Mammy

Louisy and the other slave women sometimes simmered big batches of stew in large
open kettles outdoors, but this didn't smell
at all like meat and vegetables.

She peered timidly over the black iron
rim. "What are you cooking? It smells horrible!"

Vange and Bitsy glanced at each other
and burst out laughing. "You'll never believe this, Barb," Vange said, "but we're
making coyote stew. Josh killed a coyote —"

"Coyote stew!" Barbara shrieked as she
drew back. "You mean, you really —"

"Girls!" Aunt Prudy frowned. "Please
don't scare Barbara out of her wits. She's
had enough to trouble her, since coming to
this prairie country."

Bitsy gave her head a sad little shake.
"Sorry to bewilder you, Cousin. Actually,
it's Indian gumbo. You know, bits of dog
meat, a handful of wild onions, and a turkey
feather or two . . ."

"Bitsy!" Aunt Prudy's voice was stern.
"That's enough." She turned to Barbara
with a slow smile. "You must learn not to
believe everything these girls tell you. But
you asked what this is. Well, we're making
soap. We save dabs of bacon fryin's and
whatever tallow we can spare and add lye
sifted from wood ashes. After it's cooked,

we pour it into pans and cut it into bars. It takes a good bit of soap to scrub the sod and grime from this family's clothes, you know."

Barbara nodded. She had vague memories of the darky women making the plantation soap supply, but she had never watched.

"One more pile of wood, and you can stop, girls," Aunt Prudy addressed the two gigglers as she kept stirring the foamy liquid. "Then join Aggie in the cornfield grubbing cockleburrs. Can't let them pesky weeds get ahead of us." Turning to Barbara, she asked, "Have you heard from Matthew lately?"

"No." Barbara shook her head. "Maybe next time the mail comes to town —"

"Why don't you saddle up Petunia and ride to the post office? I heard Silas was in Council Grove yesterday and may have brought some letters for us."

"Thank you, Aunt Prudy. I'll do that."

Barbara went indoors for her straw bonnet and hurried to the corral to saddle the horse. She had learned to ride as a child, for her father had kept a stable full of horses. *At least I'll make myself useful by getting the mail,* she thought. Life was dull and boring without anything to do. If only she'd have a letter from Matthew. She hadn't heard from him since coming to Kansas, and she was uneasy.

Minutes later, she galloped down the short lane to the narrow rutted road beyond. To the north prairie a faint trail marked the grass with blue lupines and wild mustard broken by wide-rimmed wagon wheels and hoof prints. She knew John and Rosie Frazer lived a mile up this trail, for she had visited their tiny cabin several times. Along the well-marked trail that led into town, the grasses blazed with wild columbine, their scarlet flowers cupping faces to the sun. Already some vegetation had turned stiff and hard, for the hot dry days of summer were waning.

A warm breeze fanned her face and she pushed back her straw bonnet. The day would probably be hot again, and she rode faster, eager to reach the cool grove of trees near the Billings cabin.

Just as she pulled up before the front door, Aunt Keziah stepped from the doorway and shook out the red-checkered tablecloth.

"Mornin', Barbara," she called out cheerfully. "Comin' after the mail?"

Barbara slid down from the horse and tied it to a hitching post. "I wondered if there was a letter from Matthew."

"We'll see. Come on in."

As she followed the tall, plump aproned figure into the store-post office, Barbara sniffed the stale smell of morning coffee and dried bean pods from overhead rafters.

"Let's check the mail right away." Keziah bustled behind the counter and brought out the mail pouch. She thumbed through the small stack of letters briskly, then shook her head.

"Sorry, Barbara. There's no mail for you, but here's a letter for the Moores. You can take it when you ride back."

With a disappointed nod, Barbara took the letter and started for the door. "Might as well go back. I'd so hoped —"

"No letter from Matthew Potter?" Hannah asked, coming in from the side door. "I'm so sorry."

Barbara nodded awkwardly. "So am I. Well . . . I guess I might as well go —"

"Why not stay awhile?" Hannah said, laying a hand on Barbara's arm. "We can visit while you're here."

"But . . . you're not too busy?"

Hannah laughed. "Not really. Rebecca Shreve and I were just piecing quilts. We can do that any day."

"We can do what any day?" Rebecca said,

appearing suddenly from the loft. "If you want to fill your chest with proper linens, Hannah, you'd better work fast. When Silas proposes marriage you'll feel terrible, not having your dowry ready."

"Oh, pshaw, Rebecca! Silas hasn't asked me yet."

Barbara took off her straw bonnet and hung it on a nail near the door. She noticed Hannah's blush on the creamy white cheeks, and looked away. How lucky for Hannah to have her admirer where she could see him almost every day.

"Come on, Barbara. Let's climb up the loft and I'll show you the quilt we're piecing now," Hannah said, starting toward the ladder.

The sudden clatter of horse hooves interrupted them and Hannah paused. Silas Locklin burst through the doorway, his ruddy face and pale mustache beaded with sweat.

"Now, Miz Billin's," he drawled as he swung around to greet Keziah, "Don't you be a-frettin', but I've been with the Kaws a-plenty, you know. They . . . they're comin' up the trail right now for a social call." He pushed back his gray felt hat and wiped his brow with the back of his left hand.

"A visit . . . here?" Hannah's hands flew to

her thick blond braids and she pinned them snugly to her head. Then she grabbed the gray sunbonnet from its nail and jammed it over her head. "*Here* . . . Silas?"

Barbara cowered beside her. Then she found her voice. "I . . . I'd better hurry on home," she said raggedly, reaching quickly for her straw bonnet.

"Don't go." Silas raised his hand. "There isn't time. Just stay here and you'll be fine. I promise."

She moistened her dry lips and looked at Keziah Billings. The woman's florid face betrayed no emotion, but Barbara noticed her hands fumbling nervously under the commodious apron. Hannah and Rebecca stood beside Barbara like a pair of frightened rabbits.

"Now, now," Silas went on placatingly. "I know Indians, be-gol, and these Kaws just want to see how white folks live. Just treat 'em nice and polite and you'll do fine. Don't let on you're scared."

The three girls, cowering along the east wall of the cabin, stared fascinated at the approaching Kaw entourage. The Indians marched single file into the cabin — 13 squaws and two chiefs — silent and stolid. Barbara's mouth grew dry again. She fumbled for Rebecca's hand and gripped it tightly. Hannah's hand shook as she grasped Barbara's right shoulder.

The Indians walked around the room, murmuring in low, gutteral voices. "Come see um. Come see um."

Barbara stood petrified. *Indians! In the Billings' cabin!* She couldn't believe it. There they stood, only a few feet away, gaping awe-struck at everything in the large room.

Silas bowed, then motioned cautiously to Keziah. "Now, be-gol, be on your toes, every one of you," he whispered from the side of his mouth.

"Be-gol, we will," Keziah mumbled. She beamed at her uninvited guests and pointed to the few chairs that stood about the room. "Won't you . . . please sit down?"

The squaws scrambled for the chairs, and one squatted on the floor with great aplomb. As she did so, her filthy deerskin shift slid up above plump knees. While Indian women pointed and muttered among themselves, Silas listened for a minute, then turned to Keziah.

"They want to see your things. Why not show them your quilts and quilt blocks?"

"Of course." Keziah beamed again, bowed slightly and climbed nimbly up the ladder to the loft. Barbara, still frozen, watched with eyes that refused to focus. All she could see was the cabin full of Indians. That the chiefs wore no war paint barely seeped into her befuddled mind. Matthew would never believe this. No one would.

Minutes dragged by. The two chiefs stood silent, arms folded across their chests. The Kaw women's moccasin-clad feet shuffled impatiently. They uttered unintelligible words in low tones that sent chills down Barbara's spine. She felt Rebecca stiffen beside her and she gulped. Silas leaned nonchalantly against the counter. How could he be so calm and cool?

Just then Keziah popped from the opening above, her full skirts billowing. In her arms she carried a colorful pile of materials — several pieced quilts and some quilt blocks already stitched neatly by hand in scraps of pink and blue, purple and red, ready to be sewn together. She tossed them on the counter, hesitated, and handed a block to each squaw. The women held them up and scrutinized both sides, grunting as they saw the neat seams on the backs of the blocks.

A quiet murmur filled the room as they nodded. One said, "White squaw nice make."

Barbara threw a frightened glance at

Hannah, whose hand had loosed from her shoulder. She seemed to have grown quiet and relaxed. Maybe Silas was right. Maybe all they wanted was to see "white squaw things."

She caught Keziah's glance directed at her and moved forward slightly. "You . . . want me, Aunt Kizzie?" she asked, her voice still quivering with fear.

"Yes, girls. Let's serve our guests. This is a social call, remember? Barbara, you help me fix coffee while Hannah and Rebecca get out the batch of molasses cookies I baked yesterday. They're in the stone crock in the lean-to."

Barbara followed Keziah to the lean-to and took the can of coffee the older woman handed to her. By now the panic had drained from her, leaving her weak and palpable.

"Better scrounge up all the tin cups you can find. We may have to take a few from the store shelves," Keziah said. "And get out the sugar bowl and cream pitcher from the corner cupboard. We must be proper hostesses."

Keziah returned to the fireplace and stirred the ashes, then filled the copper kettle with water from the dipper in the pail that stood on one end of the counter.

Barbara watched as she measured out the coffee and hung the kettle over the fire. The squaws eyed her curiously.

Before long the aroma of boiling coffee drifted through the cabin, and the women sniffed hungrily. Barbara and Rebecca picked up the cups and handed one to each Indian. As Keziah poured coffee into the cups, Barbara followed with cream and sugar. She winced at the thought of using the delicate china creamer and sugar bowl. Most of the women gleefully dumped sugar into their steaming cups, but when she offered cream, they shook their heads.

"No cow."

As Hannah came with the plates of molasses cookies, each squaw snitched two or three and nibbled almost daintily.

After a few minutes the women got up and nodded with wide-toothed grins. One shriveled little gnomelike squaw scudded up to Barbara and patted her brown head.

"Nice squaw?" she grunted, and the squaws beside her nodded and beamed. "White Turkey maybe like."

Horrified, Barbara shrank back. To think one of the filthy squaws had dared touch her hair.

As they started for the door, each squaw held up her left hand to Keziah, counted the fingers, then with the right hand raised, grunted, "Umph-umph," and added, "Come see um, come see um."

Silas turned to Keziah with a slight jerk of his head. "This means you're expected to return the call in five days."

Keziah bowed and nodded. "Yes. We will come see you."

The girls watched silently as the Kaw delegation plodded single file down the path until they vanished among the trees. Then they looked at each other in relief and sighed in unison. Hannah jerked off her sunbonnet and unpinned her braids.

With a mocking grin, Silas Locklin moved away from the counter where he had been leaning during the entire scenario just enacted before their eyes.

"Miz Billin's," he drawled with an amused smile, "you promised to visit them. Be sure you do, on the fifth day, be-gol, or you may be sorry." With a tender glance at Hannah, he swung around and stalked out the door.

For a long minute Barbara stared at the trail down which the Indians had gone. When she was sure they were far enough away, she turned to the three women who were talking in low voices as they refolded the bright quilts and counted quilt blocks.

"Well, I guess . . . I'd better go home," Barbara said. "This . . . this has been some morning, hasn't it?"

Keziah smiled impishly. "That it has, Barbara. Good thing Beecher and Edith were playing at Griffiths' today. I don't know how they would've taken all this, but the nightmare isn't over. In five days we must return their visit as we promised . . . if Silas goes with us, of course. You'll join us, Barbara, won't you?"

"Oh, no!" Barbara drew back. "Not me. Why, did you see how that one squaw patted my head? I thought I'd die. Never in a thousand years will I visit a dirty Indian tepee!"

With a quick goodbye wave over her shoulder, she picked up her straw bonnet and hurried out for her brief ride to Uncle Daniel's farm. In a daze she let Petunia's reins hang slack. *Will I ever get over feeling scared and intimidated by the wide open prairie?* she wondered.

When she rushed into the Moore cabin to tell the family, Uncle Daniel was seated at the table, his face solemn, and his deep blue eyes somber with that faraway look. The family stood around him, intent on his words.

"Word just came by stage to Council

Grove. Quantrill has sacked Lawrence."

"Sacked Lawrence?" Aggie echoed, her plain features aghast with horror. "What do you mean, Pa?"

"He and his guerrillas staged a dawn terrorist raid as they stormed into the town a few days ago. They killed over 150 people, including women and children, and burned the town."

"Oh, no!" Aunt Prudy drew back in horror.

"Who's Quantrill?" Bitsy asked, stooping over and leaning her elbows on the table.

"Don't you know?" Josh said harshly. "William Clarke Quantrill's an outlaw, serving with the Confederate army."

"But why?" Vange cried. "Why would he do such a horrible thing?"

Uncle Daniel shrugged his shoulders. "God only knows. He claims he got the message from Confederate leaders in Virginia that Kansas should be laid waste. So he starts with Lawrence, the hotbed for abolitionists. It's a Unionist town, you know. Now it's nothing but a pile of smoking rubble. This act was sheer barbarism."

Barbara's face grew white. She couldn't believe her ears. Surely, Confederates wouldn't allow anything so cruel! Without a word, she turned and fled from the cabin and sped down the path that led to the river. She began to sob uncontrollably as she flung herself on the ground by her favorite log. She didn't hear Willie until he spoke.

"Now, what's all this about, Barbara?" he said gently. "Somethin' awful must' a happened for you to bawl like that. Whatever it is, I'm sure it's gonna be all right."

Barbara's weeping ceased, and she lifted her tear-wet face. "Oh, Willie," she cried, "is it true . . . about Quantrill . . . and the . . . the raid of Lawrence?"

"I guess it is. But why should it hit you so hard? Lawrence is more'n a hundred miles away —"

"Uncle Daniel said . . . he said Quantrill was a Confederate, on orders from his leaders in the East to wreck Kansas. I . . . oh, it's so awful."

"Aw, Barbara, even General Lee and Stonewall Jackson wouldn't have any truck with the likes of William Quantrill. Charlie says his raiders was Confederate *irregulars* that don't fight fair. Don't you know that?" Willie burst out. "Quantrill's out to get Kansas because he got outlawed from the Union Gray and he wants to hit back somehow, Charlie says. But he won't have any luck, you can be sure." He laid a hand on her arm and helped pull her to her feet.

Barbara's lustrous eyes widened, and she relaxed a little. "Oh, Willie," she said in a small voice, "what would I do without you?"

"Just watch out for them pesky rattlesnakes." He threw back his head and laughed.

A certain calmness came over her at Willie's words and she smiled. Willie was her friend. She had known it from the beginning.

CHAPTER 7

The September air carried a tangy, sweet blend of trampled grass and drying vegetation. Twilight, pulling its purple cloak around it, fell quietly and softly.

Barbara stood outside the south door and watched the pink melt into sullen gray ashes along the horizon. The violet hush that fell over the prairie was so indescribably beautiful that she thought, *If I were a religious person, I'd fall down and worship God!* Then the enchantment faded.

The long, hot summer had drawn to a close and soon autumn would come. Weeks had gone by with no more word of Quantrill and his guerilla band, although they still probably raided along the Kansas-Missouri border.

The Moore women were always busy in the garden, or with cooking, washing, mending and baking. For days they had spaded up dried potato plants and piled the tubers on mounds to dry before sorting and storing them in the root cellar on the west side of the cabin.

"They ought to taste good next winter, fried with bacon drippings," Aunt Prudy told Barbara, who had stood by idly and watched.

I must seem awfully ungrateful, she thought, but she had never worked outdoors before. She had tried to cut corn, sweet and moist, from the ears so Aggie could spread the kernels on the roof of the henhouse to dry, until she cut her hand and blood tinged the corn.

"Look, don't bother," Bitsy told her, taking the knife away. "We'll get it done somehow. No need to sweeten the kernels with Southern blood. Matthew would never forgive us Yankees!"

Matthew! Barbara thought of him now. She had finally received a letter. He was well, he wrote, but war was hell. Sometimes there wasn't enough food. What there was left really wasn't fit to eat. The Yanks had raided gardens and stolen whatever they could pilfer as they marched through Kentucky and Tennessee. But the Yanks wouldn't always hold the upper hand. He hoped she was well, and that her uncle was providing for her in the new land.

Barbara sighed. Yes, she had to admit that the Moore table always had plenty of food. The fresh garden vegetables, tender, fried prairie chickens and Aggie's green apple pies appeared on the table as if by magic. I'd never make a homesteader's wife, she told herself. She wasn't cut out for heavy work.

As she turned to go back into the house, she overheard Vange and Bitsy chattering and giggling as usual.

"I told you, Bitsy," Vange's voice came from under the oak where the two girls were sprawled on the grass after a day's work outdoors, "that Silas had marriage on his mind, the way he squirreled Hannah Butterfield around. But she's scared to pieces of Indians while he practically lives with them."

"Well," Bitsy drawled with an exaggerated imitation of Silas' voice, "He's shore as anythin' got what he done come fer, begol."

Vange laughed. "Strange, though, I hear they'll live with the Billings. We'd miss her, though, if they moved away."

"Would you move away if someone charming came dashing across the prairie and asked you to follow him west?" Bitsy asked pointedly.

"I . . . don't know. That's in the Lord's hands, Bits. Pa reminds us to pray about such matters, not just laugh them off."

"I know. We seem to laugh at everything else. But by the time it happens, I'll be an old maid." Bitsy sighed like a tired old woman.

Barbara joined the two girls under the tree. By now the stars had come out and evening fell like a gentle curtain.

"I heard you talking about Hannah and Silas," Barbara said, seating herself gracefully on the grass beside them. "I think she needs someone stalwart and strong like Silas who'll fight for her."

"Oh, absolutely. That's why they're getting married tomorrow. Having an Indian scout in the Billings family has its uses — especially when the Kaws begin hobnobbing with the settlers," Bitsy retorted. "I still can't get over it, Barbie — you in the Billings' cabin when that band of cutthroats marched in and took over as neat as you please."

"They weren't cutthroats!" Barbara snapped. "One squaw even patted my hair and said I was a 'nice squaw.' "

"Oh, sure," Vange added sweetly. "Is that why you washed your hair the minute you got home?"

Barbara felt red color seep into her cheeks. "I only meant . . . but it wasn't the very minute. That . . . that was the day your father told us about Quantrill."

"We know. No offense intended. Well,

anyway, we're all invited to the wedding, the very first one in the settlement since we came," Vange said placatingly. "Isn't that something? The wedding plans must've happened awfully sudden."

"That's 'cause Elder Buck from Emporia is coming to visit the Shreves, so they decided to tie the knot while he's here," Bitsy said. "Even if the Elder's a Quaker."

Soft footsteps sounded behind them, and in the pale, silver moonlight Aggie's gangly figure stood before them.

"Better get to bed, girls, if you want to look pert for Hannah's wedding."

Vange and Bitsy yawned and struggled to their feet, and Barbara followed as Aggie led the way toward the kitchen.

"I guess you heard what happened at Hannah and Silas' infer — the engagement party," Aggie put in, her voice lifting.

"No. What happened?" Vange and Bitsy chorused.

"Well, it seems Aunt Kizzie wanted to bake a cake for the event but there were no eggs in the settlement."

"They never tried raiding our henhouse," Vange said.

"So they settled for cornbread?" Bitsy ventured, and Vange giggled.

"Hank Roberts rode horseback into the

next county and got some."

"Eggs? Ha. I'll bet they were scrambled by the time he got back," Bitsy said whimsically. "If you've ever seen young Hank Roberts ride, you'd believe it."

After Barbara crawled up into the loft that night, she lay awake for a long time, listening to the crickets' creaky fiddling among the cottonwoods, and thinking. Could life go on in this prairie country, with its fears like Quantrill, the back-breaking work and the battle with the elements? Uncle Daniel had been staunch; by God's grace they could do it. Hadn't He led them here? Aunt Prudy insisted a person could always do what he had to do. One thing Barbara had discovered since coming to live with the Moores: God seemed to be a natural part of their daily lives as though He was visibly present. Even Vange and Bitsy, in their more sobering moments, admitted that they prayed. To Barbara, God had never been real. He had seemed so far away when she needed Him. Was Uncle Daniel right? *Had* God led them here?

Her eyelids grew heavy, and finally she dropped off to sleep to dream of Matthew and their wedding under the magnolias. Only, when she walked down the grassy, flower-strewn aisle of some spacious lawn toward him, he suddenly faded away. She awoke with a start and rubbed her eyes.

Aggie was already up, slipping out of her flimsy cotton night dress and into her drab brown percale.

"Rise and shine, girls," she sang out. "Remember, we're going to a wedding!"

The Moore household was soon astir with good-natured grumbling from the girls and ribbing from Josh. From the kitchen below, the aroma of fried bacon and fresh cornbread drifted up to the loft. She hurried into her clothes and hopped down the ladder. There was a flurry of crawling into their best after breakfast and rattling by wagon into town. Barbara had debated between wearing her green-sprigged delaine or the dark green bombazine.

The Billings cabin was already milling with guests, and Barbara followed Vange and Bitsy into the long store-post office room. Rebecca Shreve showed them to a squat bench in the front, then squeezed herself beside Barbara.

"Haven't seen you around, Barbara," she whispered above the murmur of voices.

"I . . . we've been busy," Barbara said.

"Heard from Matthew?"

Barbara nodded. "He's well, but the fighting's still going strong."

"I guess it will be until this war's over. By the way, you should've gone with us the day we returned the Kaw visit." Her eyes twinkled.

Startled, Barbara caught her breath sharply. "You went along?" Rebecca nodded. "What happened then?" she asked, her curiosity suddenly aroused.

"Oh, you'd never believe this, but Silas insisted we go. Of course, he went with us, and Hannah wore her bonnet, naturally. The chief's number-one squaw seated us all on the ground of the biggest tepee. Very polite. Then the squaws brought in their crafts — bead-work, bright colored blankets and pieces of pottery. Oh, you should've seen how proud they were! We exclaimed over everything and admired it all. We were really convincing."

Barbara smiled faintly. "They must've been pleased that you came."

"Oh, they were. But you should've been there, Barbara. One little shriveled crone kept asking about the pale-face squaw who had served them coffee. That was you, of course. She kept mumbling about a white turkey."

"I told you I wouldn't come, didn't I?" Barbara snapped.

"Yes, you did. But when they served their

refreshments, Barbara, I thought I'd die!"

The wedding service was about to begin; Elder Buck now moved to the front of the room and fumbled with his Bible.

"What did you have to eat?" Barbara whispered, and someone turned and glared at her. "I'm sorry. I didn't mean to disturb."

Rebecca glanced up to see if Hannah and Silas had come in, then laid her lips against Barbara's ear. "Some concoction brewed of ginseng and other herbs, I guess. I told Aunt Keziah we couldn't drink it, but she said we had to."

"At least you didn't die from it," Barbara ventured in a light voice.

"Shhhhhh!"

At that moment Hannah and Silas took their places before the elder, and the marriage ceremony began. Hannah looked young and sweet but countrified in her new lavender-sprigged lawn, carrying a bouquet of red prairie lilies. Silas, his mustache neatly trimmed, stood solemn and tall beside her, dressed in new buckskins.

Barbara's thoughts drifted back to the flower-strewn aisle of her dream wedding under the magnolias.

Then she heard Elder Buck's voice speaking in the traditional Quaker tongue, "Wilt thou, Silas Locklin, take Hannah

Butterfield as thy lawfully wedded wife?" Barbara focused briefly on the ceremony before her.

"I do."

"And wilt thou, Hannah, take Silas Locklin as thy lawfully wedded husband?"

Barbara didn't hear Hannah's soft answer for her mind went back to Matthew Potter on the battlefield. Oh, God, she prayed, keep Matthew safe! If only she could have married him before he had been called to fight. Even a Quaker elder like Buck to perform the ceremony would have suited her.

After the wedding service, William Billings announced jovially that there was plenty of fresh apple cider and crocks of molasses cookies for the guests under the trees. Rebecca left Barbara and flitted through the crowd to help serve. Barbara followed Vange and Bitsy as the girls hurried to congratulate the couple.

Hannah's eyes shone as she received the best wishes of the two exuberant Moores.

"Hannah, don't let Silas out of your sight beyond the Kaw camp!" Vange warned.

And Bitsy added, "And remember, never take off your bonnet. With Silas, you can never tell when an Indian may pop in." Barbara squeezed Hannah's arm. "I wish you every happiness," she said huskily.

Hannah's eyes grew misty and she threw her arms around Barbara and hugged her tight.

On the way home, Vange and Bitsy were full of chatter as usual. "I almost died when they 'wilted' their vows!" Bitsy choked between spasms of laughter.

"Funny thing," Vange chirked, "I fully expected Silas to say, "Be-gol, I shore do!" Both girls shrieked with laughter at the idea.

"When I get married," Bitsy said dreamily, "my wedding will be under a grove of cottonwood trees. They sigh and whisper, almost like soft organ music." Abruptly she changed the subject. "Wonder where Charlie and Willie were. Will that man ever catch the hint about finding a wife?"

"I guess not," Vange added ruefully. "Unless we come right out and tell him."

"Sure wonder what kept them away," Bitsy mused.

Barbara was quiet. Thoughts of Matthew drove her into a deep silence, and when she scrambled from the wagon and changed hastily from the green bombazine into a blue print, she started for the door.

"I . . . I want to be alone for awhile," she told Aunt Prudy. "There's so much to . . . to think about . . ." she stammered. "About Matthew and weddings," she added shyly.

"Just run along and have a good cry, dear," Aunt Prudy said, tying a fresh apron around her tiny middle. "I understand."

Barbara sped down the path that led toward the river and her favorite log. Maybe Willie would be there to talk. She'd tell him all about the wedding, and of her hopes and dreams. She had missed the boy, although just last week he'd come to tell her about the haunts of prairie chickens and grouse. He always taught her something new. When she talked with Willie, he seemed to understand. Just why, she wasn't sure. Perhaps because he usually had something to teach her and accepted her as she was. And he always told her to come back. He was her one true friend on the prairies, and he never laughed at her or made fun of her like Vange and Bitsy sometimes did.

Before she sat down, she looked around carefully. He'd warned her about rattle-snakes lurking behind stones and logs, although Willie had said they liked to sun themselves. Finding nothing to alarm her, she sat down carefully on the log and spread her skirts around her as Mammy Crissy had taught her and laid her straw bonnet beside her.

"Even though I'm out here in this wild country, I'll never forget I'm a lady!" she reminded herself aloud. She had learned earlier to leave her hoops at home. They were definitely out of place here.

Before her mind drifted to Matthew and their wedding on some Southern colonial lawn, she heard the sound of hoofbeats from the opposite side of the river, and she stiffened. Indians? Willie had told her there were only harmless Kaws in the area. At the sound of the splash of the horse on the crossing, Barbara jumped to her feet, her heart pounding.

As the rider neared her, she saw it was Charlie Warren, his felt hat askew on his dark curls. He looked deeply disturbed, and stopped when he saw her.

"Charlie? Is anything wrong?" she asked, fear in her voice.

"Barbara," he muttered in a ragged voice, "I'm on my way to town for Grandma Griffith. It's Willie. He's awfully sick. We've no doctor —"

"Willie? Oh, no! I'll hurry to your cabin and stay with him until you get back!" she cried, snatching up her bonnet and jamming it on her head.

Before he could say another word, she ran toward the crossing. A layer of rocks covered the bottom of the shallow creek where water rilled its way through the prairies. She drew off her slippers and lifted her skirts as she stepped gingerly across the stream and climbed numbly up the low bank. Slipping her shoes back on her feet, she glanced around quickly.

In the glen beyond the creek she saw the small log cabin. Smoke curled up lazily from the chimney and feathered into the bright blue sky.

Hurrying up the path to the door, she stepped over the threshold. In the dimness of the cabin she pattered across the stone floor to a crude bed along the west wall. She could barely make out Willie's boyish figure tossing on the rumpled sheet. His freckled face was flushed with fever and a rasping sound tore from his throat.

Barbara threw herself on the floor, knelt beside him and stroked his hot forehead.

"Willie . . . Willie . . . It's Barbara. Please, *please* lie still. I won't leave you, Willie. I . . . I'll stay right here."

Tears stung her eyes and ran down her cheeks. As Willie began to cough and his face contorted with misery, Barbara's panic increased.

"Oh, please, Willie. Don't . . . don't die, Willie. *Don't . . . die . . .*"

CHAPTER 8

Barbara snatched a wooden pail from the shelf and ran to the spring behind the cabin and dipped fresh, cold water. The liquid sloshed over the rim of the pail as she hurried back indoors.

Grabbing a small square of cloth from a pile of sturdy crash towels she found in a corner cupboard, she folded it, plunged it into the water she had poured into a gray enameled basin, wrung it until it stopped dripping. Then she flew to Willie's side and laid the folded wet cloth on his forehead.

I must cool his feverish brow, she told herself. That's what Mammy Crissy had done when she'd had fever as a child. I've already lost Whatley. I can't lose Willie, too.

Willie stirred restlessly and moaned. Sometimes his body shook with fits of coughing. His eyes were closed, and he seemed unaware of anything. Now and then a choking sound tore from his throat. Oh, dear God, what was wrong with him? Why was he so ill? Why was there no doctor in the settlement? Why didn't the sheepman hurry back with Grandma Griffith? Why hadn't he had sense enough to go back to Illinois and civilization instead of homesteading here on the wild, trackless prairie?

As the wet cloth felt warm to her touch, Barbara soaked it in more cold water, wrung it out, and put a fresh compress on Willie's face. His breathing grew more labored.

"Willie . . . Willie . . ." Her voice came in ragged murmurs. "Please, Willie, *please don't!*"

She scarcely heard the hoofbeats of Charlie's roan and a bay thundering up the path toward the cabin until a wiry, gray-haired, little sparrow of a woman dressed in a faded blue percale burst through the door, jerked off her sunbonnet and rushed toward Willie's cot. Charlie followed, and stood apart, his arms folded across his chest.

Barbara hovered anxiously over the foot end of the cot, her hands trembling. Grandma Griffith probed and tested in quick, birdlike movements, her black shoe-button eyes snapping.

"What . . . what is it?" Barbara whispered, breaking the deep silence.

"It looks like diphtheria," the woman said without looking up. "You'd better go home, gal, before you catch it. It's most catching."

"No, no. I won't leave! I've got to stay with Willie. Please, please let me stay. I . . .

I'll do all I can to . . . to nurse him. Please?" Her luminous blue eyes widened with pleading.

"No, gal, it's too dangerous. You'll get sick, too," she said firmly.

"Willie needs me!" Barbara cried. "Charlie can't tend his sheep and take care of his fields and Willie too. I've got to stay. *Please!*"

Grandma Griffith glanced up at Charlie, and a long look passed between them.

"What do you know about nursin'? Can you keep him cool — change his sheets and do whatever's necessary?" the tiny frontier woman asked, looking directly at her.

"I've already placed wet, cold compresses on his forehead. I'll do whatever you say, Mrs. Griffith."

Her black eyes narrowing, Grandma Griffith looked once more at Willie's writhing figure on the cot.

"It won't be easy. There's lots more to nursin' than cold compresses. It's turpentine and lard plasters, and all we can do to bring about relief. If you ain't a frontier woman now, you will be when this is over."

Barbara drew back sharply. *What does she mean?* she wondered. *That I'll grow dowdy and frumpy or whatever frontier women even-*

tually become? I've already given up wearing hoops. Or . . . does she mean the experience will help me grow?

Moistening her lips, she nodded slowly. "I understand. As long as Willie needs me, I'll stay. And I'll do my best. You won't be sorry."

Willie broke into a paroxysm of coughing, and Grandma Griffith quickly turned her attention to the sick boy.

"Get some more cold water," she ordered. "His fever's climbin'."

Grabbing the pail, Barbara started for the door. Charlie was behind her in one giant step, and snatched the pail from her shaking fingers.

"You don't have to do this, you know, Barbara," he said, his voice low and very, very serious.

"But I want to! Willie's been the one real friend I've found here. I can't fail him. I don't care what it costs!" With that, she snatched the pail from him, ran to the spring and filled it. It felt cool in her own warm hands, sweaty with tension.

Water sloshed over the rim of the pail into her slippers as she hurried back into the cabin. Already the room reeked of turpentine and steeping chamomile tea, and for a moment Barbara grew nauseous. She quickly got hold of herself and set the pail on its shelf.

Willie's rasping cough and ragged moans rose above Grandma Griffith's tender ministrations. Charlie had gone out to check on the new lambs, she told Barbara.

"It's for sure he can't look after Willie hisself, and I can't stay here long. There are others . . ." she paused. "I only hope you know what you've let yourself in for, gal!"

Barbara was silent as she watched how deftly the older woman wrung out the cloths and laid then tenderly on Willie's burning forehead. I must learn all I can, she decided. I'll smell to high heaven of turpentine and herbs, but Willie's my job, she reminded herself when the odor threatened to overwhelm her.

After Grandma Griffith had left instructions about sponging Willie's hot body and told her to boil the sweat-soaked linens and bed clothes, she jammed the faded brown bonnet on her head.

"Don't forget to boil the sheets and nightshirt, gal," she said brusquely, fire in her sharp little eyes. "That's the best way to kill the bug. Tell Charlie to fill the iron kettle behind the cabin with plenty of water and build the fire under it for ye."

"You mean . . . me, boil the clothes? I have never —"

"Time you learned, gal. Anybody livin' out here on the prairie must pull his weight, and that includes wimminfolk. I'll be back in the mornin'." Without a backward glance, she hurried out to her bay, untied it from the cottonwood sapling, quickly mounted and rode away.

Bleakly Barbara watched her go. Panic gripped her. What did she know about nursing? What if she failed Willie? I don't even know *how* to boil a sheet she reminded herself. But she couldn't let Willie down, no matter what. With a quivering sigh she went over to Willie's cot. He looked so pathetic, his usually merry face pinched and drawn, and the wracking cough making him convulse spasmodically.

Barbara was frantic. What should she do? Fresh cold compresses on the forehead . . . more turpentine and lard for his throat and chest . . . and mop the sweat that oozed from his body. . . . It kept her moving constantly.

She didn't hear Charlie behind her until he spoke. "Look, Barbara," he said, his voice gray with tension, "I can manage through the night. Why don't you go back to the Moores? Maybe your Aunt Prudy, or Aggie, can replace you in the morning."

She jerked around to face him. "I'm not leaving Willie until he's better, you hear? And maybe I don't know much about nursing, but I'll do my best. You can't make me go back. Just you try!"

Charlie stared at her, then shook his head and picked up his straw hat. "All right. I'll fix us a bite to eat after I finish the chores."

"I'm not hungry," she spat out. "Besides, I can't leave Willie's bed —"

"If you don't eat, you'll get sick yourself. Then what will we do? If your strength leaves, you'll come down with what Willie's got. How would you like that?"

Her eyes blazing, she turned away. "All right. Go on and finish your chores." She bent over Willie and felt his forehead. It burned hot as ever.

Barbara ate a few bites of Charlie's lamb stew for supper, but it nauseated her. It wasn't the food, for Charlie had flavored the stew with aromatic herbs that seemed to bring out the taste. Somehow she didn't feel like eating as long as Willie tossed and turned, coughing and choking.

When twilight crept over the prairies with an evening chill, Charlie lit the candles. The sharp wind of early autumn blew through the half-open door and the flame guttered in the cool air. Barbara sat unmoving at

Willie's side, and left him only for fresh cold compresses. Charlie huddled in his chair, his summer-blue eyes watching her.

Suddenly he got up and came toward her. "Please lie down on my bed and rest, Barbara. You're worn out already."

She shook her head so violently that the pins flew from her braids and wisps of rich brown hair blew around her cheeks.

"No, Charlie," she said in a fierce voice. "I can't leave Willie!"

"But you need rest —"

"Just leave me alone!"

Without a word, he drew off his boots and headed towards the bed.

"I'll lie down for awhile then," he said in a tired voice. "If there's any change be sure to let me know."

"I will." She nodded briefly, then turned once more to stroke Willie's hot, flushed cheeks.

How long would he be held in the grip of fever, and the rasping, choking paroxysm that shook his body from time to time?

As she looked out the east window, she saw that the skies had grown suddenly black, and the wind began to rise. The air blowing through the open window lifted the little brown curls around her brow and she hurried to shut the door.

The fury of the storm increased. Out in the open country it hammered at the flat, resistless grassy plains and wrenched at trees and bushes; it screamed and howled in anger along the draw and buried its violent rage upon the cabin in the glen.

She didn't know what to do as the night dragged on. All she could do was listen to the sounds of the writhing wind and Willie's choking and coughing that seemed to tear him apart.

Charlie, who had fallen asleep after an exhausting day, stirred restlessly and sat up. She saw his distraught, huddled figure in the brief flashes of lightning. "Is it storming out?" he asked, rubbing his eyes. "The candles —"

"The wind blew them out," she said tonelessly, and he groped in the dark and relit them. Then he carried them away from the blowing wind that creaked and whistled through the chinks in the cabin.

"Any change?" he asked, coming toward Willie's cot.

She shook her head. Weariness had sapped her strength and she sagged into a chair.

"Please lie down now, Barbara," he said again.

"No." Her voice was low but firm. "The

wind will keep me awake. Besides, I couldn't sleep . . . I can't leave Willie —"

"But you're exhausted. If you'd sleep for an hour."

"I'm all right. Please don't ask me again!"

Shaking his head, Charlie turned away. "I've never seen anyone as stubborn as you."

She smiled a little. He was learning something about her she had hardly known herself.

"About . . . about the Fourth of July picnic," he began hesitantly.

Barbara stiffened. She'd tried to forget that he'd wanted to make up to her. "Forget that picnic," she snapped. "And any other notions you may have. I'm engaged to marry Matthew Potter and don't you forget it!"

He paced back and forth, ignoring her, pausing to look at the tossing trees outside, then at his restless brother on the sick bed. Then he stood at the window and stared outside for a long time.

"Wind's dying down a little, I think," he said as though their previous words had never passed between them. "It's growing pink in the east. Maybe the sunrise will bring about a change."

"I hope so," Barbara whispered, pushing

at her disheveled hair that fell into her eyes. She stooped over Willie and felt his face. It was as hot as ever, and his linens were soaked with sweat. As carefully as she could, she put on fresh sheets and tossed the sweat-stained bedding on the floor.

"In the morning I'll boil them," she said dully.

"I'll haul the water and build the fire for you under the kettle."

Barbara felt as limp and lifeless as a rag doll, and she probably looked worse. But this was no time to think of herself. Sometimes Willie began to choke until she thought he would never catch his breath.

When dawn broke, the eastern sky was aflame with pink and gold, and the wind had died. The ground was strewn with great branches that had been torn from the cottonwoods and the little sapling near the cabin had snapped in two.

Barbara heard Charlie go out and knew he was looking after his chores. She hovered over Willie like a mother hen with one chick; yet there was no change.

An hour later, after sampling Charlie's breakfast of cornbread and molasses, she went out to boil the infested bed clothes. The hot water, as she tried to wring out the sheets and night clothes, scalded her hands, and she cried with the pain while she draped the bedding on the storm-battered shrubs to dry.

Grandma Griffith was there when she came back into the cabin, and she hurried quickly toward the tiny bird-like woman with the little buttonhole mouth.

"Do you think there's any change?" Barbara asked anxiously, holding her red, raw hands behind her.

"No change, but he seems to be holdin' his own." She eyed Barbara quizzically. "You haven't slept any, have ye, gal?"

Barbara shook her head. "Charlie begged me to, but I couldn't leave Willie."

"You've kept Willie's sheets changed and the compresses and turpentine treatment up. That's good," she said, turning back to the bed, "You look all tuckered out. Now will you please lie down for at least an hour? I'll stay right by Willie's side."

Barbara swayed with weariness. She ached and hurt from exhaustion and the backbreaking work of boiling bedclothes, and she leaned weakly against the table.

"Well, maybe for just a bit, Mrs. Griffith," she said finally. "But let me know if there's any change."

"Don't ye fret none, gal. I'll let you know the minute he opens his eyes."

Oh, if only I knew how to pray, she chided herself. But God had no cause to listen to her because she didn't know Him.

Dragging herself to Charlie's bed, she dropped on the hard straw tick and fell asleep almost instantly. When she awoke, she heard voices and sat up quickly. Pulling herself to her feet, she started walking toward Willie's cot. The rasping, choking sounds continued, and she drew back in fear.

Suddenly she was aware of a tall, handsome young Indian bending over Willie's cot. In one hand he held out a tin cup. As he gently lifted the sick boy's head with the other, he forced some dark, pungent liquid between the pale lips. Barbara's fists clenched and her face grew livid at the sight.

"What are you doing?" she screamed. "Are you trying to kill him?"

She elbowed her way toward the buckskin-clad Indian and tried to force him aside.

"Hold on, Barbara!" Charlie's voice came strong and clear from somewhere in the background. "This is White Turkey, one of our Kaw friends. He's brought herbs he says will help Willie."

Barbara drew back, startled. To trust an Indian with something as serious as diphtheria! Were these people crazy?

White Turkey paid no attention to her until he had forced the last of the liquid down Willie's swollen throat, who coughed and sputtered with every mouthful. Then he turned to face her. His glance fell on her raw, red hands which she had forgotten to hide. Swiftly he drew something from his leather pouch and smoothed it gently over the blistered fingers.

"White Turkey friend," he said in a husky voice. "No hurt little brave. *Pescua* help make better. And *aloe* make Prairie Flower hands better." Then he swung around and glided silently from the cabin.

Glancing around bewildered, Barbara gulped one or twice. "White Turkey." The Kaw squaw had muttered something about a white turkey. Grandma Griffith had left, and no one was there but her and Charlie and Willie who still lay gasping on the cot.

The first long day drew to a close, and the second day dawned, gray and dreary as the first. Summer had gone briefly and the chilly gray morning of the third day broke.

Barbara had scarcely left Willie's side, except to tend to his needs. Her hands had healed remarkably fast. She had just returned to the cabin with fresh cold water when she thought she heard Willie's voice.

"Barb'ra? . . . You're here? What . . . what are you doing?"

She set the pail down with a jounce and flew to his cot. "Willie, you talked! You're feeling better?"

He grinned feebly, and his white, wan face looked like a caricature of a clown. "I'm . . . hungry. What's to eat?"

She ran toward the door and flung it open. Charlie was just herding his sheep toward the pens on the ridge, his coat buttoned up to his chin.

"Charlie! Charlie!" she screamed. "Come quick!"

He sprang over the rail fence and ran toward the cabin, his face white.

"Willie . . . Willie's says he's hungry. Oh, Charlie, Willie's going to be all right!"

For a moment Charlie stood still, a look of tenderness on his face as he fastened his gaze on her tired face. "Thank God," he said fervently. Then with a bound, he hurried into the cabin and grabbed his brother and held him tight.

Barbara never knew where the rest of the day went. It flew by, and even the chill gray prairie seemed to shimmer with golden light. By evening, as Willie sat up for his cornbread and milk, Barbara picked up her straw bonnet.

"Well, I guess you won't need me any more," she said with a wistful smile after she had folded the last clean sheet into the chest that stood under the window.

"We'll always be needin' each other, Barbara," Willie said with a sudden lilt in his voice. "I'm glad . . . I found a sister again, after Nellie May. I've sure needed one," he added sheepishly.

Happy tears blinded Barbara's eyes and her step was springy as she sped down the path that led to the crossing. She wore one of Charlie's heavy flannel shirts, for the evening air was chilly.

The Moore girls were just finishing the supper dishes when Barbara burst through the south door of the cabin. She didn't realize how tired she was until she dropped into one of the barrel chairs and let out a long, slow breath.

"Well, that was quite an ordeal you went through, we hear," Bitsy greeted her cheerfully, slamming flatware into a drawer. "Even wearing Charlie's shirt to warm your poor lonely heart."

"I'm sorry I couldn't let you know where I was," she said lamely, ignoring Bitsy's trite remark and toying with the frayed cuff of the left sleeve, "but when Charlie told me Willie was so ill —"

"He stopped by long enough to tell us you were at his cabin, the day he rode after Grandma Griffith," Aunt Prudy said quietly, setting the empty milk pans on the table to be rinsed with hot water. "But when we heard that Willie had diphtheria — Barbara, do you realize how catching it is? Beecher Billings died of it just yesterday, and there was a private burial. And Edith Billings is very sick now. You know, you're exposed and could get it yourself."

Barbara's face flushed. "I . . . didn't stop to think. All I knew was that Willie needed me."

"Charlie and Grandma Griffith said you were a fine nurse," Aggie said gently as she hung the dishpan away and spread the dishrag over it to dry.

"Oh, it must've been romantic, living for three days under the same roof with Charlie," Bitsy said with a dreamy sigh. "I bet —"

"Romantic?" Barbara laughed bitterly. "When all I did was try to keep death's angel at bay? Bitsy, are you daft?" She jerked off Charlie's shirt and flung it on the table. "Here's the sheepman's shirt . . . and welcome to it."

She jumped to her feet, lifted her skirts and climbed the loft. All she wanted was to sleep and sleep. And to dream of marrying Matthew. If she didn't die of diphtheria first.

CHAPTER 9

A slow, steady drizzle had fallen on the prairies for several days. It seemed to have washed color from the landscape and left a gray, wet world in which the earth and sky blurred and ran together.

Barbara stood at the south window, watching the dreary drops pelt and patter on the pane. It was a welcome relief from the hot, dry spell that had plagued the plains during the past weeks. A small sharp gust of wind swirled the wet drops around the edges of the glass and she noticed a tendril of ivy twist and curl as it crept up the seasoned log wall.

With a sigh she turned away. "Sometimes I think the sun will never shine again," she murmured to no one in particular. "It seems I've been here so long." She sighed again.

Bitsy and Vange were seated at the table, snipping away at quilt pieces which Aggie and Aunt Prudy painstakingly stitched into blocks by hand. Uncle Daniel and Josh sat near the wood stove and mended harness. Was there ever a time when the Moore family wasn't busy? Where were the carefree, relaxing days Barbara had known on the plantation, enjoying parties and outings with her friends, before the days when the war had reared its ugly head?

Vange looked up from the gay red bit of calico she was snipping. "Oh, I don't know, Barb. I doubt that the rain will bring the war to a close sooner in the South."

"Just wait 'til you experience one of our prairie winters," Bitsy warned, biting her lower lip as she cut out a neat, gray triangle of percale. "In a day or two you'll forget we ever had a rain. Besides, what would you do if the rain stopped?"

Barbara came to the table, pulled out a chair and sat down. "Oh, I don't know. I guess I'm a bit anxious to know how Willie is. I hope he hasn't caught a cold in this damp weather."

"Charlie's got plenty of sheep tallow, remember," Bitsy chuckled. "It's good for whatever ails you, you know. As soon as the rain lets up and the creek is down, Charlie'll be by on his way to town for supplies."

With a dry smile Barbara picked up a scrap of blue calico and fingered it idly. "If you had an extra scissors I could help cut quilt pieces. Maybe the day would go by faster." As an afterthought she added, "But what would Charlie's going after supplies have to do with me?"

"You could flag him down and ask about Willie," Vange said, handing her scissors to Barbara. "Here. I'll let you use mine while I stretch awhile. This weather makes me drowsy." She got up, threw back her arms, and went to the window.

"Why should I flag down the sheepman?" Barbara flared, snipping carefully around the cardboard pattern. "I'll leave that to you, Bitsy."

Bitsy giggled. "Oh, and what would I say? 'Your nurse Barbara Temple wants to know how her patient is.' Why, Charlie would think I was crazy. Or you, for that matter. You're so lucky you didn't come down with that terrible diphtheria. Are you ever stubborn, Barbara Temple. Here, cut out two triangles of this gray, but snip carefully. They have to fit together exactly right."

"Besides, you can ask him on Sunday when we go the Thomas Wise place for the box social," Vange suggested, leaning her arms against the windowsill.

"Box social?" Barbara sniffed with disdain. "Who says I am going to an old box social. I don't want —"

"Surely you know what a box social is. The girl fixes a box of food and the boys bid on it. Whoever buys your box is the one you eat it with. Neat idea, huh?" Bitsy chirked.

"But you know I can't cook."

"No problem. Aggie's little apple tarts and crisp, fried prairie chicken and raised doughnuts should tempt any young feller," Vange offered sagely. "Or you could try to cook something for a change."

Barbara bit her upper lip. Vange had to be joking. She drummed her fingers on the table before replying. Better play along with them. She didn't want to be caught in the middle again. Her cousins had the knack of making her feel . . . well, ignorant and helpless.

"I'll let Aggie fix whatever she wants, although I can't see why you want me to go."

"Don't be a snob, Barb," Vange retorted. "You just said you missed your outings, and here's your chance to get out. Since you've been stuck out here on the prairie you might as well make the best of it. Well, the rain's letting up, I think." She came back to the table and sat down.

"Here's your scissors, Vange," Barbara said abruptly, shoving the shears toward her cousin. "Guess I've cut enough for one day. I think I'll go up and write to Matthew. Believe me, I'd rather be with him than on this stupid, soggy, gray prairie."

She got to her feet and started up the loft, feeling a trifle foolish. Her uncle's family really tried to make her feel at home, and she was grateful. But it wasn't easy, living in this wild strange country where it either rained all day or the wind blistered the prairie. She'd never get used to it.

A few drops still pattered on the bark roof as she went to her trunk and drew out her writing pad and pencil. Word had come to the Kansas newspapers in early July about the battle at Gettysburg in Pennsylvania. Although General George Pickett's charge had failed and casualties were heavy, with over 2,000 Confederates killed, Barbara was thankful that Matthew had not been there. From what he wrote, he was with General Lee at Chancelorsville in May, where the South claimed a sweeping victory. Surely the war would end soon. It couldn't last much longer.

She scribbled furiously, her pencil flying over the pages of her tablet. She told him about the hot, dry days of August, the incessant rains and the crops Uncle Daniel's family had harvested. There was little else to write. She didn't mention Willie and his dreadful illness.

Sunday afternoon gleamed clear and bright with just a hint of a crisp October breeze. Barbara, astride Petunia, eased her gaily-decorated box into the wide, leather saddle bag then followed Vange and Bitsy on Dolly and Prince as they galloped down the trail toward Marion Centre.

Already a crowd of young people had gathered in Billings' grove, waiting to ride north out of the settlement toward the Wise homestead together.

Charlie was there, riding tall and straight in the saddle on his roan's back. He waved his big gray felt hat at Barbara and grinned.

"Willie said to tell you he'll be waiting for you by the river tomorrow afternoon," he said in an absurdly casual voice. "I think he wants to show you a big walnut tree he found the other day."

"Is he . . . all right?" she asked stiffly, slowing her mount. "I mean, is he home all alone?"

"Willie's a big boy. After checking the sheep pens, he'll ride into town and hang around with Chub Butterfield till we get back. The Moore girls threatened to shanghai me if I didn't show up," he said, grinning.

Barbara gave a curt nod, then whirled Petunia around and joined her cousins who were already following Silas and Hannah Locklin, Hank Roberts, Rebecca Shreve and the Griffith boys and the others as they headed down the trail.

The shimmering prairie stretched toward the wooded headlands that lay in deep purple vales where the ground was golden with fallen cottonwood leaves. Bittersweet bushes dripped with coral beads, and the fiery red sumac blazed among the orange-brown upland that yawned ahead.

"Winter isn't far off," Barbara overheard Charlie's strong voice. "Listen!"

"Wild geese?" Rebecca Shreve asked.

"Canadian honkers."

There was talk and chatter of everything under the sun except the war. Rebecca reined in beside Barbara, her round face merry and bright.

"I hear you nursed Willie Warren a few weeks back when he was so sick with diphtheria," she said. "You were lucky you didn't catch it."

"Oh, I'm a strong woman," Barbara scoffed. "Where I grew up we're brave. And our soldiers are brave and strong too." Her voice was proud.

Rebecca drew away briefly. "I'm sure of that," she said gravely. "Here one has to be. And the prairie breeds even greater strength! God was good to you, wasn't He? When my cousin Beecher died —"

"Oh," Barbara's face flamed. "I'm so sorry, Rebecca. I didn't mean . . . I'd forgotten he . . . that the diphtheria took him. How's Edith?"

"She's doing fine. But for awhile we didn't know. Like it was with Willie. God sure was good, for my little cousin survived." Rebecca's face took on a pensive look, and Barbara urged Petunia ahead quickly. She wasn't sure she could accept death as calmly as these frontier people. She rode ahead and stopped abruptly on the crest of the hill.

Below, near the draw that dipped toward Clear Creek, pale yellow sunshine filtered through the screen of haze among the timber. Stalks of goldenrod burned like candles along the banks. As she rode on, the miles sped past while the horses cantered down the incline.

When the Thomas Wise cabin came into sight, the clatter of horses' hooves quickened. Josh drew up beside her and helped Barbara dismount when they pulled to a stop in the fenced-in yard.

"Mmmm, something smells delicious," he said, reaching for Barbara's box that she slid out of the saddle bag. "Whoever buys your box is in for a rare treat. You must've outdone yourself, Cousin."

"You know very well Aggie fixed what's in my box, Josh!" Barbara retorted. "I've never learned to cook, and you know it."

"Well, it's never too late to learn." After Josh handed the box to her, she hurried after Vange and Bitsy. Her two cousins had already made themselves at home in the roomy cabin. Young, rusty-headed Tom Wise waved his arms in welcome.

"You've all had a good hour's ride over the trail and I'm sure you're starved," he called out, his ruddy face glowing in the dim cabin. "All you lassies place your boxes on the table. We'll begin bidding at once."

Barbara turned to Vange. "You mean, I'm actually going to share my box with whoever buys it?"

"That's right."

I hope it won't be that blond with his ridiculous cowlick, Barbara decided, noticing the young men in the crowd. She was still trying to sort out the Shreves and Griffiths and the Cobles from the rest. *I don't know why I let Vange talk me into coming. Nearly everyone's a stranger,* she thought. Aggie had backed out at the last minute.

Titters and laughter followed as each box was sold and couples paired off to find some shady nook on the Wise place to eat what was in the box.

Hank Roberts bought Rebecca Shreve's and Jack Griffith bid on Elizabeth Shreve's until he claimed it. Vange found herself paired off with Roddy Coble, a newcomer to the settlement. Bitsy hovered at Barbara's side, wiggling like an over-anxious schoolgirl. "I hinted to Charlie about mine," she whispered. "He can't miss it. I wrapped brown paper and tied a sprig of goldenrod on top."

Barbara drew her breath sharply. "But so did I! I just hope —"

"Oh, he'll never know if we decide to switch."

"How much am I bid for this box with the yellow posies?" Tom called out. "If all our girls around here could cook like Aggie Moore —"

Poor Aggie, Barbara thought, *why didn't she come?* Everyone knew of her culinary skills. And she'd have not lacked for a suitor today.

She saw Charlie's hand shoot up high. "I bid 50 cents."

"Sold!"

Barbara turned and grinned at Bitsy. "Looks like you'll have your wish. Sheepman Charlie just bought your box."

Bitsy's smile faded when she saw Charlie grab the box. She turned to Barbara with an amused expression.

"No, that's not my box, Barbie. I put a

sprig of mint on mine, not goldenrod. I just wondered what you'd say!"

"Come on — whose box is this? Who's the gal who brought it?" Tom yelled. Barbara shrank back. "I . . . but I don't want . . . to . . . to eat with . . . with him," she sputtered. "Here . . . please take my place, Bitsy!"

"No," Bitsy shook her head. "I won't cheat. Better go on, Barbie. Charlie's s'posed to share your box with you."

Barbara edged herself toward the door. She'd slip out and hide. This was preposterous. She wouldn't eat with Charlie Warren if he was the last person in Kansas!

"Hey, Barbara. Is it your box I bought?" Charlie called out. "Bitsy says so."

Her face flamed. "You can have it yourself," she fumed. "I . . . I'm not hungry."

How dare he think of it when he knew she was engaged to marry Matthew! He'd tried to catch her eye ever since she came. She hurried through the door and ran down the trail, her full skirts brushing the tall prairie grass that grew in tufts between the wagon tracks.

A large warm slab of rock lay beside the trail and Barbara sat down. She spread her green bombazine skirt around her and bit her lower lip. This outing was a real bust, and she shouldn't have come. Charlie had known all along it was her box, she was sure. He'd probably seen it when she slid it out of the saddle bag. What colossal nerve!

"Barbara."

A voice spoke behind her and she turned. Charlie stood there, holding out the box. "I bought this box and I'm to share it with the person who fixed it. It's yours, isn't it?"

She nodded furiously. "Yes, it's mine, but I don't want to eat with you!"

"Why? What have I done that's so awful? I thought that when you helped me care for Willie —"

"That was then," she broke in. "Besides, I didn't fix the food. Aggie did. I know I shouldn't have come today. You and I can never be more than . . . neighbors. Don't you see?"

He shook his head helplessly. "But as neighbors, can't we share a meal? What's wrong with that? You're so stubborn —"

"Please understand, I'm going to marry Matthew Potter. I just don't want anyone else hanging around. Go on. Enjoy Aggie's fried prairie chicken and fresh doughnuts by yourself."

He looked at her with a puzzled frown and left.

Well, at least I didn't have to eat with him.

Yet the thought of Aggies's delicious cooking made her hungry.

Half an hour later Barbara picked herself up from the rock and made her way back to the Wise cabin. By the time she reached the door, the young men were untying the horses from the hitching posts.

"Time to get going so we get home before dark," Josh told her as he led Petunia toward Barbara and helped her into the saddle. "Did you have a good time?"

She eyed him sharply and nodded. "I guess so." No need to tell him what had happened.

On the way home the group sang song after song. The prairie caught their music and sent their voices rippling over its clear, wide spaces. The glory of the autumn day was ending in the grandeur of a crimson sunset shaded toward the north by a threatening thundercloud.

"Let's race," someone shouted, and the ponies and horses lined up to start. Just then a whoop, a savage yell sounded just ahead.

A tall young Indian on a brown-and-white pony rose from the edge of the draw and dashed toward them. Girls screamed and looked frantic. For a moment the ponies were thrown into confusion, and some mounts became unmanageable as the young brave headed for Barbara and leaned toward her. It was the same Indian who had come to Charlie's cabin just a few weeks before.

"Prairie Flower!" he called out. "Twelve ponies. White Turkey give 12 ponies!"

She let out a piercing cry, and he darted away. Jack Griffith hurried to her side, a wide grin on his craggy face.

"That was White Turkey," he said.

Silas Locklin was there suddenly. "He wants to give 12 ponies for you, Barbara Temple. Hey, that's a marriage proposal, be-gol!"

Barbara's face grew white, her hands clammy with sweat.

"Oh no," she softly groaned. First, the sheepman Charlie Warren. And now this. To be courted by an Indian was the last straw!

CHAPTER 10

November turned raw and cold after the first clear, frost-snapping mornings. Great flocks of ducks flew in from the north, settled briefly on the Cottonwood, then winged in V-shapes to the south. Thin, opaque ice glazed the surface of the small creeks, and the river ran black and sluggish beyond the timber.

Barbara, bundled in layers of jackets and Uncle Daniel's greatcoat, laughed as she followed Willie's nimble steps along the creek banks.

"Right there. Up ahead," he shouted, pointing to a stately tree. "The best black walnuts along the Cottonwood."

"Well!" she panted as she scrambled up beside him. "So, here is the tree. I'm sorry I couldn't make it sooner, but I helped my cousins pick apples. But where are the nuts?"

"Down on the ground. See?"

Her gaze dropped to the cover of crack-ling dry leaves underfoot. "*Those* black things? They don't look like nuts. They're ugly."

"Wait 'til you taste 'em. You have to crack

off the black shells and dig out the nutmeats. You'll never taste anything yummier."

"How do you eat them?"

"Oh, they make the best molasses and ginger cookies. Or the best fudge. Here, let's pick up a bunch."

"I didn't bring a pan, Willie."

"My gunny sack's plenty big."

Barbara's laughter trilled in the brisk morning air. "You think of everything!"

"Well, if we're goin' nuttin', we need somethin' for the nuts, don't we? Makes sense, don't it?"

The plop of nuts into the sack interrupted their chatter for the next 15 or 20 minutes as Barbara helped Willie gather his nut harvest.

"I was afraid the squirrels would've carted them all off by now," Willie said after he had picked up all he wanted.

"But what will they eat if we steal their food supply?"

"Don't worry. By now they've cached all the food they'll need. Besides, I've left a few."

He led the way as he forged ahead, lugging his burlap sack along the dry brown bush that skirted the river. "Come on. I wanna show you somethin' else."

Barbara huffed after him, shivering a little in the cold air. "You mean — there's something more?"

"The prairie has lots of surprises." He paused and peered at a small hillock among a pile of fallen logs. "Here it is. See that hole? Badgers."

"B-badgers? Are they . . . wild, like coyotes?"

"Oh, they're not that big, of course, and sure not as bold. They burrow deep inside these little hills. But they're interestin' critters. Helpful, too. They feast on gophers and rats and other pests. I like to watch 'em when they come out."

"What do they look like?"

Willie pushed back his red wool knit cap and scratched his tousled head. "Well, they're about two feet long and have a squat body and short, thick tail. They've got powerful claws which they use for diggin' and their fur is shaggy gray tipped with brown."

Barbara stared at the hole. "And I suppose they won't come out and show themselves while I'm here?"

"Like I said, they're kinda shy." He grinned. "But it's interestin' to watch them." He moved on.

"Do you come here often?" Barbara asked, panting to keep up. "I mean . . .

156

aren't you afraid of . . . Indians?"

"There's mostly Kaws around here. Didja know they're called 'People of the South Wind'? Besides, I kin read a few Injun signs. I know the Kaws won't hurt me none."

Barbara grimaced, remembering White Turkey and his bold ride toward her on the way home from the box social. Then she grinned in spite of herself. *People of the South Wind.* That figured. Kansas had plenty of wind.

"You don't think . . . I mean." She paused awkwardly and shivered again. "You see, White Turkey came after me a few weeks ago. I —"

"Ya cold? You're shiverin'. Oh, White Turkey will never hurt you, Barbara. He likes you almost as much as Charlie does."

"Charlie!" Barbara rapped out the name sharply. "I . . . I don't have much use for your brother, Willie."

"But why? What's Charlie done to you? He's a great brother. I know he wouldn't —"

"No, maybe he wouldn't. It's just that somehow I can't stand him. You know I'm going to marry Matthew Potter when the war ends. If Charlie has any ideas —"

"He knows that Barbara. But he likes to be sociable as long as his sheep are looked after. That comes first." Willie set out on a fast clip, and Barbara had to hurry to keep up. Her teeth chattered.

"I just had an idea," Willie burst out when they reached the Cottonwood crossing that led to the Moore cabin. "Let's go to our cabin and warm up. While we're there why don't we bake some molasses cookies . . . just you 'n me?"

"Bake cookies?" Barbara gasped. "But I don't know how."

"I got Ma's old recipe box. We kin read, can't we?"

"Charlie would never —"

"Charlie's out choppin' wood on the north branch crick. He wouldn't even know. Or care either. C'mon, Barbara. Let's have some fun . . . just you and me? Hey, besides, you're freezin'. You gotta warm up."

Barbara hesitated. Sure, she was cold, but the idea of baking cookies scared her half silly. What did she know about ovens and dough? She remembered Josh's quip the other week about it being time she learned to cook.

"Oh, Willie," she spoke slowly. "I know I sound stupid, but I never learned anything at home. We had darkies to do all the work. Sometimes I feel a little foolish and helpless.

Do you really think I could do it?"

"Sure, you could. C'mon, let's get started."

Half an hour later Barbara had warmed up and Willie had cracked a small bowl full of nuts. After she had struggled with the soft, molasses dough, Willie helped her roll it out on the table, cutting rounds with a cracked coffee cup.

As the aroma of molasses and walnuts drifted from the piping hot oven, Barbara felt a thrill sweep over her. She could hardly wait to tell the Moores about her new experience.

When she crossed the creek an hour later, carrying a plateful of freshly baked cookies which Willie had insisted she take with her, she held her head high. It was her first real accomplishment. She couldn't wait to write Matthew.

CHAPTER 11

When Barbara burst through the south door of the Moore cabin bearing her plate of cookies, her cousins were already setting the table for the noon meal. The clatter of flatware punctuated their laughter and lively chatter.

"Would you believe Mehitabel and Ezra?" Vange was saying as she slammed the cracked pottery plates on the scrubbed oilcloth. "They've just — hey, Barb, what have you been up to?"

The warmth of the kitchen sent tingles into Barbara's cold cheeks and she set the plate of cookies on the table. She stood back and surveyed them proudly.

"This."

"This what? Where'd you get the cookies?" Bitsy said, grabbing a cookie and nibbling somewhat daintily. "Hey, they taste great. Mmmm. Walnuts, too. Who baked them?"

A smile tugged at Barbara's lips. "I did. That is, Willie and I. He . . . Willie thought it would be a good idea while we warmed up in the cabin after our walnut hunt."

"You mean *you* slaved over a hot stove

to create these luscious things?" Bitsy gasped.

"Now, Bitsy," Aggie clucked from the cookstove where she was frying a pan full of jackrabbit. "Barbara isn't completely help-less."

"But — they're terrific! Here." Bitsy grabbed two cookies and jammed one into Aggie's mouth and the other into Vange's. "See what I mean?"

Barbara watched as Aggie and Vange chewed speculatively. Would her cousins still think of her as a spoiled Southern girl who didn't know a thing?

Vange nodded, appreciation in her blue eyes. "Oh, they're absolutely fantastic. Barb, why didn't you tell us you could do something so marvelous?"

"I . . . I didn't know it myself," she said shyly. "But when Willie and I picked up the walnuts, he said baking a batch would give us a chance to warm up."

"And where was Charlie? Was he im-pressed, too?" Bitsy asked tartly.

Barbara crinkled her nose. "He had no idea we were messing up his kitchen."

Aggie wiped her floury hands on her brown apron and grinned. "Well, if the sample I ate spoils my appetite for dinner, it's well worth it. Barbara Temple, welcome to the culinary department of the Moore cabin!"

The girls laughed, and Vange set the sugar and salt shakers on the table. She placed the plate of remaining cookies on the shelf almost reverently.

"Our dessert. And a very special one, too. But as I was saying when Barbara burst into our lives bearing her great and wondrous gift, I don't know when I've seen a more grateful pair than the Fosters as William Billings loaded them down with supplies from the store. They almost worshiped him, I think."

"Who are the Fosters?" Barbara asked, removing her wraps and hanging them on nails in the corner.

"Ezra and Mehitabel. They're a couple of negroes who have moved into the little stone cabin north on the banks of Mud Creek. I hope you'll meet them too."

"Negroes!" Barbara spat out. "Nothing but runaway slaves."

"Maybe not. Slaves have been free to come and go as they choose."

Throwing back her head, Barbara snorted. "Really, I have no use at all for that Abraham Lincoln. He's an ignorant country bumpkin without any sense at all. He's not a gentleman. Why'd they come to Kansas?

Their place is in the South!"

At her outburst Josh stalked into the kitchen, his face glowing from the cold. He marched up to Barbara and placed his hands on her shoulders.

"I won't have you speaking of Mr. Lincoln like that, Barbara. I love every inch of this great state of Kansas, and I'm proud Kansas has room for these poor negro folks. Sure, I love my kin in the South, but I believe they're wrong in trying to break up the Union. I think President Lincoln did what was right for the whole country when he freed the slaves."

Barbara pushed Josh's hands away. "Oh, you people make me so mad! You seem to think that plantation owners just sit around being waited on. My folks cared for all their people. We took care of their children and their children's children. They were a part of our lives."

"But when you break up slave families by selling them to someone else —"

"Most plantation owners didn't want to break up families, but sometimes they had to, or go bankrupt," Barbara flared.

Without a word, Josh turned abruptly and jerked off his jacket and cap. Barbara drew back. Josh had been warm and friendly from the first, and it hadn't occurred to her that he had ideas of his own. For a little while she had felt accepted by her uncle's family because she had baked a batch of molasses cookies. Now she realized she could never really be a part of them as long as their ideals and beliefs were so different.

She was silent during the noon meal, and shut her ears to Vange's chatter about Ezra and Mehitabel Foster whom she had met at Billings' store that morning. Apparently the settlers were welcoming them with open arms. But Barbara was sure the couple belonged in the South with their masters. Many darkies were smart as anybody; yet they *needed* their white owners as much as the plantations needed them. That's how it was meant to be.

As Thanksgiving Day drew nearer, the Moore women bustled with plans. There would be days of baking and cooking, for John and Rosie, Charlie and Willie had been invited to share the festive meal.

Barbara, briefly having felt accepted because of her display of kitchen know-how, withdrew. Several times she noticed Aggie opening her mouth as if she wanted to ask Barbara to help, then closed it again. *They can't forget I'm a plantation girl who isn't supposed to know anything,* she thought. Well, she wouldn't bother to offer her help. But the cookie-baking episode had taught her one thing: she could learn how to cook, and it wasn't so hard either.

The day before Thanksgiving Aunt Prudy and Aggie hovered between stove and shelf and table with pots and pans and crocks of flour and tins of lard. The cabin grew redolent with the aroma of ducks basting in the oven, prairie chickens, stuffing with dumplings on the back burner of the stove, kettles of boiled, dried corn dotted with fresh butter. Two large sweet potato pies sweetened with wild honey cooled in the lean-to.

Vange and Bitsy scrubbed the kitchen from cupboards to the wide plank floor until the boards shone white.

Barbara stirred restlessly in her bed and sat up on Thanksgiving morning. Already she heard breakfast sounds down in the kitchen. She slipped into her blue-flowered print with the long puffed sleeves and narrow bands of blue piping around the ruffles. Brushing her thick brown hair, she coiled it loosely into a bun and fashioned a snood over it.

Clambering from the loft, she hurried to the table where bowls of fried potatoes, sausages and platters of fried cornmeal mush sent steamy aromas to her nostrils.

In spite of her feelings of detachment after

the altercation between her and Josh and Vange's apparent admiration of the pair of darkies, Barbara was hungry. The family had already begun to eat, for everything must be cleared away before the Thanksgiving guests arrived.

Barbara ate hurriedly, then stacked her plate with the rest of the tableware to be washed.

"Wonder if anyone else is dropping by for service?" Vange wondered out loud.

"Like Roddy Coble, maybe?" Bitsy said, dipping the dirty plates into the pan of hot soapy water. "I hope you didn't invite him to stay for dinner. We'll not have enough grub if we feed every newcomer in the settlement."

"Of course, I didn't invite Roddy!" Vange snorted, pushing the broom furiously as she whisked the crumbs away. "He knows he's welcome any time. But he and Alex Case plan to ride out to Cottonwood Crossing to check Cousin Lank's cattle."

"Well, as long as you keep your greedy little paws to yourself and leave Charlie to me —," Bitsy flung out with a smirk. Aunt Prudy shushed the girls quickly.

"Don't start that again, Elizabeth," she said sternly. "We want Charlie and Willie to feel welcome. Remember, they have no folks. Don't scare them off by being pushy."

Bitsy made a wry face behind her mother's back and began to wipe the yellow oilcloth cover. An amused smile touched Barbara's lips as she watched her cousin. Bitsy was welcome to the sheepman. Her concern with the Warrens was Willie.

Half an hour later the room was tidy and chairs and benches placed in rows. Uncle Daniel, seated at the table, rustled the crisp pages of his Bible, probably looking for his Thanksgiving text.

The door burst open and John and Rosie Frazer rushed in, laughing and stomping their feet. Aunt Prudy took their wraps and they sat down. Minutes later Charlie and Willie arrived.

Barbara, seated on the end of the bench, patted the place beside her. Willie slid next to her.

After singing several hymns, the small congregation waited for Uncle Daniel to lead the short Thanksgiving service. He read several psalms of thankfulness, then prayed.

Barbara's mind wandered. What did any of these homesteaders have for which to be thankful? Or anyone, for that matter? The Civil War had pulled families apart, and property was often stolen or confiscated.

Yet he was naming his blessings one by one.

"For Your leading, Lord, and Your constant presence, we're grateful. We also give thanks for Your abundance to us in this new land, and for Your protection . . . and above all, for Your Son, our Savior Jesus Christ . . ."

After the brief service, the men went outdoors to check on the livestock while the women set the table and prepared the food.

Barbara offered to slice the firm brown loaves of wheat bread. Although the slices came out uneven when she started slicing, she carefully finished off the task with almost even slices from the last loaf.

The wind had died to a murmur when the men came into the house. The slow trickling of constant female chatter finally stopped as Uncle Daniel bowed his head to say the table grace. After the "Amen," brisk conversation, then laughter swept over like the prairie wind of which there was no stopping.

The topic of conversation turned inevitably to the war, between servings of succulent roast duck and crisply fried prairie chickens.

"I hear over 6,000 Kansas men have been assigned in all categories to help fight," John Frazer said between bites of the unevenly sliced bread and forkfuls of fluffy mashed potatoes. "Governor Robinson has ordered out all of 13 regiments alone, not to mention the 19th Cavalry."

John was a quiet man, but when he spoke, everyone listened.

"We're lucky that Kansas is not a battle-field," Josh muttered in a low voice.

"Oh, yes, she is!" John said with a fierce-ness that was unlike him. "The war, espe-cially along the Kansas-Missouri border, rages very hot at times. John Brown and his men —"

"Abolitionists," Uncle Daniel cut in tartly, helping himself to more dried corn.

"But the border ruffians are doing their dirty work, trying to make Kansas a slave state. We don't need them to tell us on which side to fight!"

Uncle Daniel cleared his throat. "I've always hated war," he said gravely. "I would do anything in my power to avoid it. But I must stand for the Union, although Presi-dent Lincoln said in his inaugural speech that he would not recognize the power of any party to break the contract of the Union."

Bitsy spoke up quickly. "I'm for the North, of course, Pa."

"Not the North, child," Uncle Daniel said. "The Union. The whole United States must bind the North and South together in a strong, free country."

"If it hadn't been for the Jeff Davis rebellion —" Josh began, and Barbara opened her mouth, her face white.

"Rebellion!" she stormed. "Our Confederate states were driven! I think you Yankees are just plain crazy, all of you!"

A silence settled over the Thanksgiving table, and Barbara hung her head. It made her furious to think that this group of people thought they had all the answers.

"Barbara," Uncle Daniel spoke softly and kindly, "I'm sorry we've overstepped our tactfulness in discussing the war at this table. You have every right to feel as you do. Please forgive us if we've seemed ungracious."

She opened her mouth to answer, when a knock sounded at the door. Josh jumped up and hurried to open it. William Billings' large frame filled the doorway.

"I brought over a letter for Miss Barbara Temple," he said, holding out a worn, dirt-stained envelope.

"For me?" She scrambled to her feet and flew toward him. She was sure the letter was from Matthew. She tore open the envelope and read the words hastily. Then she gave a low cry.

"Barbara?" Aunt Prudy was beside her in an instant. "Is anything wrong?"

The room was suddenly silent. Barbara moistened her dry lips. "Matthew's been . . . wounded, although not too badly. He was with General Bragg in at the battle of Chickamauga in the northwest part of Georgia. The . . . losses were heavy, but he says they've driven the Union soldiers away. So there! Do you still think the North will win?" she flung out. "The war will soon be over. You'll see!"

Willie leaned toward her. "I suppose you'll leave as soon as it's over?"

"The very minute it's over, I'm taking the stage for home!"

His blue eyes clouded, and his merry face grew grim. "Then I hope it lasts a long time."

CHAPTER 12

Christmas dawned bleak and gray with sleet crackling against the windows. When she scratched the frosted panes, Barbara saw only snow-packed prairies, and snow-laced timber along the river. The first winters for the settlers had been severe, but the one of '63–'64 seemed even worse.

Since the first of December a fierce storm had blown up and dashed itself into a three-day frenzy before its hysteria wore itself out. The hard-packed trails were ridged up two or three feet above the surface of the ground. Ice-winged prairie chickens perched on snow-covered bushes and floundered in the deep drifts. For weeks the wind had howled across the bare plains and piled the snow waist high in places.

The whole month was one endless fight to care for livestock, dig away drifts and cut stacks of firewood. Uncle Daniel and Josh worried about the feed holding out. Each time a storm slowed, they planned to turn animals out to forage for dried grass, but the storm seldom stopped. It seemed to Barbara the stomp of snow-crusted boots and clink of shovels were always in her ears as the men dug a trail to the barns to feed the farm animals.

Food became scarce. Every night they ate porridge made from a hard boil of cracked corn after it had cooled. With it they had milk and molasses.

Now as the family gathered to celebrate Christmas, they exchanged simple gifts of handkerchiefs, pincushions and warm knitted mittens and scarves. Later Charlie and Willie staggered through the snow, Willie proudly bearing a catfish he had caught through a hole in the ice of the Cottonwood.

In the reddish glow from the logs of the fireplace, they munched buttered popcorn and played jokes and charades. It was a Christmas unlike Barbara had ever experienced. She felt suspended in limbo, without feeling; at times, homesickness for the South wrenched through her like a physical pain.

Yet somehow this Christmas wrapped itself around her like a shawl that warmed her heart. Vange and Bitsy were up to their usual jokes, Bitsy quipping that the world's greatest glacier was spotted by a man with good "ice sight" and Vange insisting that knitted socks were first used for hand warmers but soon went down to "defeat."

The girls rocked with laughter at Josh's ". . . prairie chickens in a cottonwood tree" from a parody on *The 12 Days of Christmas*.

After the new year of 1864, the sun shone warm and snows melted; water ran sluggish and black under the icy surface of the Cottonwood. A few days later the prairie was held in another frigid blast of winter wind. Barbara hovered endlessly by the fireplace. Sometimes she thought she could never be warm again. She read and reread the few cheap novels she had brought from Georgia as she toasted her toes in the warmth of the fire.

One evening in late February a loud rap sounded on the cabin door after Woodson's sharp bark. When Uncle Daniel got up to open it, the candles on the mantel guttered in the wind as three young men stumbled in, half frozen.

Roddy Coble, his handsome face red from the biting frost, introduced his friends who held out frostbitten hands toward the fire.

"This here's Alex Case," he said, pounding the black-haired mustachioed young man on the back. "And that tall, gangly Iowan is Reuben Riggs. He's built a cabin right up the trail toward Lost Springs."

Riggs bowed deeply. "At your service, folks. If you need a lawyer to represent you, notice the shingle above my door."

"Doesn't he remind you of Abe Lincoln, the Great Emancipator?" Alex chortled.

Everyone laughed, and a smile tugged at Barbara's lips. It wasn't exactly funny, but it was a break in the dull monotony of the long dreary winter. Even the mention of President Lincoln hardly fazed her. The cabin was snug and warm, and with the talk and laughter all around she felt almost serene and secure.

As usual, the conversation soon turned to the war. "I hear General Grant has driven back the forces on Missionary Ridge," Riggs said with an air of authority, "where the losses were tremendous. Over 700 of our Union soldiers were killed and nearly 5,000 wounded."

"That cuts back our army pretty deep, doesn't it?" Josh asked.

"Yes, it does. Our governor is calling for more enlistments. Fighting is tough, and it's hard not to rush and join them."

"Our Kansas Ninth has been a well-traveled regiment this past year," Alex added.

Josh leaned forward, his chin on his hands. "And all I do is turn sod and chop wood," he said somewhat bitterly.

Barbara turned her head sharply. Was Josh thinking of enlisting? Thus far, her uncle's family had not actually participated in fighting. When she saw the fire of patriotism burn in her cousin's eyes, she shivered a little.

As the three men prepared to leave, Vange followed them to the door. Roddy Coble drew her aside for a few whispered words, and she blushed as they spoke. Soon they bustled out the door in a barrage of laughter and farewells.

Joshua Moore was quiet for the next several days. Barbara figured he was battling with the thought of enlisting in the army, and it made her edgy. But if he needed anyone's advice or sympathy, he never let on.

She soon forgot her fears because he didn't mention it as the weeks wore on.

One mild afternoon in early March, when the snows had begun to melt and the prairie lay soggy underfoot, Rosie, her face pink from the cold under her bright cap, burst into the cabin and flung her brown cape on a chair.

"Guess what! I just had to run over and tell you." Her words fairly bubbled. "John and I . . . we're going to have a baby next fall!"

Vange and Bitsy looked up from their perpetual quilt blocks, their eyes locking.

"Oh, dear, oh, dear," Bitsy murmured with a malicious grin, "I'm too young to be an auntie."

"What about me?" Vange said, shaking her glorious auburn head.

"I'm younger," Bitsy argued.

"Who cares? It's John and Rosie's baby," Aggie retorted. "It's Rosie who's too young to be a mother."

Aunt Prudy gave a quiet, grandmotherly nod, and Barbara stared at Rosie who looked very young with her softly-braided hair. It was hard to imagine Aunt Prudy cuddling a grandchild. Wouldn't it be sort of awful to have a baby? There was more to getting married than romance, Barbara pondered.

She recalled negro women wailing and screaming as they gave birth to little kinky-headed babies in the cabins beyond the sheds on the plantation and how her mother had taken a personal interest in each one. Would Aunt Prudy make over Rosie's baby in the same way?

Aggie laid aside her sewing and got up to stir the fire. "This calls for a celebration. We've got some dried plum cakes and I'll fix a pot of coffee to go with it."

"Well, ours won't be the first child born in the settlement," Rosie added. "I hear Silas and Hannah are expecting an addition in late summer."

"Already?" Bitsy screeched. "I don't see how. Silas is forever riding after the Kaws!"

"Bitsy! That's not very delicate. But we'll start knitting bootees and caps right away," Aunt Prudy said, laying aside her shears and sorting through her bag of yarn. "You take good care of yourself, Rosie."

"Oh, Ma, I will!" Rosie said, an excited flutter in her voice.

"Already one grandchild," Aunt Prudy said dreamily.

"And when Vange marries Roddy —"

"I'm not going to marry him," Vange snapped. "That's what I told him the night the men were here."

"Why not? You don't wanna be an old maid," Bitsy teased. "I know I don't."

"Well, Roddy's not the right one for me. Don't ask me how I know. I just do."

A heavy silence hung over the room at her words. Barbara thought, *Why, with her and Matthew there had never been a time when they hadn't planned to be married.* She hoped Vange knew what she was doing in turning down a handsome catch like R. C. Coble. But perhaps Vange had prayed, as she and

Bitsy had mentioned that night last summer.

Rosie's exciting news colored the daily fabric of their lives in the coming weeks. Baby quilts, squares of flour sacking for diapers and knitted caps and bootees became constant topics of conversation as scissors snipped and needles flew.

When Josh announced that he was riding into Council Grove with Henry Blanchard on a two-day trip for supplies and garden seeds, Aunt Prudy hastily scribbled items on a scrap of brown paper.

"Make sure the flannel's nice and soft, Joshua," she said, shoving the paper into his gloved hands. "It's none too soon to cut out little kimonos and sacques to sew, so bring plenty."

"I'll practice crocheting edgings on your pantalets, Vange," Bitsy said after Josh had left. "By the time I've learned to do a neat job —"

"You leave my pantelets alone!" Vange shrieked.

"If you hadn't turned down Roddy Coble, think how nice you'd look, climbing on his horse with a graceful swish of your skirt," Bitsy said dryly. "Or are you still waiting on that handsome brave?"

Vange glared at Bitsy, and Barbara turned

away. To hear her cousins' good natured banter sometimes grated on her nerve. Talk. Talk. Talk. If Aggie joined them, they sounded like a bunch of saucy blue jays in the timber. At least, that's what she'd heard Josh mutter.

When the last snow had melted on the south side of the stacks, the chickens, scratching wildly in the wet straw, seemed to think spring had come.

Josh returned from Council Grove two days later. Unpacking his saddle bags on the table, small brown parcels of peas and beans and sweet corn and turnips spilled from the contents. Then he drew out a bolt of soft, white flannel.

"It's the softest they had, Ma," he said, winding the string from the package into a spool to re-use.

"It's fine," Aunt Prudy said. "Aggie can get busy this very afternoon cutting out baby garments."

Josh seemed preoccupied as the family sat down to their meal that night, Barbara thought. Finally he spoke.

"The recruiting officer was at the tavern when we got there," he said. "I . . . couldn't help myself, Pa. I signed up."

"You . . . you'll join the army?" Uncle Daniel said, smothering a plateful of cornbread with molasses.

"Yes. It's the 'year of decision' for the Union, as they say. Most Kansas regiments are engaged in fighting. The Eighth's been returned to Chattanooga, and I'll be joining the Tenth in Tennessee. Or maybe I'll help wipe up the guerillas in Missouri."

A sharp, indrawn breath escaped Aunt Prudy. "But the guerillas are so reckless. Don't forget what they did to Lawrence!"

"I want to see this war ended, Ma," Josh said stubbornly. "If I can do something to help bring it to a close . . ."

Barbara shut her ears to the war talk. *If only it was over,* she thought. Then she could go home and forget about this wild, windy prairie and its dedicated settlers.

"When do you leave, Joshua?" Aunt Prudy asked, quietly buttering a piece of cornbread and nibbling nervously on the crusty top.

"Tomorrow."

The word struck the room into silence. Barbara felt her muscles tighten and a bitterness seeped into her mouth for she had always liked her cousin Joshua Moore. Suddenly she hated him.

"I suppose," she began icily, "you're fighting for the North?"

"Yes."

"Yankee!" She spat out the word. "I hope to God you and Matthew never meet!"

She turned and fled from the cabin. Coatless, and without her bonnet, she stormed out along the river path, her lustrous long curls streaming behind her. Away, away from the forces that were destroying her life, her ideals. *I should've known,* she thought. *Josh would want to fight against Matthew.*

She scarcely noticed the heavy silence in the pale evening until suddenly a coyote howled from somewhere along the creek. Another answered faintly from a distance, and an owl hooted in the timber. Already shadows were crowding into the undergrowth. Woodson, the Moores' dog, had followed her and perked up his ears at the howls and hoots as he sniffed around the bushes.

"Hey, where ya goin' so fast?"

Someone spoke out in the semi-darkness, and Barbara drew back, startled. Then she recognized Willie, who had merged with the shadows of the river.

"Willie!" she gasped.

"Anythin' wrong? Where's your cape? You'll freeze out here."

She tried to read his face in the dimness, then shook her head.

"Willie, Josh got home from Council Grove . . . with news that he's joining the army!"

"Well, the country needs volunteers, don't it?"

"Not for the North! Don't forget, I'm for the South. So how can I forgive —"

"You can and you will," Willie announced firmly. "We all want this war to end, one way or another, don't we? You'll go back and tell him goodbye like you outta."

"No! I can't."

"What if Josh is killed? Or loses an arm or somethin'? If he wants to fight for what he believes, why should you try to stop him? Wouldn't you stand up for what you believe?"

Barbara didn't answer. What if she never saw Josh again? Her heart stopped its frantic pounding and she looked up at the yellow cowslip moon that had crept up over the bare branches of the cottonwoods. Woodson nuzzled her legs as she moved toward the young boy.

"Willie . . ." Her words were low. "I don't know what you're doing out here, but I think I'm glad you were. I needed you tonight . . . someone to listen to me. Almost as though Whatley was here."

"Well," he chuckled. "Oh, Charlie said he thought he heard one of his ewes out here. And with those coyotes howlin' too close for comfort, I offered to look. And I find you, one poor lost lamb. You all right now?"

"Yes." Barbara nodded. "I think I am. But Josh . . . what he's doing . . . I can never accept."

"Sorry, Barbara. Well, it's gettin' late. Better toddle back to the cabin. You're freezin' out here. Go on now."

As she walked shivering back into the cabin, Barbara bit her lower lip. She couldn't say goodbye to Josh tomorrow. For how could she agree with his *cause?*

CHAPTER 13

Barbara made herself conspicuously absent when Josh left for the army. The three Moore girls seemed quieter than usual, but not for long. Too soon they chattered and laughed between hemming flour sack squares for diapers and stitching dainty edgings around the little squares Aggie had painstakingly cut out and sewed, using the newspaper pattern Aunt Prudy had dug out of her old chest that stood at the foot of the bed in the east bedroom.

"If Rosie doesn't have twins or triplets, it won't be Aggie's fault!" Bitsy grouched after she threw the seventh hemmed diaper on the table. "Why, you're not even giving Rosie a chance to sew for her own baby."

"Wait until you get married and one after another 'stairstep' arrives," Vange warned. "You'll be mighty happy for Aggie's needle and thread."

"That's ages away," Bitsy scoffed. "By then I'll be rich enough for a store-bought layette."

"Who wants flimsy store-bought stuff?" Aggie put in dryly. "And how do you know Charlie's sheep will produce enough wool for you to get so uppity?"

"What's Charlie's sheep have to do with it?" Bitsy fumed.

Vange and Aggie laughed themselves silly, and Bitsy flounced up the loft in a huff.

Barbara sighed. If she weren't so clumsy with a needle she might have offered to help, but sewing was completely out of her range of abilities. Letters from Matthew were infrequent, but the sun shone brighter when word came that he was alive and well again.

One bright spring morning when Uncle Daniel came in from a trip to the blacksmith shop in Marion Centre, he was full of news.

"Looks as though we're finally going to have a school," he announced. "John Snow has loaned some logs for a schoolhouse. There's to be two sash windows, a puncheon roof covered with dirt and a door to the west. It's to be built half mile north on the east side of Clear Creek. Men are working on it already."

"What about a teacher? What good is a school without a schoolmarm?" Aggie asked.

"Rebecca Shreve has consented to teach," Uncle Daniel said.

"You hear that, Bitsy?" Vange called out. "You're not 16, so here's your chance to acquire more sense."

"Me? But I have to help Ma with the work. You know that!"

Aunt Prudy punched down the bread dough with a vicious whack. "As long as Vange and Aggie are around, I can spare you. One less person to giggle and chatter would suit me fine. Besides, I thought you hated hemming diapers."

Bitsy gave a delicate snort and turned to Barbara. "What do you say we both go?"

"Go to school?" Barbara's brow furrowed. She had thought her days of education were ended when Miss Mallory's Academy in Atlanta had closed due to the war. Of course, there would be no music, no fine arts, no ballet and cotillion dancing. But it would give her something to do. Life was boring as it was. "Maybe I will. I can help Rebecca, if nothing else."

"Good. When the schoolhouse is finished and school begins, we can ride out with Willie," Bitsy said with a toss of her gold head. "Both of us on Petunia."

Several days later the thin, bitter air of winter again rasped like sandpaper and taunted the earth with its biting chill. The next day a balmy south wind fanned across the prairies. The changeable Kansas weather defied understanding.

With the feel of the spring breeze in her face and the aroma of fresh-turned loam in her nostrils, one morning Barbara rode out to see the new schoolhouse. More and more new families had settled in the community. Barbara decided to stop at the Billings store to ask for mail first. There was always news to pick up, too.

Crates of eggs and a few bolts of cloth, barrels of molasses, sugar and salt, and dried beans, crackers, herring, and codfish and strips of buffalo jerky gave the store an air of distinction.

When she came into the store, she noticed Grandma Griffith at the dry goods counter debating between a bolt of dark blue print and a brown fabric, sprigged with tiny yellow flowers.

"Let me see —" she said as her black shoe-button eyes squinted. "I think I'll take the blue. More practical." She turned, obviously hearing Barbara's footsteps behind her. "Oh, it's you, gal. Been doin' any nursin' since last fall?"

Barbara stiffened. "Oh, no." She shook her head. "I'm not a nurse, you know, Mrs. Griffith. I . . . I just helped take care of Willie."

"Well, you didn't do so bad at that. But of course, any gal on the frontier must pull her

188

weight. My daughter Molly Hoops and husband Evin and the two young'uns will arrive here in a few weeks. Told her to be prepared to live where there's no doctor. And be sure to bring along her doctorin' book."

"Where are they coming from?"

"Indiana, same as us." She lifted a pail of fresh eggs onto the counter. "Here, count 'em, William. I think there's enough to pay for the yard goods. Need an extra dress and apron for when I go out to deliver Hannah's baby."

William Billings, who was counting out the eggs, paused and looked up. "We're mighty obliged for offerin' to deliver our first grandchild, Miz Griffith. If only Silas hadn't dragged Hannah out to Cottonwood Crossin' with its Injuns pokin' their heads into windows and scarin' the womenfolk half silly."

"Indians?" Barbara cut in sharply. "I didn't know there were Indians around."

"Guess they're more curious in those parts, what with Lank's cattle. One night when Hannah was home alone washin' the dishes, she looked up and seed a grinnin' Kaw face at each of the six window panes. Sure hope the scare ain't harmed the baby none."

Barbara tossed her head. "Well, that's

189

stupid. People around here are so backwoodsy that they'd believe anything!"

With a delicate snort, she started for the door, then stopped short. A negro man and woman sauntered through the door and the round-faced woman wearing a drab gray cotton dress smiled at Barbara. As Barbara whirled around and rushed out of the store, she thought bitterly, *I suppose they're more negro slaves running away to Kansas. Why couldn't they have stayed in the South where they belonged? I wish I was there right now . . .*

She headed Petunia northeast below the bluff where a well-worn path led up to the new schoolhouse. Having seen the negro couple at the store, her thoughts were wrapped up in the sudden reminder of the war-torn South. The last letter from Matthew told of bad droughts, poor food and always the great loss of life. Soldiers were worn out. He didn't know how long they could hang on.

She skirted the log across the gurgling stream and climbed up the bank. The schoolhouse sat on the edge of the timber amid a tangle of wild grapevines and scrub oak. Trees formed a backdrop for its dark logs, and the gentle prairie sloped away from the open doorway.

The sound of sawing and the fresh smell

of newly-cut logs met her as she slid from Petunia's back and stepped through the doorway. The building was about 10 by 14 feet, with a dirt floor. A dry goods box stood on the far end, probably to serve as the teacher's desk, and the seats were of freshly-cut split logs.

A wave of revulsion swept over her and she turned away. Imagine, being educated in such a primitive institution of learning! The war had to end soon. Perhaps she needn't attend school here after all.

As she and Petunia started back through town and headed down the trail, she caught sight of White Turkey's familiar figure riding toward her. He was still far down the road, but his red tunic and black hair were unmistakable. Twelve ponies indeed!

Kicking Petunia's ribs, she whirled around and turned south. She knew Widow Margaret Strawhacker's small cabin was nestled around the bend of the Cottonwood, where she lived with her son. Barbara headed straight for the Strawhacker cabin. As she galloped along she recalled the sad story of how Dan Strawhacker had died, leaving Margaret and 14-year-old William Henry to shift for themselves on the raw prairie.

Rounding the bend now, Barbara noticed

the snug, cozy little log cabin set among the cottonwoods and oaks. A beaten path led toward the door and a half dozen horses were tied to the hitching posts. She wanted to get away from White Turkey and hurried inside without knocking.

Several bearded strangers dressed in buckskin and dun-colored shirts were at the breakfast table.

"Oh." Barbara paused awkwardly on the threshold. "I . . I was rushing to get away from White Turkey."

"He didn't hurt you, did he?" the broad, sandy-haired man interrupted.

"Oh, no, sir. But I was afraid —"

"You're safe here," the man said.

"He . . . he offered 12 ponies for me once!"

The man smiled a little. "My name's Kit Carson. This here is General Harney, and those men on that side of the table are James Steele and Thomas Murphy. Over there near the fire are Colonel Bent and Jack Leavenworth."

Margaret Strawhacker took the bewildered Barbara's arm and led her to a chair near the window. "Forget about White Turkey and his 12 ponies, child," she said. "Silas prob'ly told him you're spoken for." She turned her attention to serving breakfast.

"We're stopping here on our way to Atchison to meet with several Indian tribes on the Arkansas River to try to secure safer travel along the Santa Fe Trail," Colonel Bent explained as he took another bite of cornbread. She noticed chunks of buffalo meat on his plate.

"God bless Widder Strawhacker for givin' us such a fine breakfast," added Carson. He got up and went to the door, peering out far across the horizon.

The widow came up behind him. "What do you think our chances are of starting our town and making a go of living here?"

Kit Carson looked at her with pitying blue eyes. Then his face softened. "Well, it seems nature has done everythin' for your country that can be done, or that you could possibly expect. The only drawback is that you may never experience it. If the Indians ever want to raid your settlement, there's nothin' to hinder them from cleanin' you out in an hour. But if they never do, you'll be all right."

Barbara shuddered a little at the Indian scout's words. Yet somehow she felt safe with this group of men. By now White Turkey would have ridden far out of sight, she was sure. She waited until the men went out, sprang on their horses and rode down the trail. She hoped they would succeed in their peacemaking mission with the Indian tribes.

"I'm sure they will. But that won't concern me," she tried to reassure herself. "I'll soon be back in Georgia, where I can forget all about Indians and White Turkey and this wild country." Twelve ponies indeed!

CHAPTER 14

The summer of 1864 was long and hot. News from the war front was not good. Rumors surfaced that Jefferson Davis' life was in danger, Corinth had been evacuated, Memphis deserted and Richmond captured. It seemed the rebels at Corinth had fled farther south to avoid being thrashed by General Halleck. The Union armies were not gaining as rapidly as the settlers in Marion Centre had hoped. But General Sherman, in command of the divisions of the Mississippi, was laying waste to the country, destroying railroads, ordering the rails twisted, burning cotton and bridges. Still, nothing came to a head.

The Moores had hoped that when General Grant was given chief command, he would wind things up in a hurry, but Grant seemed to do little better than Halleck. Aside from knowing Josh was fighting for the North, Barbara cared nothing about the news from the Union front.

As the scorching wind blew across the prairie day after blistering day, pictures marched across Barbara's mind in one endless procession of horror. The battlefields of the South stretched too far away for her to hear the booming cannon or see the gaping wounds or smell the foul odors, but her imagination was fertile. If only the war ended before anything happened to Matthew. Yet the prospects were bleak. The fighting seemed destined to hang on forever.

Barbara, Bitsy and Willie had gone to school for a very brief session. The settler children were needed to help in the fields, and the term had closed after two weeks.

The homestead bustled with activity in spite of the heat. Uncle Daniel with John Frazer's help, dug wells, harvested meager crops of grain and put up stacks of prairie hay for winter cattle feed. Inside, the Moore women were busy with the never-ending tasks of baking, cooking, washing, ironing, sewing and scrubbing.

Deep cracks appeared on the dry prairies as the hot winds sent shimmering waves of heat over the land. Grasses grew brown and brittle while gardens shriveled. Everything edible must be prepared for storage. Honey, crab apples, wild grapes and plums, prairie chickens, quail, wild geese, ducks and rabbits were prepared. The women of the prairie canned whatever food couldn't be dried to be used in the cold months ahead.

In the evenings, after the brassy winds had died and a soft, quiet coolness stole over the prairies, the family often sat outdoors in front of the cabin, talking about the war or community events. When it oppressed her, Barbara slipped away and sauntered toward the river. Now and then she met Willie, and they sat on an old log to talk, but not until Willie had scoured the area for a rattler.

Once a coyote made off with two of Aunt Prudy's hens, and to hear her cousins lament, Barbara was sure the acid of their fury should have been enough to kill the murderous varmint. "Why, that thieving, conniving beast!" Bitsy grumbled. "Ma needs those hens to provide eggs for the family. I have half a mind to —"

"To confront that thieving, conniving beast?" Aggie cut in with a smirk. "Come now, what would you say?"

"I . . . I'd tell that sly fox to leave Ma's hens and Charlie's sheep alone!"

"I didn't know Charlie had lost any," Vange said dryly.

Bitsy grimaced. "Well, as far as I know, he hasn't. But that doesn't mean that a mean coyote won't try."

Her reply sent Vange and Aggie into spasms of laughter.

"I figured Charlie was in the picture somehow," Aggie said after she caught her breath.

The long days dragged by. The girls' harping, teasing, laughing, chatting were never absent. Sometimes it lifted Barbara's spirits and made her smile; other times it grated on her nerves so much that she saddled Petunia and rode away across the prairie. Of course, when the mail came in from Council Grove, she always had a good excuse to ride to Billings' store.

One August morning, before the sun sent its chariot into the brassy sky to pour more heat over the day, Barbara rode up the dusty trail to see if the mail held anything important. Only a few letters for Uncle Daniel and a church magazine had arrived. She choked back a wave of disappointment.

Grandma Griffith was in the store, weighing a few scrawny potatoes in her hands.

"I don't know how we'll manage this winter," she muttered darkly, her black shoe-button eyes snapping. "We're plum out of 'taters, and company here, too."

A pert young woman wearing a faded pink sunbonnet and thin blue calico dress placed her arms around the older woman's shoulders.

"Don't you worry, Ma. We don't have money, but I'm sure we won't starve. The Lord hasn't failed us yet, and I don't expect Him to fail us now."

"I know," Grandma said wearily, "but at times . . ." She spied Barbara standing at the mail pickup corner and hurried toward her. "Oh, you haven't met my daughter Molly Hoops, have you, gal?"

Barbara held out her hand. "How do you do, Molly? I'm Barbara Temple."

"Nice to know you, Barbara," Molly said in a slow, warm voice. "Evin and I and our two girls pulled from Indiana a few weeks ago. Where do you live?"

"With my Uncle Daniel and Aunt Prudy Moore about a mile or so northwest. I . . . I come from Georgia, so this prairie country is very . . . strange to me."

Molly laughed. "I know what you mean. When Evin and I walked a mile south to our claim, and I gazed over the bare prairie and the distant bluffs, I thought, How on earth will we make our living here? We don't even own a team of horses or have enough money to pick up our goods from Atchison! My brother George has been awfully good to us though. We've been living with George and Betsy while Evin has been helping other settlers with their work. In turn, they'll help us put up our cabin."

"Yes," Barbara said with a faint smile, "the settlers are good about helping each other."

"I'll be glad to get settled. Evin and Hank Roberts are going to Atchison with a team of oxen to pick up our goods soon. After our cabin is up, we can move in."

Grandma Griffith placed the handful of potatoes on the counter. "I guess this is all I can afford this time, William. We'll scout around for pokeweed by the river for our supper tonight. Tastes better with a few 'taters thrown in. By the way, William, I trust Hannah's doin' fine?"

"Yes, and the baby's doin' good, too," he responded gruffly with a bit of embarrassment at the idea of talking about babies.

"Oh! Did Silas and Hannah's baby come?" Barbara asked.

"She did," Grandma Griffith said. "A girl named Anna Belle born a week ago. I guess maybe you hadn't heard, although the Moore girls always know everythin'! But there so much excitement at the time that we didn't know how things was goin' to turn out."

"What happened?"

"I knew the child was due so I rode up to Cottonwood Crossin' a week ago with

Henry Blanchard. The baby no more'n put in her arrival when a couple of men rushed into the ranch house and yelled, 'Indians are comin'. Barricade the doors and keep out of sight!' The men climbed on the roof with guns. Sure enough, about a hundred Indians rode up, demandin' cattle. While they bickered with Lank and the men on the roof, I grabbed the axe with one hand and the coffee pot with the other. Pourin' a cup of coffee, I shoved it toward Hannah. 'Here, drink this,' I told her. Well, the Indians won that round, ridin' off with 30 head of cattle, but no lives was lost. Although one of Lank's men got a nick in his arm."

"You mean *Indians,* so near here?" Barbara gasped. "Did they leave?"

"Oh, yes. But that axe never left my side. Just let an Injun poke his head in the door and he'd have been sorry. It about scared the daylights out of Keziah, so she sent William to Moores' ranch with a wagon and brung me and Hannah and the wee child back here."

"Oh, Ma, you never told me how brave you were!" Molly cried, cradling Grandma Griffith's head against her shoulder.

Barbara tucked her mail into the wide pocket of her blue gingham and with a nod to the two women, she left.

As she rode Petunia toward the west, the sun's rays were already beating down on her straw bonnet. It would be another scorching day. She thought of Hannah and the tiny baby in the stifling heat of the living quarters above the store. How could one cope when faced with such primitive conditions? Aunt Prudy maintained that one could handle anything if one had to. *Will I ever have to confront trouble the way these people on the prairie are confronted almost daily?* she wondered.

It was easier to shrug off those disquieting feelings and think of something else, like riding in a carriage along the wide avenue among magnolias on Atlanta's quiet streets, wearing a blue silk dress and holding a matching parasol over her head. It was the best way to forget about raiding Indians and the burning summer wind.

She decided to ride by the river for a breath of cooler air. Maybe Willie would be waiting for her. Suddenly she heard Bitsy's shrill voice:

"Bar-b'ra, we've found blackberries!"

I guess I should help pick, she decided, but it's so hot. Still, the bushes along the water would offer welcome shade.

Sliding from the horse, she tied it to a limb of a scrub oak, and made her way carefully through the brush. The sound of chatter and laughter led her directly to the blackberry bramble where Aggie, Vange and Bitsy, lips and fingers purpled with berry stains, were plinking the ripe berries into their pails.

"Come on, join the fun." Vange shoved a pail into Barbara's hands.

"Just think of the luscious pies and the jellies to spread on your cornbread next winter," Aggie reminded her.

"And the purple stain on your teeth," Bitsy added and then began to sing lustily off-key to the tune of "Lavender's Blue":

"Blackberries blue on the bushes today;
Blackberry pies Aggie will make Saturday . . ."

The other two girls joined her, Vange's voice sweet and clear, Aggie's thin and high, while Bitsy with her slightly off-key soprano rolled her blue eyes with every note. Barbara tied Petunia nearby, then picked berries in silence amid this small group of gay carollers.

After the pails were full, the girls started back for the cabin. Barbara led Petunia toward the barn and stabled her. When she came into the kitchen, the girls were washing the berries while Uncle Daniel sat at the table munching a piece of corn-bread.

With all the laughter and chatter, Barbara hardly heard the horseman riding up until she heard the creaking of the screen door. It was flung open so suddenly that its jarring almost knocked her against the wall.

A man stood on the threshold, wild-eyed, breathing hoarsely. "Indians are coming!"

The chatter died as sharply as the snap of a brittle branch from a cottonwood. Everyone stared at the man, and no one moved for a minute. The news hung in the stillness like the silence of the prairie after a crash of thunder.

Uncle Daniel laid down his half-eaten bread. "We've heard that story before," he drawled with a wry smile.

"It's true this time," the man's voice rose into a screech. "A man run his horse all the way from Wichita. They're on the rampage along the Arkansas River, killin' and burnin' everythin' as they come!"

He whirled around and sprang on his horse, and they could hear the clatter of hooves on the trail as he headed toward Marion Centre.

Barbara thought, *I had almost begun to believe we were safe. Uncle Daniel's words when he first picked me up: 'A peaceful prairie country . . . Indians friendly,' he said. And then the men at Widow Strawhacker's who came to make peace with the red men . . .*

There was no song and laughter now. Not a minute had gone by, but it seemed like an hour in that frozen silence. The three Moore girls and Aunt Prudy were white-faced and Barbara's hands grew clammy with fear.

Uncle Daniel jumped to his feet and grabbed his gun and straw hat. "We'd best head for the Shreves'. They've got a stone wall on the west side of their cabin to ward off Indian attacks. Hurry and grab some food. We'll leave as soon as I can bring the team around," he said as he stormed from the cabin.

With wiry little Aunt Prudy and the versatile Aggie in charge, Vange, Bitsy and Barbara scooped together a pitifully small food supply.

"No Indian's going to make off with my wild strawberry jam!" Aggie said stoutly as she grabbed several jars from the cupboard shelf.

Bitsy snatched up a box of baby clothes. "Ain't no Injun making off with Rosie's baby things! I hemmed too many diapers to let the redskins make off with them."

Vange and Barbara snapped up pails of unwashed blackberries. "Nor our berries," Vange grumbled.

Uncle Daniel called the collie and picked him up in his arms. "Neither will they get Woodson!"

Minutes later, the family scrambled into the wagon mid a welter of quilts and blankets which their father insisted they needed. He drove the team as fast as he could toward town. When the wagon turned in at the Shreve enclosure, the sturdy log cabin loomed like a safe haven. Other settlers had arrived, with people rushing indoors.

A heavy silence and low whispers and a sense of fear permeated the small cabin. The only audible sound was the high-pitched wail of Hannah Locklin's baby daughter.

Three young boys — Jack Griffith, Johnny Hallet and Elisha Shreve — offered to go outdoors and look around.

"Maybe you'd better head east, since they're bound to come from the west," Johnny warned.

"Maybe it was antelopes Bill seen, Johnny," someone suggested.

"Antelopes, nuthin'! I'm sure I saw 'em,

too. I know Injuns when I see 'em!"

"Be careful, boys!" William Shreve cautioned as the trio slipped out the door. Barbara huddled in one corner, scarcely breathing. *Will I get out of this alive?* she wondered. *Will I ever see Matthew again?* Somewhere in the background she heard sounds of people praying. *Could Uncle Daniel's God manage this?* she mused bitterly.

Fifteen minutes later the three boys burst through the door. "You better scuttle out to Cottonwood Falls quick. We seen moccasin prints and signs on the other side of the Cottonwood River," Johnny burst out.

"Could've been Kaws," someone suggested, but the boys shook their heads.

In a mad scramble of bodies, people climbed into their wagons and with the sound of fierce gee-hawing, the vehicles left the Shreve cabin. By common consent all were sticking together, bound for Cottonwood Falls for the safety of a small fort. Something was ominous about the long snaky caravan winding across the prairie that led up hill and through the valley of the brown grassy meadow to the east. The creak of wagon wheels, the faint clank of harness, the swish of horses' hooves through the deep prairie growth were something Barbara would never forget.

If Indians came at all, it would be from the west, the boys had said, so someone constantly turned his head and looked back. Barbara thought, *If we live through this, I'll never wander away from the cabin again.*

Then a new fear hit her. Willie! Willie and Charlie weren't in the group. If something happened to Willie, she'd never forgive herself for not warning them. But they had been in such a hurry. Had the rider failed to warn the two in the cabin in the glen?

Night began to fall and the moon swung up over the horizon like a giant silver cartwheel and scattered white magic over the hills. The slow creaking of wagons lulled Barbara and made her drowsy. I'll never sleep again, she vowed as she stifled a yawn. Not with Indians on the warpath. She drew off her straw bonnet and held her bare head on her arms.

Suddenly she awoke to the aroma of sausage frying and the scent of strong coffee brewing and she sat up abruptly.

"What . . . what about the Indians?" she gasped, remembering the terror of the past hours.

"Indians seldom attack at night. We'll sleep on our blankets and a lookout will keep watch all night," Uncle Daniel said.

Barbara crawled stiffly from the wagon

and stretched her legs. She could almost enjoy the soft evening air if the situation were different. If only she knew Willie was safe . . .

Other settlers had built cooking fires, and she saw that the wagons had pulled into a circle. Just then the messenger who had brought the news of the Indian attack, dashed up and slid from his horse.

"What is it, Bill?" George Griffith was on his feet instantly. "Any more news?"

The man rolled his hat in his hands nervously and lowered his eyes. "Yes, and no. I guess there was no Indian raid after all. It seems that some young fellers decided to run down the rumor. They rode out to the river and learned that a white boy and an Indian had actually scuffled and exchanged shots, but there was no real fight. The fellers rode back to town at breakneck speed, firin' their guns, tryin' to play up the incident. They got drunk, and the story got started about a raid." He paused sheepishly. "There's no reason you can't all go back home."

The sighs of relief that came from the encampment sounded like the wind whispering among the cottonwoods.

"Well, let's sleep first," Uncle Daniel suggested. "Ready to stop for prayers, girls? We have much to thank our Lord for."

This time, Barbara was ready to join them. Maybe the Lord did manage things after all.

CHAPTER 15

In September the rain came, lashing at the brown prairies with a violent fury. For more than two hours it blew down in sheets, flung from heavenly buckets, dashing water in spasmodic handfuls against the window panes and seeping into the cabin through the dried chinking between the logs. Long, flickering flashes of lightning, accompanied by drum-rolls of thunder battered the earth until finally the storm had spent itself into a small, persistent wetting shower.

After the skies cleared and the sun broke on the fresh, rain-washed earth, Barbara stepped outdoors. As she started down the short lane toward the trail, her black slippers made squishy sounds on the muddy path, and she lifted her full skirts of the green-sprigged delaine high to keep from spattering the starched crispness. She saw the stalks of goldenrod that always reminded her of lighted candles along the trail.

"Oh —," she caught her breath sharply as she reached the roadside. "What quaint flowers!"

Their golden flames lifted to the bright

sunshine seemed as freshly-scrubbed as Aggie's kitchen floor.

"Halloo!" A voice called from behind her and she whirled around.

"Willie Warren! What are you doing here?" she cried. "And how did you get across the river? All that rain . . ."

He grinned sheepishly. "Oh, I clumb over the east bend on a fallen log above the rushin' water so I could hop across. It flooded our glen, too. Charlie's not happy about that. But I come because I wondered if you know when school's to start."

"Maybe not 'til October. It seems there's still much field work to keep the older students busy."

"I see," Willie said, pushing back his sandy hair. "I hear Molly Griffith will be our teacher, at least, until she gets married."

"Married?" Barbara echoed. "Molly's getting married?"

"To Roddy Coble. I guess after Vange gave him the gate, he started seein' Molly."

Barbara turned away, thinking about Matthew. She hadn't heard from him for so long. Of course, mail didn't always come through. But once the war was finally over and she would return to the South, she'd miss Willie. *He's the one real friend I've got,* she thought.

"You're sorta quiet. Did I say somethin' wrong?" he asked, looking at her with troubled eyes.

"N-no, Willie. I was just thinking that you're my best friend. When the war's over and I leave, I'll miss you," she said in a low voice.

"Well, I'm thinkin' maybe you'll stay."

"Stay!" Barbara flared. "Why should I stay?"

Willie shrugged his shoulders. "Maybe I meant I hope you'll stay."

She smiled coyly. It was one of the nicest compliments she'd heard in a long time.

October came with sunshine filtering in pale yellow through a screen of haze. Maples blazed their vibrant color through the timber, and cottonwoods were wrapped in smoky tones of greenish-bronze.

Bitsy, Barbara and Willie rode their horses to school when it finally opened. Miss Griffith, her thick coils of dark hair piled on the top of her head, sat behind the dry goods box desk. It was romantic to think of Miss Molly and Roddy Coble and the forthcoming wedding. Matthew, with his sandy hair and merry gray eyes the color of Rebel uniforms, pushed into her thoughts again.

The roomful of scholars recited aloud like

a noisy brood of chickens. Barbara settled down to her studies, and the weeks passed without incidence.

November turned raw and cold. Great flocks of ducks flew in V-shapes from the north, rested briefly on the Cottonwood and winged their way south.

President Abraham Lincoln was elected to his second term as President on November 8th. Uncle Daniel and the Moores seemed elated. It made little difference to Barbara one way or another.

"Can you think of him meeting with those big Eastern politicians, breaking into one of his backwoodsy stories?" she scoffed.

"Yeah, with his feet on his desk!" Bitsy added and Vange and Aggie burst into gales of laughter.

"Wish I could've voted," Bitsy said in her usual brash way.

Uncle Daniel looked up, his blue eyes stern. "I guess by nature women weren't intended to vote."

"I'll bet Pa could find that in the Constitution: 'Be it declared that women shall not vote,' " Bitsy muttered, and Vange rocked with laughter again.

"Or in the Bible," Vange added between chuckles.

"But the President has plenty of horse

sense," Uncle Daniel said, frowning. "He's got gumption, too, tackling the profound problems of our nation during this grave period in time."

What good does all his gumption do, Barbara thought, *if he can't put an end to this awful fighting?*

One early, bitterly cold Saturday morning the girls were awakened by Uncle Daniel's booming voice from the kitchen.

"Hurry on down, girls. It's something important."

Barbara, stirring in the warm cocoon of the heavy wool comforts and feather tick, uncovered her head. Already Vange and Aggie were scrambling into their clothes, shivering with every jerk. Bitsy sat up and yawned.

As Barbara began to dress, her cousins were ready to climb down the ladder. Joining them in the icy kitchen shortly after, Barbara learned Uncle Daniel and Aunt Prudy had gone and the girls were bundling into their heavy jackets and scarves.

"What's up?" Barbara mumbled, still half asleep.

"Rosie's baby is about to come. John stopped by to get Ma, and Pa's off to Marion Centre to pick up Grandma Griffith," Aggie explained, hurriedly wrapping a long knitted scarf around her ears. "It's beastly cold out and Pa wants us to do the barnyard chores. Think you could fix breakfast?"

Barbara stifled a yawn. "I'll try, but I won't promise any wonders."

"Well, you can boil water, can't you?" Bitsy said, pulling on long knitted mittens.

"Don't worry. I won't let you down," she called out after them as they slammed out of the lean-to door and headed toward the barns.

The cold wind blew around Barbara's back like an icy trickle of water down her shivering spine. She shook as she threw another handful of fagots into the testy black stove and added another log to the fireplace.

Now . . . what next? Pour water into the gray enameled coffee pot for coffee. Stir up cornbread for breakfast. Fry sausages. There was ice in the water bucket and she was forced to chop it with a heavy iron spoon. She got out the mixing crock Aggie and Aunt Prudy used, and searched for cornmeal on the shelf of staples beside the stove. A new wrinkle crept between her eyes. How much cornmeal? She had no idea, but she'd have to guess. A few cupfuls should do. She added water and a bit of salt and beat the dough vigorously. Then she poured it into the black square pan and shoved it into the oven.

When the water in the coffee pot began to boil, she dumped in two tablespoons of browned rye which the Moores used for coffee. In seconds it boiled over the rim and hissed on the hot stove top. The odor was fetid and stifling.

A scorching scent seeped from the oven, and she yanked at the oven door. A wave of black smoke spewed out and she slammed it quickly.

"Oh, drat!" she wailed. "Why did I ever promise to fix breakfast? I wanted to help, but everything's ruined . . ."

At that moment she noticed the sausages were beginning to turn black. She grabbed the handle of the skillet with her bare hands and jerked it from the front to the rear of the stove. Pain stung her hands and she grimaced at the red, searing marks on her palms. The room was growing dim with smoke that filtered from the blackened cornbread in the oven.

Nothing had gone right with the breakfast she'd tried to cook. She sat down on a chair and cradled her head in her arms and cried.

Just then she heard stomping in the lean-to and the girls burst into the kitchen, carrying pails of foaming milk with hands stiff and cold. Barbara's sounds of sobbing continued.

"Barbara!" Aggie cried, slamming her milk pail down and placing a hand on the quaking shoulders. "What's wrong?"

"I've ruined everything!" she sobbed. "Just when I wanted . . . so much to help."

Vange and Bitsy looked at each other, then Bitsy muttered, "just as we figured when we smelled all that smoke like the inside of an Injun tepee!"

"We thought maybe you were fixing buffalo jerky," Vange retorted, and Bitsy added, "which we've never been able to accomplish. Congratulations, Barbie; you've succeeded in something."

A wave of red color swept over her face. She knew they were teasing as usual, but it only made her feel worse. In minutes someone had grabbed a hot pad and dumped the scorched cornbread out the back door. Soon the coffee was bubbling merrily with real coffee smells, and the sausages, not as badly burnt as she'd feared, were simmering lightly in their own drippings.

While Vange and Bitsy strained the milk through squares of white cheesecloth, Aggie whipped up another batch of corn bread and slapped the pan into the oven.

Wearily Barbara set the table, wincing with pain as she took down plates and flatware from the cupboard shelves.

When the meal was ready and the girls sat down to eat, Barbara merely pushed the food around on her plate.

"Barb! What's happened to your hands?" Vange asked suddenly, obviously noticing the red streaks on her palms. "You burned them, trying to fix breakfast, didn't you?"

Aggie jumped up and hurried to the shelf and returned with a jar of something. "Here. Let me put some skunk fat on the burns," she said, picking up Barbara's painful hands.

She snatched them away. "Skunk fat? Never!"

"But it'll soothe the pain," Aggie went on, taking the soft white hands into her calloused brown ones. "You did a brave thing, trying to cook breakfast when you've had little experience. Looks as though you could stand a few cooking lessons."

The skunk fat soothed the red burns, and Barbara looked up. "Do you mean . . . you'd teach me? I guess it's time I learned something."

"We'll be glad to help you. Just don't you worry," Bitsy chirked. "And with your poor, singed hands, you'll be excused from doing dishes for awhile. Aren't you lucky!"

Barbara thought, *They're so kind, even if they're funny. They could've been mad because I ruined breakfast. It's high time I did something decent once in awhile.*

As the cousins breezed through the morning chores, Barbara sat at the table and listened to their incessant chatter and spurts of laughter.

"Sure hope Rosie isn't having a hard time," Vange said, suddenly sober, as she scraped the soot from the top of the stove. "If I'm going to be an auntie I don't want Rosie to kill herself to make it happen."

"Remember, I'll be an auntie, too," Bitsy scoffed. "I hope we can get word to Josh. I can just hear him in his next letter: 'Dear Ma and Pa and lady-uncles'!"

The three collapsed with laughter and Barbara grinned. She had begun to feel like a part of the family after all these months, in spite of their differences. Maybe it was time she took part in their fun and games, too.

The day dragged on, with Aggie piling bags of flour and pans of molasses on the table as she rolled out four tins of dough for dried apple pies, pans of wheat bread and sweet rolls. While Bitsy donned her heavy wraps and brought in armloads of stovewood for the cookstove and fireplace,

Vange tackled the cleaning. All the kitchen shelves received a thorough scrubbing as well as the bare plank floor. Barbara, her hands wrapped in unbleached muslin bandages, could do little but watch as she had done so many times before. She'd played the southern belle for so long. Somehow she was beginning to appreciate the efforts of pioneers to carve out their lives on the raw prairies.

The Seth Thomas clock on the mantel ticked away the minutes and hours with no word from John and Rosie's cabin. The girls grew silent, and Barbara knew they were all concerned about their sister. The silence that hung over the usually noisy cabin seemed unusually deep.

Suddenly there was a loud stomping in the lean-to. As the door burst open with a gust of icy air, Uncle Daniel and Aunt Prudy staggered in, their faces raw from the cold.

Barbara noticed their grim faces immediately. Something was evidently wrong. She sprang from her chair and hurried toward them.

"Is anything wrong?" she asked.

Uncle Daniel's jaw muscles worked tensely and Aunt Prudy turned her face away.

"Rosie had . . . has a boy . . . Samuel John," Uncle Daniel spoke in a thin, haggard voice.

"A boy?" she echoed.

The three girls flew around like a flock of squawking chickens. "How big is he?" "Does he have Rosie's honey-colored hair?" "Is he bald?" "Is John bustin' his buttons?" Questions tumbled all over each other.

Uncle Daniel pulled off his greatcoat and peeled the knitted mittens from his hands. Aunt Prudy, her little face pinched and tired, her wispy hair sagging at its pins, drew off her wool cap and shrugged out of her quilted wrap.

"Rosie . . . had a very bad time. Grandma Griffith did all she could. But —"

"But I thought you said *has* a boy. What —" Aggie countered.

"The baby's health is damaged. He . . . he's ill, and always will be." Aunt Prudy's voice was low and sad.

Uncle Daniel cleared his throat. "Aggie, you'd better pack up right away and go help Rosie. She — your sister — needs you. I'll drive you over on the wagon when you're ready, then I'll take Grandma Griffith back home."

Barbara pulled a chair close to the fire and led Aunt Prudy toward it, pushing her into it gently. Why, Aunt Prudy was getting old! She was a grandmother now, and grandmothers needed to rock. If only there was a rocker.

Aunt Prudy sighed deeply. "This past night has made me feel as ancient as Sarah, Abraham's wife. But you have to get along in years, so I guess one does what one has to do and accepts what one can't help. And, of course, trust the Lord and hang on."

Barbara felt a stab of pity for the pioneer women who must brave rugged life along without proper medical care because no doctor was available. She thought of Rosie and how she must have agonized to bring her firstborn into the world, then to learn he would never be normal.

Dear Lord, she prayed, *give her grace and strength. Let all be well somehow . . .*

CHAPTER 16

The week passed. A sullen gray cloud bank rose up in the west, and the balmy breeze that had blown from the warm south all day whirled suddenly around to the north, whipping angrily down the dim road.

As the wagon headed northwest along the river toward Cottonwood Crossing, Barbara crouched down on the straw-filled wagon box, pulling the buffalo robe around her. Vange and Bitsy took turns stomping their feet to keep warm, for the hot soapstones had long lost their warmth. They bumped their heads together and laughed as the wagon swayed on the bumpy road.

"I'm sure I can hear the buffalo thunder," Bitsy muttered and the girls laughed again.

Then she began to sing lustily:

"Over the river and through the wood, to Cousin Lank's ranch we go. The horse knows the way —"

"Aw, shut up!" Vange growled. "Right now, I'd settle for a wood stove with a fire, instead of buffalo robes and rumbling over this rattly trail to the Crossing."

"How m-m-much f-f-farther?" Barbara asked, her teeth chattering.

Bitsy shrugged. "Who knows?" She picked up the words of the song again:

> "The horse knows the way to carry the
>   sleigh —"

"At least, I hope the team knows where we're going. If Cousin Lank hadn't begged us for so long to come for Th-Thanksgiving . . ."

"Poor Rosie and John and Aggie, cooped up alone in their tiny cabin with that dear sick baby!" wailed Vange. "We should've fixed our ducks and sweet potato pies and gone to eat with them. They'd have enjoyed the grub, if not our company."

"Don't worry. Aggie will see that they're well fed," Bitsy muttered. "And anyway, Vange, it's time we did a bit of socializin' this winter. Except for school, we haven't seen anyone all fall."

"Not even Charlie and Willie," Vange said. "Usually they come by at least once a week to sample Aggie's cooking. This year they're probably stuck with Charlie's same old mutton stew."

Barbara's teeth chattered as she listened

half-heartedly to the girls' chatter. They had been on the road since daybreak. She wondered how tiny Aunt Prudy kept from freezing to death on the wagon seat beside Uncle Daniel.

Abraham Atlantic Moore and his wife Nancy had invited the family for Thanksgiving dinner at the ranch. Because Lank was Mama's cousin, Barbara knew she must appreciate the gesture of her kinfolks. But the bleak November wind that moaned over the grassy plains made the world seem even more grim and gray. She'd heard that Evin and Molly Hoops were working at the ranch, Evin helping with the cattle while Molly cooked for the hands. They had left their cabin on the south banks of the Cottonwood below the town for winter in an attempt to earn money. The prospect of seeing the sprightly Molly brightened Barbara a little.

Her face felt chiseled out of ice by the time she noticed the wagon slowing down the lane that led to the ranch. Before long, the team stopped and she was lifted, cold and stiff, from the wagon to walk on icy, wooden legs to the warm house.

Indoors, in the large ranch kitchen the aroma of turkeys basting and brown beans simmering in the iron pots met the chilled

Moore family as they staggered through the door.

Molly Hoops rushed around with warm blankets and pillows and soon propped Barbara up before the fireplace. Vange was stomping her feet as she lifted the lids from cooking pots, while Bitsy sniffed hungrily and blew on her icy fingers.

"I hope my stomach's thawed out in time for dinner," Bitsy muttered, unwinding her long woolen scarf from her head. "Molly, I hope you have plenty of food."

Molly's merry voice jingled. "Don't worry, Elizabeth. I've worked on this meal for days, besides cooking for the ranch hands. Since Mrs. Moore is visiting her folks, the Watermans —"

"How many hands are there now?" Uncle Daniel asked as he stomped into the kitchen. "Lank has quite a spread here."

"Evin and the usual help," Molly said, laying a starched white cloth onto the large table. "There's a new fella named Barry Keaton who came out on the stage a few weeks ago. Barry's on his way to Denver to work on a newspaper, but since the road ahead's all snowed in, he's helping here through the winter."

"Traveling by himself?" Uncle Daniel asked, peeling off his greatcoat and hanging it on a nail in the rafter above him.

"If you mean is he married . . . no, he's not. He's a very nice young man, So polite too, and always ready to ask the blessin' on the food. How's Rosie's baby?"

Aunt Prudy's pinched little face fell. "Poor Sammie cries a lot. I feel sorry for the wee thing. Rosie and John, too."

"That's the part about pioneering we have no control over. Inadequate medical help, bitter cold weather. If the good Lord sees fit to give us healthy young'uns, we're thankful," Molly said, spooning wild grape jelly into an amber stemmed goblet.

Vange helped Molly set the plates on the table while Bitsy and Aunt Prudy dished up the food. Barbara began to feel warm and drowsy, and pushed the heavy blankets away. *I thought I'd never get warm again,* she thought, *but here I am, hungry enough to eat a whole turkey.*

A sudden stomping in the lean-to announced the ranch hands, their faces crackling with frost as they marched into the kitchen. Throwing their coats onto a pile in the corner, they nudged their way to the warmth of the fireplace. The musky scent of leather and horseflesh drifted through the cabin, mingling with the familiar smells of real coffee and food simmering on the cookstove.

Barbara noticed the long hair, the clipped mustaches, and wondered how men could spend long hours in the bitter cold, rounding up and feeding cattle.

Evin Hoops gave his wife a hug as the other hands slapped their palms together while huddling around the fire.

One young man stood out sharply above the others. This was probably Barry Keaton. He was tall and dark, with his hair neatly trimmed. He wore a red-and-blue checked flannel shirt and blue denims that were stuffed into his boot tops. Barbara saw him look around the room, and his glance lock suddenly on Vange's animated face. Vange blushed furiously clattering with cooking pots as she piled mounds of fluffy white potatoes into huge crockery bowls. Barbara felt a strange feeling tingle through her — as though this was a special moment for Vange and Barry.

Minutes later Lank Moore announced that dinner was ready, and told the houseful to be seated. Molly took the chair nearest the cookstove, Barbara sat between Vange and Bitsy, with Cousin Lank and Uncle Daniel beside Aunt Prudy on the far end. The ranch hands sat on the opposite side. Evin and Molly's little girls were sandwiched between their parents.

After Uncle Daniel had asked the blessing, the heavy platters of food made the rounds. There were huge plates of wild turkey and dressing, thickly sliced venison dripping in its own juice, fluffy mashed potatoes, baked sweet yams swimming with dots of butter, baked beans, dishes piled high with dill pickles and bowls of buttered beets. Fragrant slices of brown wheat bread were stacked in mounds.

Vange, helping Molly with serving, kept the coffee cups filled and the gravy bowl full.

"This food's fit for a king," Barry Keaton said, looking at Vange as she filled his cup for the third time. "Makes me wish I could stay here forever, instead of moving on."

She set down the coffee pot on the stove, "And *are* you planning to move on?" she asked, her voice a trifle unsteady.

"I'm a reporter on my way to Denver to work on the daily newspaper," he said, lifting the coffee cup to his lips again. "But the passes are snowpacked, so I'll just spend the winter here, helping Lank with the cattle. Maybe by spring . . ."

Barbara couldn't help overhearing their light conversation. Her cousin never looked prettier, Barbara thought, her face flushed from the warmth of the room and the glorious auburn ringlets escaping from her braided coronet.

"That's . . . nice," Vange said. "It must be wonderful to write for such a big newspaper."

"Well, I was correspondent in New York for a year on Horace Greeley's paper, but Greeley urged me to go on west. He feels I'd do better there."

"Horace Greeley!" Vange exclaimed. "You knew Mr. Greeley? Isn't he the editor of the New York *Tribune*?"

"And isn't he against President Lincoln?" Lank Moore put in wryly, reaching for another slice of bread.

"Oh, no, sir. Not now. He supported Mr. Lincoln, even saying the end of the Union was preferable to any compromise with slavery. When he . . . when he tried to deny Lincoln's nomination because he felt Mr. Lincoln's mistaken deference to slavery, I left his employ. He said that I should go where the slavery question didn't come up. Greeley is most zealous, but sometimes his zeal has gotten him into trouble."

He paused and looked straight into Vange's eyes. "And somehow I'm glad I came this way." He grinned, his smile lighting up his pleasant features.

Barbara's heart skipped a beat. She hoped it was because of Vange that he looked so happy.

The afternoon passed swiftly. After the girls had helped Molly with the dishes and put the food away, there were pans of buttered popcorn and molasses taffy, and much delightful chatter and laughter around the fire, Barbara almost forgot about the long, nearly 18-mile ride that lay ahead. Especially when she saw Vange and Barry deep in conversation at one end of the large kitchen. Little Carrie Hoops hovered behind the stove, probably eavesdropping on their visiting.

At four o'clock Uncle Daniel announced it was time to leave for home, and went out to harness the team. He brought the wagon to the kitchen door, and with hot bricks for their feet, the womenfolk bundled up and piled in. Vange was the last one to crawl over the side of the wagon, for it took her longer to say goodbye — mostly to Barry.

The bitter wind had died down and the cold seemed less penetrating than it had on the way to the ranch.

Vange seemed full of eagerness. "Oh, Barbara!" she whispered. "Is this how it was with you and Matthew? That you just *knew* you'd met the right one?"

Barbara was quiet for a few seconds. With Matthew and her it hadn't happened suddenly. They had always known that some day they would marry. There had never been any question.

She moistened her lips. "Yes . . . yes, of course, Vange. I always knew Matthew and I would marry some day. And . . . and we will!"

"Of course, you will. It's just that I've never met anyone quite like Barry," Vange added breathlessly.

"Does this mean you're leaving Charlie to me?" Bitsy lilted. "I only wish I could get him to look at me like a moonstruck calf the way Barry looked at you, Vange."

"Moonstruck or not," Vange murmured softly, "I think I liked it."

Shreds of cloud caught fire, and the flame and tumult of the windy sunset spread over half the sky. The late afternoon ran slowly, heavy like honey, then twilight began to fall as the wagon rumbled homeward over the dry ruts.

It was dark when the wagon pulled to a stop before the snug Moore cabin. A glimmer of light shone from the south window. It was strange that Woodson's welcome bark didn't greet them.

Charlie Warren stood in the lighted

doorway of the cabin, his thick wool cap pushed back, and his dark curls falling over his forehead.

"Trouble!" he called out before Uncle Daniel could ask. "Indians, confound 'em! Drove off your cattle this afternoon."

Uncle Daniel's forehead wrinkled. "You saw them?"

"I heard shouts and yelling. By the time I got here, they had the critters down the trail. There was nothing I could do knowing you don't argue with an Osage. Woodson's missing too."

"Are you sure they were Osages?" Uncle Daniel said, his jaw taut.

Charlie nodded. "I saw them close up. They sure weren't Kaws."

"Didn't even bother to shut the gate, did they?"

"I was just coming to check, then decided to build a fire in your cabin. Knew you'd be frozen when you got home. Too bad Woodson may wind up in an Osage stew."

"Where's Willie?" Barbara cried, crawling over the side of the wagon. "Is he all right?"

"Willie's fine. I left him in charge of the sheep. They're in that little glen beyond the creek, out of sight. Otherwise —" he paused awkwardly.

"At least your sheep are safe," Uncle Daniel cut in, helping Aunt Prudy from her perch. "Guess we're still prone to forget about those thieving Osages."

Charlie stood aside as the family trooped indoors. Barbara followed Vange and Bitsy to the fireplace. She wondered if Uncle Daniel and the girls could've kept the Indians from raiding even if they had been home. Then she caught her breath sharply. Why did it have to be Uncle Daniel's livestock and dear old Woodson, instead of Charlie's confounded sheep? Couldn't he have frightened off the Indians somehow?

"I hope he's not feeling smug," she muttered under her breath, then hastily upbraided herself. Charlie Warren was a good neighbor, and he knew the code of the prairie. One man against an Indian spelled certain death.

CHAPTER 17

November dragged by, cold, dark and dreary. December stole in, bleak with gray clouds and great logs crackling in the fireplace. The space in the kitchen became cramped with the quilt frame for Vange's wool comforts and quilts crowding along the east wall. For Aunt Prudy to go into her bedroom, she had to squeeze her tiny figure between the frame and the wall.

Although there were no cattle to feed, Uncle Daniel kept busy fixing fences, mending harness and chopping wood. He had come across one young, fresh heifer in the woods which the Indians apparently had missed, so at least there was milk to drink.

Vange and Bitsy sat hunched over a bright patchwork quilt, their needles flying. Barbara sat idly by and watched. Needles had never fit into her hands, and she wasn't ready to try now. Bitsy scowled as she jabbed her finger with the needle again.

"Rats! At this rate Vange won't get married until her grandchildren are grown. We'll never get this quilt done by spring."

Vange threw her sister a long, scornful look. "Oh, yes, we will. Things would move faster if you didn't prick yourself so often and used your common sense when you thread a needle. It takes you a hunter's moon to thread a needle."

"Well, if you hadn't insisted on such dainty stitches, I could use a darning needle!" Bitsy grouched. "And if you'd have picked a husband from Texas, where it's warm, instead of someone who insists on dragging you beyond Greenland's icy mountains, we wouldn't have to throttle such warm stuff together. Maybe you should ask White Turkey for some buffalo robes —"

"Bitsy!" Vange rapped out sharply. "Wait 'til you get married. Will you be satisfied to sleep under a buffalo robe instead of Ma's nice wool comforts and soft quilts?"

Bitsy grunted as she pursed her lips and finally pushed the thread through the eye of the needle. "All right, but what we really need around here is Aggie. She'd have this quilt whipped together in no time."

"Don't begrudge Rosie Aggie's help with little Sammie," Vange said. "Someone has to rock that poor child almost day and night, you know."

Barbara sat up suddenly. She really wanted to help Vange. "Maybe I could go to Rosie's and rock the baby so Aggie can come home and help you," she said in a small voice.

Both Vange and Bitsy looked up, startled. Aunt Prudy, who was setting bread dough in the pans to rise, whirled around.

"That's a splendid idea, Barbara," she said. "But what of school?"

"I mostly help the teacher anyway," Barbara said, "and this is a slack season for lessons, with the cold weather and all."

"It would free Rosie to look after the house while you rocked Sammie, and Aggie could help here at home where she's needed so badly," Aunt Prudy went on.

The idea was still new to Barbara. Although she had visited John and Rosie's cabin frequently, caring for a sick infant was another matter. Still, it was one way she could be useful. She had long failed to carry her share of the load.

"You'll miss our constant chatter," Bitsy reminded her promptly. "And all the news. But never mind. Our golden silence might make you appreciate us more."

The golden silence of the girls' constant chatter and laughter was quickly shattered with the sick baby's constant crying and moaning, Barbara discovered later that afternoon when she reached the small cabin on the north prairie. The wooden cradle

John had built was piled with feather ticks and warm, knitted blankets; yet the baby fretted and whimpered almost constantly.

"We've learned that he's most comfortable when he's rocked," Rosie told Barbara as she pushed her gently into the solid walnut rocking chair near the fire. Then she laid the baby in Barbara's arms. The wizened little face was screwed into a contortion of pain, and the pitiful sounds filled Barbara with near panic.

She began to rock gently, crooning softly as she rocked. The whimpering grew no less. Helplessly Barbara touched the thin little face and brushed back the silly brown hair from the pain-darkened eyes.

She looked up at Rosie, bending over a washtub of baby clothes, wringing out a clean, sudsy diaper.

"Does he . . . do this all the time? I mean, cry this way?"

"Most always. Now and then he sleeps for a spell. But the pain is never absent."

"Is there anything . . . anything at all you can do for him?"

Rosie slapped out a square of flour sacking and shook her head. "Nothing. Perhaps if we lived in a city where a specialist could check him, there might be some help. But Sammie would never survive a trip to

St. Louis. Especially not in winter."

Tears blurred Barbara's eyes. It wasn't fair. If babies came to this world to hard-working settlers, at least they should be healthy. Why had God allowed this poor little mite to be born so ill?

As she held the thin little body against her breast, she choked back her tears.

"What's . . . what's going to happen to this baby, Rosie? You've had such dreams."

"I know," Rosie said, drawing her breath in deeply. "John and I were so happy when we found we were going to have a child. But we also knew the risks."

"The risks?"

"Here on the prairie with little medical help . . . and me with my problem —"

"What problem, Rosie?"

Rosie smiled weakly. "When I was a child I was badly hurt falling from a horse. I was internally injured. The doctor back in Indiana warned me against having children. But we . . . we trusted the Lord —"

"And now He's let you down, hasn't He?" Barbara said quickly, bitterly. "If God would've allowed it, the baby could've been all right, couldn't he?"

"No, no," Rosie said, her voice straining. "We . . . we can't question God. He tells us in Second Corinthians that His grace is sufficient for us; that His power is made perfect in weakness. Somehow, some way the Lord wanted us to have this child. I still don't know why. But seeing him wracked by pain sometimes is unbearable, and there are times when I think I can't stand it." She paused, and leaned against the kitchen table, her eyes like pools of pain. "Sometimes I even pretend to be a strong believer, but I'm not fooling anyone. That's when I need the Lord's strength more than anything. Not for myself, but to give to my son."

Barbara looked at the baby in her lap, the constant painful cries scarcely ebbing. A gray sadness hung over her, not only because of Rosie and the baby, but because of something else . . . something she couldn't define.

Rosie had resumed her scrubbing motion on the washboard in the little tub.

Rocking, rocking, Barbara swayed gently back and forth, her heart melting with pity for this pathetically ill child in her arms. *O God, why can't You do something?* she cried. *If You could lead Uncle Daniel's family into this wild land, away from their family, can't You at least heal this tiny baby?*

Moistening her lips, she asked, "Have you prayed for a . . . a miracle? I mean, God could heal this baby, couldn't He?" she continued, suddenly wanting to hold out hope.

"We know God can perform miracles," Rosie said, keeping up her rhythmic scrubbing against the rough board. "If He chooses. Yes, we have prayed. But —"

"If I were you, I'd rant and rage and shake God and make Him listen!" Barbara burst out hotly. "If this were my baby —"

"No," Rosie cut in gently, "We have left it in His hands. For awhile I felt as you do. But I have learned to give this burden of the sick child to Him. He says, 'In quietness and trust is your strength.' As long as He provides that . . . ," Rosie's voice trailed off.

Barbara felt numb. Not for herself but for Rosie and John. As though they had no other course but to leave it to God — a God who didn't listen, who didn't care. And I can't do that, she decided.

Sometimes she helped Rosie feed the baby, trying to spoon the thin gruel of barley and milk into the tiny mouth. She was amazed at Rosie's cheerfulness, her attitude of acceptance. And yet Barbara's feeling of sadness persisted.

One cold brittle afternoon she walked the mile to the Moore cabin for a change of scene, although John faithfully supplied her with news of the outside world. Vange's trousseau and the mounds of quilts and comforts were stacking up, and the girls were up to their ears with laughter and talk. Aunt Prudy gave her a warm hug, her little face pinched and more tired-looking than usual.

"If Vange makes one more quilt, Barry will need the U.S. Cavalry to lug her and all her worldly goods to Denver!" Aggie said with an exaggerated sigh. "How's Sammie? The same, I s'pose."

"Yes." Barbara smiled wanly. "When I rock him and croon and sing, I forget about that war out there. If only there'd be word from Matthew."

"The moment your letter arrives, we'll send it out by special dispatcher," Vange said. "Namely me. Which is our fastest horse these days, Bitsy?"

"Petunia's getting very restless. I think she misses Josh. Too bad Woodson's gone. We could train him to carry messages."

"Never mind. You'll get your letter, Barbara. Here." Aggie wrapped up a loaf of fresh brown bread and a crisply baked dried apple pie. "Take this back for supper. You'd better skedaddle 'fore it gets dark."

Barbara wound the blue wool scarf around her neck and buttoned her coat. "It's been good seeing you all. I hope we'll be together for Christmas."

"Oh, we will . . . whatever Christmas we'll manage," Aggie said as Barbara set out into the late afternoon. Already shadows were crowding over the prairies. The land, slightly higher nearer the trail, rolled into faint swales like solid waves of a tawny sea.

I'll miss Vange when she gets married and moves away, Barbara decided. Of all the cousins, I think I like Evangeline the best. But she'd probably feel the same if it were Bitsy or Aggie who went away. Maybe that's why she felt so sad. Christmas was only a week away. The usual bustle and scurry at the Moore cabin had given away to preparing for Vange's wedding. But with Josh gone and Baby Sammie so ill, there seemed little interest in Christmas plans.

Willie trundled over one afternoon to John and Rosie's cabin before the holidays to see Barbara.

"I've missed you in school, Barbara," he said after he had tiptoed softly around Sammie's crib.

"You can see I'm needed here now, Willie," she said gently. "Are you having a Christmas program?"

Willie shook his head. "Not really. We're recitin' pieces and singin' a few carols. Miss Griffith says she's too busy gettin' ready for her weddin' to think about a program. Do all weddin's take that much fuss and bother?"

Barbara laughed softly, "Some do, I guess. Vange is up to her teeth in wedding plans. When Matthew and I get married, we'll probably plan a beautiful wedding in a little church with magnolia bushes blooming all around it."

"But the war ain't over yet." His voice was short.

"No, it isn't. Still, that won't make me stop dreaming."

"Well . . ." he pulled on his cap and started for the door. "See ya at the Moores' on Christmas, Barbara?"

She smiled faintly. "Sure, Willie. Sure."

A few days before Christmas, word came that Josh had been wounded in battle and was captured on October 19th while he was with General Sheridan at Cedar Creek. The news threw a pall on the Moore family. Even Rosie's composure seemed shaken.

"If only the war would end soon!" Barbara fumed at the supper table. John had taken his turn at holding Sammie and he rocked steadily for a moment before replying,

"Seems the Rebs were surprised when Sheridan got wise and there was a big fight.

Read about it in the St. Louis paper when I was at Council Grove the other day. The North lost more'n twice as many men as the South, but they forced the Rebs from the field. That's probably where Josh got wounded and captured."

"I . . . I never really wanted anything to happen to Joshua," Barbara said, spooning a kettle of vegetable soup into a huge bowl for supper. "He should've stayed home, and he'd have been safe."

"But he did his duty, just as Matthew is doing his," John remarked.

Matthew . . . Barbara's heart lurched with fear. When would she hear from him? How much longer would this rotten war last? *Dear God, please let it be over soon.*

"I hear Roddy Coble and Molly Griffith are getting married about New Year's time," John went on to change the subject.

A spurt of anger flared through Barbara. "Yes, everybody's getting married but Matthew and me!" she flung out bitterly. And the strange feeling of sadness swept over her again.

CHAPTER 18

Christmas came and went without the usual bustle and stir. Barry Keaton had arrived on horseback from Lank Moore's ranch to spend the day. Charlie and Willie came to eat Christmas dinner, then left. Since Rosie and John were unable to take little Sammie out, the Moore family bundled up and spent the afternoon in the little cabin on the north prairie, toasting chestnuts and munching buttered popcorn.

Barbara's feelings of sad loneliness persisted. The baby whimpered and cried, in spite of Aunt Prudy's constant rocking, as though Christmas meant nothing at all. And it seemed that way to everyone, although Vange and Barry apparently had eyes only for each other. Even the thought of Matthew was cut off from Barbara like a curtain. She began to believe he had been captured, or surely she would have heard from him.

The new year of 1865 stole in softly in the wake of a heavy snowstorm. Snow piled against the windows and drifted across the wagon trails, smoothing out the ruts as by a cold hand. A low wind sang in the chimney, and along the snow-packed timber, trackless prairies covered the river like a white silent hood.

Pale yellow light from tallow candles on the shelf sputtered, and the reddish glow from the cottonwood logs in the fireplace added to the deep, eerie stillness.

Vange and Barry planned to be married in April. The wagon train which they were to join would trek more freely over the packed trails after the snow melted.

"And to think I pricked my fingers to the bone trying to hurry up all those warm covers for Vange!" Bitsy wailed. "If Vange as much as needs one more embroidered pillow slip —"

"We're ahead of schedule," Vange cut in with a lilting laugh, her chin dimpling. "At least, Barry can't say he chose a bride who wasn't prepared to brave the cold with him."

"All I can say is I'm glad Aggie can hustle up her own bedcovers if she ever gets married," Bitsy grouched. "I hope I never have to stitch another quilt as long as I live."

"How about yourself?" Aggie prodded, biting off the last bit of red yarn with her sturdy white teeth as she finished up the tag end of the comfort.

"If I ever get married —" Bitsy began, "*If* I ever get married, I'll stage a regular sewing bee. I'll invite the Billingses, the Shreves and Griffiths. We'll make short work of outfitting my trousseau, for those Butterfield girls have mounds of quilt blocks ready to go." She paused and eyed Barbara sharply. "As for Barbie, we're lucky she won't demand a dowry of down and doo-jiggers. In the South everything must be cotton."

Everyone laughed over that, for laughter came more easily again, although there had been no more word from Josh. He was held up daily in prayer. Surely the Lord would keep him safe. Someone had finally written him about Woodson.

Aunt Prudy had spent the day helping Rosie with the baby, but suddenly she was back, her brown face paler and more pinched than usual. Barbara threw a worried glance at her aunt.

"Aunt Prudy, is anything wrong?" she asked. Vange and Bitsy looked up from their sewing.

"The . . . the baby's got lung fever. It's only a matter of time." She paused, her watery blue eyes misting.

Lung fever! Barbara's hands flew to her throat to stop its pounding. Aunt Prudy said she had come for onions the family had hoarded. She swiftly packed the last of them in a flour sack. They had been careful so the onions didn't freeze. Now they were to be baked to make compresses for the baby's chest.

For five days Aunt Prudy stayed at John and Rosie's cabin, holding the child on her lap most of the time near the red-hot fireplace. Barbara came over one afternoon and offered her help since school had not resumed after the Christmas holidays.

"Over there. Get the goose grease from the corner cupboard and start rubbing," Aunt Prudy said sharply. Her hair had sagged from its pins and her eyes were bloodshot from loss of sleep. Sometimes the baby's breath came so fast it sounded like a whistle made from the willows by the draw.

Barbara's heart ached as she watched the wizened little body shake and turn blue. She wondered how Rosie could take it now, with her so-called "faith."

"Take him, Lord," Barbara overheard Rosie whisper once while she watched Sammie suffer one night. "It's all right . . ." Suddenly, the fever subsided and the normal pinkness crept back into the pinched little face. The crisis soon passed, and the family returned to its normal routine.

Without warning, the weather turned mild. Snow began to thaw, and the cabin dropped four-foot icicles. Wagons were forced to ford slushy creeks and crawl up muddy hills. Some hillocks seemed half-brown mud and half-white snow that reminded Barbara of a Guernsey heifer's hide. Winter sparred with spring, although it was only mid-February.

School was scheduled to open on Monday, and the settlers moved out of their winter cocoons. Bitsy and Barbara donned warm scarves and mittens and rode Petunia through the muddy trails toward the log schoolhouse. Willie often joined them on their ride to school. Rebecca Shreve was back behind her dry goods box desk, poring over textbooks since Molly Griffith was married. It had been Barbara's privilege to teach several new songs to the scholars.

"There's a new one we sang back home, called 'Yankee Doodle Dandy'," she said. "It's a lively tune. Go ahead and stomp your feet and clap your hands, if you want to." She probably didn't dare teach them "Dixie."

Rebecca seemed delighted. "You have a knack for getting the children to follow right along," she said, busy with slatework. "Tomorrow we'll work on valentines for a party at the end of the week. You can show the children how to make pretty hearts from colored paper."

"Colored paper?"

"Believe it or not, my mother brought along half a roll of bright green flowered wallpaper from Indiana. We've never decided what to do with it as it's hardly enough to cover even one wall of our cabin. Maybe some cupids and hearts would be nice, if we make a pattern."

School the next morning flew by as the scholars snipped heart shapes and cupids from Rebecca's wallpaper and a scrap of red Barbara had found in her trunk.

Rebecca dismissed classes at noon since Willie and Charlie had gone to Council Grove for supplies, and the Griffith boys were cutting wood at home. The Miller girls were to go home early to help their mother. Barbara urged Bitsy to take the horse and ride on home.

"I'll come later," she said. "The walk in this crisp air won't hurt me."

"Why don't you go, too, Barbara?" Rebecca said, putting away the slates and red paper.

"I'll bank the fire and come home as soon as I finish," Barbara replied.

"Better hurry. The sky is growing darker out."

"I'll come soon."

She heard the slam of the door as Rebecca left, then smiled at a sudden idea. If she folded a square of white paper four times, she could make cutouts that looked like lace and glue the lacy cutout onto the red hearts. Tomorrow she'd bring a handful of flour and mix it with a bit of water to make paste.

In her busyness, she scarcely grew aware of the creeping darkness. When a gust of wind rattled the windows, Barbara looked up. She saw low, scudding clouds blowing in rapidly from the northwest. Jumping up, she banked the fire and flung on her wraps. When she pushed open the door, a cloud rolled low over the prairie, hissing and spitting sleet.

Barbara cowered against the blast as she set out for the trail that led toward the Moore cabin. The strong wind and raging sleet completely wrapped around her. Snow whirled into her nostrils as needles of sleet cut her face. She dug her mittened hands deeper into her coat pockets and found nothing but more snow. She wanted to cry out but her breath wouldn't come as she trudged forward.

"I can't be too far . . . from home," she panted. "I should be able to . . . make it. Surely the prairie won't go back . . . on me . . ." As she bucked forward, another blast of snow-filled wind blinded her. She saw only darkness ahead.

Stumbling against a dark object, she sank to her knees. It was a rattling dry bush somewhere along the trail, and she crouched and clung to it, not wanting to let go of her scant shelter.

I've got to keep my head, she thought. *What would Uncle Daniel do? He would pray . . . O God, I don't even know to pray. How can I have Rosie's faith in a God who doesn't seem to care?*

A great blast of wind hurled her against the limbs of the bush, scratching her face. With dull dismay, she realized she was too numb to feel pain.

Quite suddenly her mind cleared and she knew what she must do — follow the creek until she reached a cabin. She heard sleet pelting on the ice-covered stream and started toward the sound, but her freezing legs refused to move, and she sagged to the cold ground.

Then she heard another sound, one of breaking snow crust and the smell and noise of a horse coming nearer.

"Hel-p!" she cried feebly against the shrieking wind. No one could hear.

Moments later to her surprise, a man swung from the horse and bent over her.

"Good God, Miss, what you doin' here?" his words sounded hollow in the biting wind.

She shrank back, not recognizing the man's voice. Without a word, he hoisted her to her feet and flung her upon the horse in the saddle in front of him. With the shriek of wind in her ears and pellets of ice in her face, she let herself grow limp with the cold and the slow jogging of the horse. The road ahead seemed like a solid sheet of nothing; she had no idea where the man was taking her, and she didn't care.

Suddenly a vague outline of a fence blurred through her line of vision, and the rider pulled the horse to a stop beside a dark blob, probably a cabin.

Sliding from the saddle, he picked her up in his strong arms and shoved her through a doorway. She found herself in a tiny stone cottage, warm and mellow with the smell of firewood and crackling flames. There was a fragrant aroma of stew bubbling in a kettle. She blinked the sleet from her eyes and looked around.

Standing like an icicle before the open fire, Barbara turned at a sound beside her. She made out a round, black face beaming at her from a gigantic collar of a faded gray cotton pinafore.

"Oh," she gasped a little. Weren't these the *runaway slaves* she'd seen at the store? "You . . . you!" She spat out the words.

"We's Mehitabel and Ezra Foster, child," the woman spoke in a soft voice. "Here, lemme he'p you off with your things. Why, you plumb near froze!" She began to rub Barbara's numb fingers, then pushed her into a chair in front of the fire and tucked a blanket around her knees.

"B-but . . . ," Barbara sputtered. Why had this couple come? And what right did they have to be here? Why didn't they stay in the South where they belonged?

The man materialized out of the background and grinned with a flash of teeth. "Lucky I found you, Miss. I was ridin' home after helpin' Josiah Meek chink his cabin when I seed you stumble up ahead, a little past the schoolhouse, I figured you never make it, goin' wherever you was goin'. So I brought you here to wait out the sto'm."

"You! Where did you come from? And why are you here?" She drew herself up proudly. "I'm from Georgia, and I —"

"Land, child, what you doin' way out here? It don't really matter where you come fum," Mehitabel scolded. "We come here fum Missouri helpin' Josiah and his family get settled."

"Aren't you slaves?" Barbara asked bluntly.

"You mean, does we b'long to somebody?" The man and woman looked at each other. "Oh, no, Miss," the man went on. "Ever since Pres' Lincoln said we was free, we been free. But we ain't leavin' the Meekers. They been awful good to us. Best friends we ever had . . . even when they done owned us."

So they'd been freed. The idea of free slaves was still new to Barbara.

From a tiny corner cupboard, with a clatter of spoons and bowls, Mehitabel emerged with a steaming bowl full of stew for Barbara.

"Eat hearty, miss. When this wind die down, Ezra take you home."

"But . . . but you don't know who I am!" Barbara cried, pushing away the stew. These people meant well, and she suddenly felt ashamed. "I . . . I'm a Southern girl, a . . . *a Rebel!* Don't you understand? You should hate me!"

"Your stew's gettin' cold, Miss. It don't matter who you are. God loves you and so does we," Ezra said quietly. "You warm now?"

Barbara gulped. What was this? More of this God-loving, faith-giving love she had experienced since coming here? First, Uncle Daniel Moore and his family, then Rosie, the settlers — Yankees who loved her and made her feel welcome — and now this negro couple. Did God really make so much difference in a life?

She lifted her spoon and tasted the stew. There were chunks of buffalo meat and dried turnips, and it tasted wonderful.

Ezra was standing at the window looking out. Then he turned and came toward her.

"Wind's died down, Miss. Maybe I better take you home. Your folks be worried 'bout you. That is, if you warmed up."

She nodded woodenly. "Yes, thank you. I'll get my wrap." Suddenly she turned, and gave Mehitabel a quick hug. "Thanks for everything," she said again.

The snow and sleet had stopped and they started out the door. The prairies were without color, and the Cottonwood Valley filled with cold sunset light. The snow scene before them lay soft and dainty, with faint traces of mauve and silver, while the pale sky above shaded suddenly to crimson and purple in the west. Once more the prairie — changeless, yet always changing — enchanted her.

CHAPTER 19

The thin, bitter air of winter receded in late March as a balmy southern breeze blew over the prairie. Soft spring rains had fallen and distant gray clouds lay misted in deep blue.

When Barbara came home from school one afternoon, she felt a bounce in her step that had been absent all winter. The long cold months were over and now there was new hope.

As she stepped over the threshold of the cabin, she was surprised to see Uncle Daniel seated at the table. This was unusual, for he was usually too busy plowing for spring crops to waste time indoors. There was no sign of Aunt Prudy and the girls.

"Why, Uncle Daniel," she greeted him pleasantly. "Imagine you here. I thought crops were clamoring to be planted."

He didn't respond with his normal light banter, and she noticed the faraway look in his eyes again. Without a word he handed her an envelope. She glanced quickly at the return address. It was from Richmond, the Confederate government headquarters.

With numb fingers Barbara slit the seal, and smoothed the crackling pages. A blur of words swam before her.

"Potter, Captain Matthew. Wounded, died December 16, 1864. A valiant soldier, serving with General Hood . . ."

The paper fluttered to the floor and she sank heavily into a chair. It wasn't true. It couldn't be true. God couldn't do this to her. She couldn't feel anything now that the dreaded news had come. People cried when loved ones died, but she couldn't cry. It was as though a terrible searing fire had swept over her, leaving nothing but dead ashes.

"Barbara," Uncle Daniel stood beside her, an arm around her shoulders, "I'm so very sorry. We'd been so worried about you all these weeks when no word came. But we've prayed —"

She flung off his grip and jumped to her feet, standing there for a minute, submissive for a brief moment to God's will. Then, when realization hit, the tears began. She grabbed her blue-and-gray shawl, flung it over her shoulders, rushed out the door and down the lane. She crossed the trail and sped southeastward through the tall grasses, embroidered so brilliantly with spring flowers.

Minutes before, it had been a friendly golden prairie, lilting with color for her enjoyment. Now she ran among thistles that scratched her ankles and tore at her skirts, her heart pounding with love and hate and anger and peace. On, on she flew, to get away from the dark message that had ripped her world apart. Panting, her breasts heaving with sobs, she skimmed over the grass, headed for nowhere.

Up the rocky hillock Barbara sped. She poised for a moment on the crest and then ran down the other side. With a twist, she stumbled and fell from sheer exhaustion. She didn't feel the wrench of her foot because the pain in her heart was so great. Throwing off all restraint, she rolled in the grass and began to cry aloud, railing at a God who allowed the horror of war and death.

"God! God, why did You do this to me?" she cried, her sobs harsh and angry. She flung herself on her stomach and pounded the sod with clenched fists as though God would tell her it wasn't true. For months she'd felt a deep sadness — since before Christmas. Maybe God had tried to warn her, to let her know something was wrong. But nothing could bring Matthew back, she knew it now.

A hollow feeling thrummed inside her which echoed only the sound of wild weeping, although not even shedding one tear could bring back her hopes of a happy future with Matthew. She was trapped. Trapped by a wild, cruel prairie . . . with a lonely prairie wind which blew her grief-stricken thoughts around and around until she thought she would go mad.

Now all hopes of leaving Kansas were dashed. She had to stay because she had no other place to go. Her sobs simmered to a thin little whimper.

A rustling sound startled her, and she sat up. A rattlesnake, whirring and ready to strike, coiled about six feet away from her.

She wanted to scream, but her voice froze in her throat. In panic she tried to move, but the wrench of pain in her ankle knifed through her. What had Willie said? *Be careful where you sit, or you might disturb a rattler sunnin' hisself on a rock* . . . Her mouth grew cottony dry as she watched the rattler, fascinated. Life was over for her, for Matthew. All she saw was a pit of horror ahead.

"Oh, God . . ." The words were deeper than an anguished prayer.

"Stop, Prairie Flower! Do not move!" A deep voice spoke softly, gently, beside her. She looked up to see White Turkey spring from his pony and leap toward the rattlesnake with his quirt raised. In one stroke that snapped so quickly Barbara didn't know it happened, the whirring had stopped. The snake's body writhed, headless, on the stone ground.

Petrified, Barbara made a desperate move to get to her feet and run away, but the stabbing pain in her ankle drove her back to the ground.

In panicky silence, she watched the young Kaw come slowly toward her, his black eyes riveted on her face, and she screamed. As he reached out his hand, she shrank back. She had heard that Indians raped white women. Is this what she owed him for saving her life? For declining his proposal of marriage?

Reaching toward her, he tenderly lifted her onto his pony. Barbara was so shaken with grief and horror that she seemed drained of all emotion, all feeling. On foot himself, he led the pony through the tall, trampled grass, stepping lightly along a dim path that led toward the south bend of the river. Barbara could only open and close her mouth, the dry feeling choking her and her horror mounting.

The pony stepped carefully, not jarring her in the least, until they reached a small clearing beside the river. A handful of tepees was clustered in a grove of cottonwood trees. White Turkey pulled his mount toward the nearest lodge and reached for her.

She screamed again. Nothing could persuade her to enter the tepee with the handsome Kaw.

Just then the flaps parted and two white men emerged. She recognized one as Elder Buck from Emporia. She swayed and then swooned into his arms.

CHAPTER 20

When Barbara opened her eyes, she was lying on a pile of blankets inside an Indian tepee. The sweet smell of soft grasses and the lapping of river water was all around her, and she looked around wildly. Elder Buck was seated beside her, a strong hand on her trembling shoulders.

"Wh . . . what?" she stammered, her eyes wide with terror.

"You're all right, Miss Temple," he said gently. "Please don't worry."

The other man was standing with his back to her, and he turned to speak.

"I'm Mahlon Stubbs," he said. "Missionary to the Kaws at Council Grove. Preacher Buck and I have spent several days here in the Kaw camp conducting Bible studies."

"Bi-Bible studies?" Barbara echoed. "Here? Among the *Indians?*"

Mahlon Stubbs squatted beside her. "Some of our dear red brethren have accepted the gospel of Jesus Christ and we've been having a sort of . . . retreat here on the riverbank."

Barbara struggled to sit up, but the pain in her ankle was still sharp. Suddenly the events of the past hour surged through her and she gave a low moan.

"I, uh, it's all been so . . . so strange. I'm not sure —"

"White Turkey brought you here about an hour ago. Do you remember?"

"He . . . I . . . there was a rattlesnake, and he killed it." She grimaced, recalling how the young Kaw had carried her away on his pony. Then the panicky feeling knifed through her again. "What . . . what happened? Did anything —"

"He brought thee here to camp," Elder Buck assured her, "and thee simply passed out."

"My ankle." She thrust her hand toward her foot.

"He massaged it, fixed it up with herbs and tied it with a strip of soft antelope hide. It will be all right in a few days."

Barbara's breath came heavily. "But —"

"White Turkey is a gentleman. He has also become a believer in Jesus Christ. He would never hurt thee, you know. It was fortunate that he was looking for some fresh pokeweed for our supper when he found thee. God works in mysterious ways."

She recalled his offer of 12 ponies for her hand in marriage. Was it only a few short months ago?

"Oh," she sighed. Then the agony of the tragic message she had received cut through her again and she began to sob softly.

"Is anything wrong, Miss Temple?" Mahlon Stubbs said, smoothing the colorful blanket over her feet. "You're obviously upset about something."

How much should she share with these two white strangers? She had heard the elder preach now and then at services when he came through on his circuit. She knew he was a kind, gentle man.

Shaking her head, she drew a soggy handkerchief from her pocket and blew her nose. "I just got word. My fiancé, Matthew Potter, has been killed in the war." She paused for a moment as the full impact of the message shot through her again. "And it isn't fair! Why would God do this to me?" she raged, her fists clenching.

" 'Why' is the one question that's been asked through the ages," Buck went on in his quiet way, stroking her hand gently. "I cannot answer that. We only know God makes no mistakes."

"But that's so *unfair!*" Barbara lashed out as she burst into hot tears. "I left my country, my departed loved ones behind, and only Matthew was left. And now —"

"You have a good place to stay."

"But I'm trapped, *trapped,* don't you see?" she shrieked. "I can't go back to Georgia. There's no one left for me there."

"Then why not stay here?"

"Stay? Here?" The words tasted bitter. "Why should I stay? I have no one here either, except my uncle and his family and they're my political enemies. They hate the South. They probably hate me, too, but they're too kind to say so."

"Perhaps the Lord has led thee here, too, like He did thy uncle's family. 'He will have no fear of evil tidings; his heart is fixed, trusting in the Lord.' That's from Psalm 112. And John 3:16 says, 'For God so loved the world that He gave —' "

"No!" Barbara shook her head wildly and drew herself upon her elbow. "Trusting in God hasn't done anything for me. God took that away from me when Matthew died."

"Have you ever asked God to live in your heart?" Mahlon Stubbs asked. "Have you ever met Jesus the Christ? God's love will follow you wherever you go — from Georgia to Kansas. That's the wideness of His mercy. Everyone needs to know Jesus Christ as his Savior, not just for the future that lies ahead, but right now, for help to meet trouble when it comes."

"That's simply unrealistic! If you're

strong, you'll take trouble. If not, you'll go under," she stated. She wanted to add, "It won't do me any good to believe in a make-believe God."

For a few minutes the soft murmur of the two missionaries lingered in the background. Then Barbara pushed everything from her mind and drifted off to a quiet sleep, willing herself to drown all that had happened in the past few hours.

When she awoke, the two men were gone. She was aware of a fragrant aroma that drifted through the tepee. What time was it? She must go back to Uncle Daniel's cabin, for he would be worried. *Maybe someone will take me back,* she thought. Slowly she pulled herself to her feet and limped out of the lodge, the pain in her ankle much less. A group of Kaws, together with Elder Buck and Mahlon Stubbs were seated near the fire, eating the simple evening meal.

White Turkey spied her and moved toward her quickly. "Here, Prairie Flower," he called out. "Eat. Nice stew." A faint smile touched his lips. "No ponies!" He nodded as he brought a crockery bowl filled with a steamy preparation swimming with bits of venison, greens and wild onions as he led her beside the fire. "God love Prairie Flower," he added softly.

She lifted the bowl and sipped a bit of the stew. It was good. After the Indians had finished their soup, they began to sing, softly at first, then with a rising, throbbing rhythm. The words were a mixture of English and Kanza, but the tune was a gentle, yet wild, carefree chant:

"Jesus is wanting us to come
To Him,
To His land
Where we will live
With Him forever . . ."

The words were repeated in soft, quivering nuances.

It startled Barbara, for this was not a hymn she had heard in church. Yet the message was the same. Somehow she sensed God was there, and a quiet peace stole over her as she listened to the end of the song. She knew White Turkey had changed since she had first met him. He was different somehow. Everything was different. She had even slept in an Indian tepee after vowing she'd never visit one!

The sudden crackle of a twig sounded behind her, and she looked up. As a horse and rider came around the bend, she gave a low cry.

"Uncle Daniel!"

He paused before the fire and gestured with his hand. "Greetings, my friends. I have been looking for my niece. I heard singing and I see you have found her." The two missionaries invited him to sit beside them by the fire, but he shook his head.

"Time we'd better get back," he said.

Barbara laid down her bowl quickly and pulled herself to her feet. "I'm sorry I ran off, Uncle Daniel. If it hadn't been for White Turkey," she paused, glancing at the young Kaw who stood behind her, and a lump formed in her throat. "There was a rattler and he killed it."

"Thank God for that, Barbara. I'm glad you were found."

"How did you know where to look?"

"When you ran from the house, I knew you needed to be alone with your grief. But after an hour, when you hadn't returned, I was worried. Our prairies are wide. But as I followed your trail through the grass and came upon the dead rattler, I was sure God had sent someone to look after you. The smoke of the campfire and the singing led me here. I knew you were safe among friends."

"If it hadn't been for White Turkey . . . ,"

Barbara glanced at the Indian with a grateful smile. He stood silent with his arms folded across his chest. His eyes were soft and gentle, and she was sure he understood.

"Come, Barbara," Uncle Daniel said, "It's time to go back home." He helped her on Petunia's back. The horse cantered down the dim trail toward the Moore cabin. The twilight deepened and the clean, sharp aroma of freshly turned loam and new green shoots of grass wafted from the fields on the opposite side of the trail. A white mist had settled in the hollow along the trail toward the north prairie.

"We'll ride straight to John and Rosie's," he told Barbara as she raised questioning eyes to his.

"But why? Where are Aunt Prudy and the girls?"

Uncle Daniel drew a deep sigh. "Little Sammie died this afternoon. Very quietly and peacefully. It's our place to be there."

CHAPTER 21

The ride to the Frazer cabin seemed interminable. Barbara's thoughts were in a turmoil. So much had happened during the past hours that she thought she would go mad. What had she done to deserve all this?

First, the grim news of Matthew's death, then the fears and strange experiences in the Kaw camp. And now, little Sammie gone.

I should've known, she told herself. Sammie was awfully ill. But I loved him very much. He was so small, so frail, so sick, and he needed us all — he needed me, too. But I was too full of self-pity and prejudice to really care.

Dear God, she cried in her heart, *why must You take everything and everyone I love from me? My family, my home . . . I thought at least I had Matthew. Then You took him, too! And then — Baby Sammie. Dear God, please don't take Willie!* her heart screamed. *He's all I have left now.*

Uncle Daniel seemed very quiet on the ride, probably wrapped in his own grief. Barbara wondered what his thoughts were now.

"Barbara —," he spoke suddenly, interrupting her musing. "I want you to know how sorry I am about . . . about Matthew. I know how much you'd counted —"

"It's all my fault," she cried, her lips taut and firm. "I've let you down. You were so kind to me, and I didn't appreciate it. I see only my own stupidity, my self-pity."

"No, Barbara," Uncle Daniel said staunchly, "it wasn't your fault. It was nobody's fault. God's ways aren't always our ways. He —"

"But why should He punish you because of me?" she lashed out. "I've failed everyone — you know I have — for refusing to accept what you've offered me."

She felt she had betrayed the standard she had set for herself, and in doing so she had brought God's wrath upon all who cared about her. How God must hate her!

They rode silently until they reached the gate to the Frazer yard. As Uncle Daniel slid from the horse to open it, he motioned her to ride through.

"I'll stable the horse and help John with evening chores," he said in a voice thick with emotion.

Barbara walked woodenly to the cabin door. *What will I say?* she thought wildly. *What will I do to comfort Rosie and the others in there?*

Slowly she lifted the latch and walked into the cabin. Aunt Prudy was at the table peeling potatoes, and Aggie was frying prairie chickens as though this day was as any other. Vange and Bitsy were folding away the clean diapers and tiny lace-trimmed sacques and blankets into cardboard boxes. Rosie stood at the window, fingering the yellow cretonne curtains absently.

She left the window and hurried toward Barbara. "Oh, Cousin, I'm so sorry about Matthew!" she said, hugging her tightly.

Vange and Bitsy rushed toward her and threw their arms out. "Barbie," Bitsy wept, "Barbie, we knew when Pa brought the letter — oh, it must've been awful!"

"What can I say, Barb?" Vange said gently, stepping back. Barbara saw the deep concern in her eyes.

Aunt Prudy, looking jaded and weary, left her pan of potatoes and simply wrapped Barbara in her arms and held her as gently as a child.

Barbara drew back, puzzled. *I don't understand,* she thought. *These people have lost a child — but it's me they're comforting. They care. They don't preach; they don't judge. They just love me.*

She burst into hot tears and threw herself

on the bed and began to sob. Her tears melted together for Matthew, for the tiny baby who had wheezed its last and the kindnesses and love of her Uncle Daniel's family which she had disdained. *They love me! And I don't deserve this love,* she thought.

Someone had lit the candles and as the cabin danced with shadows, Barbara was suddenly aware of a blanket-wrapped bundle on the far end of the bed. She stopped crying and gently uncovered the bundle and gasped. There lay the little baby, still and peaceful, all whimpering and moaning ended. The pinched, wizened little face seemed quite fresh and smooth.

"We'll bury him tomorrow morning," Rosie said, standing beside the bed, a soft, gentle light on her face. "Pa is going to make a pretty box, and Aggie has promised her white knitted shawl in which to wrap him."

Barbara's fists clenched. *How can she be so calm, so collected? This is a human being, someone they loved and waited for, just as I loved and waited for Matthew. . . .* Yet there was a quiet resignation on Rosie's face that Barbara couldn't understand. What was it all about?

She slept very little in her bed in the loft that night. As the yellow cowslip prairie moon shone into the small east window, she tossed and twisted. And her dreams, when she slept at all, were a mixture of Matthew and Baby Sammie and Willie all riding away to the West in a covered wagon. And she was left behind.

The next morning she felt drained. Early she heard Uncle Daniel's hammering in the barn, and she knew he was building the tiny coffin. *I should help somebody,* she told herself. *I've been aloof and prissy long enough.* The least she could do was hug her own grief to herself and not show tears for Matthew. Tears now belonged for Sammie.

Shortly after breakfast the Moore family gathered in one corner of the garden where John had spaded up a small, rectangular spot of ground. It was a cool, grassy place, shaded from the late March sunshine by a young spruce. Uncle Daniel spoke only a few words from the Scriptures: " 'Suffer the little children to come unto me, and forbid them not: for of such is the kingdom of God. . . .

" 'For my thoughts are not your thoughts, neither are your ways my ways. . . .'

"And so we commit this child into Your loving arms, dear Father . . . until we meet again."

Rosie stood tall and dry-eyed, her hand on John's shoulder and his fingers twining around hers. It seemed the light still shone on her face. Aunt Prudy's wiry figure in her black bonnet stood stiff and erect as a young sapling, crying softly as tears cut wet paths down her leathery cheeks. Vange and Bitsy and Aggie stood solemn and quiet beside their father. Barbara crept behind them so she wouldn't see John pick up the shovel and throw grassy clods of sod onto the tiny box. *I can't even bury Matthew,* she thought, turning her face away.

Whirling around suddenly, she sped away, half-limping down the path toward the river where she had gone so many times before. She must face her own grief and sorrow that crushed her with an agony she couldn't share. She knelt by the log where she had so often sat before, as though it was an altar and she had come to pray.

Again she thought of Rosie, and the light of hope in her shining face. A hope in what? In Whom? In Jesus Christ and His eternal life? *God loves you . . . God loves you . . . For God so loved the world that He gave His only begotten Son . . .* How many times had she heard these words in recent weeks! Did this mean that, even though there were no answers to the "why" that had plagued her, perhaps *God* had His own reasons for what He planned for her future? That He still loved and directed her in spite of her troubled questions? That perhaps it hadn't included Matthew at all?

Yes, God loved her in spite of her pride, her weaknesses, her failures. It was incredible, but she had to admit it was true. Hadn't He said in Jeremiah 31:3, "I have loved thee with an everlasting love"?

"Dear Lord," Barbara sobbed aloud, "You have overflowed with unconditional love for me through Jesus Christ Your Son. No matter what I've done, or thought I'd done, You love me *just as I am!*"

Finally God had torn up her ugly cancer of pride and prejudice, and a sweet peace filled her heart. The ache and pain for Matthew was still there, and the thought of Baby Sammie in the cold, dark grave was something she would never forget, but something new, something fresh and beautiful had touched her life.

Slowly she got to her feet and walked confidently back to the cabin.

CHAPTER 22

April stole in with a fresh burst of green grass and a shower of wild plum and crab apple blossoms. Dutchman's breeches and bluebells sprouted thick in the timber above the Cottonwood. Meadow larks warbled on rail fences and frogs croaked in river bottoms.

News came that the war was drawing to a close. Petersburg had fallen on April 2d, Richmond on the 3d, and Lee had fled towards Lynchburg.

Now it was April 6th, and in less than a week Evangeline Moore would marry Barry Keaton. Barbara had watched Aggie bury herself in paper patterns and mounds of materials, sewing miles of dainty stitches on the full skirt of the yards and yards of creamy bombazine that came from Barry's mother. It was joined to the fitted basque which was the vogue of the day. Of course, Aggie had long studied the picture of the model on the cover of a women's magazine that Charity Shreve had received from Indiana. The gown was about as stylish as it could be, under the circumstances.

"I hope I have all the measurements right," Aggie pouted, her mouth full of pins, "but it's hard to figure out how to close the back. Perhaps hooks and eyes?"

"Why not a row of self-covered buttons?" Vange offered hopefully, slipping in and out of the basted dress.

"And chase me up half an hour early on your wedding day to button you up?" Bitsy glared. "Not on your life. I s'pose as a Keaton you'll demand the best." She shook her head. "Wasn't Barry's father a senator or something?"

Vange laughed. "Or something. It doesn't matter. I just want to look my best on my wedding day. But hooks and eyes will do. I think it was very thoughtful of his mother to send the gorgeous materials, even if she can't come to the wedding."

Barbara clambered up the loft and rummaged through her trunk, pulling out the blue-and-green plaid she'd worn only a few times. With a little advice from Aggie, she learned how to sew several rows of black silk galloon braid around the skirt. The braid was left over from her mother's dress-maker's notions.

"I wish I could afford a new ribbon for my straw bonnet," she sighed as Bitsy watched her struggle with needle and tread. "Mine's so drab and faded."

Bitsy placed a finger beside her nose and

thought awhile. "Oh, I know! Why not rip the blue-green ribbon from my old blue Sunday poplin? Remember the bands on the sleeves? If we wash and press them carefully, they should make that bonnet look almost like new."

"Could we?" Barbara beamed. "Oh, I do want to look nice for Vange's wedding, since I can't plan my own." She caught her breath sharply. "But it's your dress."

"Never mind. I'm going to wash the linen lace of my best sky blue delaine. We won't be 'belles of the ball' but we'll be there in our tuckered-out duds!" She gave her blond head a toss and laughed.

When Vange tried to squeeze into the tight-fitting basque waist of her wedding gown, the girls shrieked.

"Next time, wear your corset. You'll have to hold your breath for about four hours if you don't," Bitsy said sagely, and the girls dissolved into peals of laughter. Barbara found herself laughing with them.

"Why, Barb!" Vange said suddenly, "You have a very happy-sounding laugh, you know."

"Oh —" Barbara drew in her breath quickly. It had been hard to work up a spirit of fun with all the pain she hoarded in her heart. Still, she was learning Rosie's secret:

the Lord did provide grace and strength. And besides, soon Vange would be gone, along with their fun times together.

Vange, still wearing her wedding gown, stepped out the door and tiptoed to the ivy that tangled around the logs of the cabin. Snatching a soggy, dried morning glory vine, she draped it around her glorious auburn hair, then danced back into the middle of the kitchen, her hands stiffly laced across the front in a foolish imitation of the model on the magazine cover.

"Here's the happy bride, ready for her husband," she said in a mumbling monotone.

"Vange!" Aggie scolded. "Get out of that dress this instant. Don't you care if you get crumpled morning glory petals all over that dreamy, creamy bombazine? What I wouldn't give for such a dress to wear at my wedding — if I ever have a wedding."

The girls looked at Aggie. If anyone sacrificed herself, Aggie Moore certainly did.

"But what *will* you wear at Vange's?" Barbara asked, a sudden interest in her drab cousin.

"Well, I can always turn my old brown poplin . . . if I have time. If there isn't . . . well, never mind. I'm not the bride, so it won't matter how I look."

Barbara frowned. It wasn't right that Aggie had to make do with turned-over hand-me-downs which came in the mail every now and then from Cousin Bedelia of Ohio. For the second time Barbara searched through her trunk. Her mother's old soft, dark red silk with the rows of black rutching on the skirt had always seemed too old for Barbara, but perhaps if Aggie made it over for herself, the gown would do something for her cousin. Especially the high neckline with fluted ribbons edging the banded stand-up collar.

A year ago Barbara would never have given Aggie another thought, or even been willing to part with a dress that had belonged to her mother. Now she suddenly wanted Aggie to look pretty, too.

"I'll fix her hair . . . take down that ridiculous bun and coil it in a low roll at the nape of her neck," she muttered to herself, remembering her resolve the first time she'd met Aggie. Now she'd finally carry it out.

Snatching up the dress, she hurried down the loft and waved it in Aggie's brown face. "Here. Fix this thing any way you like. It was Mother's, but I'm giving it to you."

Aggie stared at her unbelievingly. Then she broke into a freckled grin as she took the dress in her rough, worn hands and fingered it gently. "Why, Barbara," she said, giving her a quick hug, "you're the nicest thing that's happened to me today!" Just then the sound of an approaching wagon rumbled down the trail and stopped at the far end of the lane. It was probably John, rattling toward the river for a load of brush for firewood.

Vange slipped out of her wedding dress and had just pulled into her gray chambray, when they heard a thump-thump on the hard-packed path.

Glancing toward the open door, Barbara gave a startled cry, "Joshua!"

The three girls dropped whatever they were doing and rushed toward the door.

"Josh! Josh! Joshua!" Cries of delight echoed with the slam of the door as the girls ran to embrace their brother.

Barbara stood at the window and watched. Josh, gaunt and thin, his tousled hair blowing in the breeze, tried to balance himself awkwardly on a crutch. His blue army uniform was worn and threadbare. Then she noticed the stump where his left leg had been, and her eyes blurred with tears. If Matthew had survived, even with a stump for a leg . . . But I must be glad Josh came back, she scolded herself. She listened to their happy chatter through the open door.

"Where are Ma and Pa?" Josh asked after he had untangled himself from the three lively sisters.

"Ma's at Rosie's helping her plant a vegetable garden and Pa's in the field, preparing to seed oats," Bitsy chattered. "You haven't asked about Barbie."

Josh seemed to hesitate. "I . . . I don't think she'll want to see me," he replied bravely. "When I left, she wouldn't even tell me goodbye."

With a start, Barbara moved out the door and ran toward him, reaching out her hand slowly. "Welcome back, Josh. I . . . I'm really glad you're here. How did you come?"

"Yes, how did you get home? Surely, you didn't walk," Bitsy began, then broke off in embarrassment as the siblings moved into the cabin. Barbara followed quietly.

"I took the Trail to Lost Springs where Stephen Wise happened to meet the stage. I asked if he'd bring me home. Didn't want to bother anybody, but I just couldn't wait to get home."

"Bother!" Bitsy shrieked. "Well, pull up a chair." She went ahead and shoved aside paper patterns and sewing notions. "That is, if you can find a place to sit. Did you know your sister Vange is going to forsake all others and cleave only to Barry Keaton, as long as they both shall live? Meanwhile we've lived with millions of stitches and scraps, quilt pieces and tea towels and pillow cases. It's been horrible!"

"You'll soon be rid of me," Vange retorted amicably. "Then let's see you shed tears over the millions of snips and scraps!"

Without a word, Josh hobbled toward Barbara and hugged her soundly. "It's good to be back. Barbara. I'm so sorry about Matthew."

She pulled back, startled. "You've . . . heard?"

He led her to a chair and pushed her into it, then sat down beside her. "I . . . have news for you. I met Matthew Potter."

Barbara felt the color drain from her face. *"You — !"*

"No, no, Cousin. I was his prisoner. He was the captain of the guard that captured us. Believe me, some Rebs can be mighty decent. When he heard I was from Kansas, he mentioned your name as the woman he loved. As soon as he got over the shock that you are my cousin, he asked if I would give you this." Josh fumbled in his pocket of his shabby blues and drew out a leather pouch. "Here. Take it."

With trembling fingers Barbara drew out

a dainty gold locket. The filigree around the edges was slightly smudged as though Matthew had carried it with him for a long time. As she pressed a tiny snap, the locket opened. Inside was a picture of her standing beside a magnolia bush. Tears sprang to her eyes when she remembered the day it was taken. It was the day he had asked her to wait for him.

"He . . . he said you were to keep it until he could give you the chain in person. That night we were attacked again. But we were rescued by our men from the skirmish, and that's when I got shot in the leg. I think he had a premonition." Josh paused. "Matthew was a brave soldier, Barbara. We . . . we both did what we felt was right for us. We both did our duty. I don't think he felt any bitterness toward us, and he never once complained about his enemies. We each had the right to see a different duty from what each of us decided was his. I . . . I'm sorry for your sake it was I who came back and not Matthew."

Barbara bowed her head as she clasped the locket in her hands. Tears trickled slowly down her cheeks. How wonderful that Josh had met Matthew and that, although they had been on opposite sides, they were not really enemies. With a wan smile she lifted her tear-wet face.

"Thank you. I . . . I'm glad you came back, even if —"

"Even if I lost a leg?" He grinned feebly as he got up and thumped back to the door and stared at the greening landscape. "My, it's good to be back in Kansas. How I've missed our prairies. And Woodson," he added in a low voice.

"Girls, we've got to get busy," Aggie said brusquely after the tearful reunion was over. "There's a feast to prepare for our soldier who is home from the war. Here, Barbara, you peel potatoes and I'll fry some ham. Sorry, but no one is around to shoot prairie chickens. Vange, you tuck all your wedding finery away and don't you dare get a single smudge on that bombazine! Faded morning glories indeed! Bitsy, you ride out to John and Rosie's and tell them all to hurry on over. Stop by and tell Pa —"

"I'll go to the field and tell him myself," Josh said with a catch in his voice as he picked up his crutch. "One of these days I'll master this thing. I'll tromp over the prairies and shoot the usual quota of prairie chickens."

"Oh, we've looked forward to crunching on buckshot again," Bitsy scoffed, and everyone laughed.

The next several days passed quickly. Josh's homecoming added a glow to the final days of wedding preparations, although Bitsy grouched that she didn't have time to spend with her brother.

Barbara felt a subdued peace in her soul, though the pain of Matthew's death lay deep. Just now she was happy to share in the joys of the Moore family. And she had Matthew's locket. It was almost like having a part of him.

Saturday morning dawned fresh and clear, the pungent smells of greening pussy willow along the draw mingled with the strong fresh aroma of loam and subsoil from the freshly-plowed fields.

Later that afternoon a rider rode over the trail, pushing his foam-flecked mount furiously. Barbara, who was hanging damp tea towels on the bushes to dry, felt her heart in her throat. More Indians? Then she relaxed. Charlie Warren was panting as he pulled to a stop. *What did he want now?* she thought with a grimace.

"Lee's surrendered, Barbara! It's all over! I was in town, just as Silas Locklin rode in from Emporia. He said word came by telegraph!"

Without another word he whirled around and dashed toward the cabin in the glen.

The war was over at last. As Barbara watched Charlie go, a numbness crept over her startled figure, and she leaned heavily against the logs of the cabin. In the distance she could already hear bells ringing and whistles blowing and the gong of the anvil in the blacksmith shop.

She bowed her head reverently, "Thank You, Lord, . . . Thank You. . . ."

For this day she had dreamed many months and years, and now it had come. But she knew that without Matthew a part of her dream would never come true.

CHAPTER 23

All morning long prairie larks twittered and chirked in the cottonwoods as a soft breeze sighed through the pale green branches.

Barbara had roamed over the prairies for an hour, gathering bouquets of wild flowers for Vange's wedding. Before the cabin stood Barry Keaton's Conestoga wagon, loaded to the hilt with supplies and Vange's possessions. They would join a wagon train at Cottonwood Crossing that night and leave for Denver in the morning.

She carried her armload of fresh, fragrant blooms into the white, scrubbed kitchen. Aggie was flitting here and there, checking to make sure nothing was overlooked. Pausing, she shooed Bitsy and Josh from the mounds of molasses cookies she had baked and stored in huge stone crocks days before, now set on platters laid on the clean shelves.

"Honestly," Aggie fumed, "you two act like a pair of toddlers just out of bed. Can't you ever think of Vange's wedding as a solemn occasion instead of gobbling up all the refreshments in sight?"

"By the way, where is the doleful bride?" Josh asked, swallowing the last crumb as he peered into the lean-to.

"Up in the loft with green apple and boiled turnip cream on her face. And don't you call Barry! If he sees her now, there won't be a wedding," Aggie muttered, straightening the crocheted doily on the edge of the mantel for the fourth time. "And Vange isn't doleful either. Bitsy, you go up the loft and tell her to wash that goop from her face; then take her down to Mama's room and start getting her into her wedding gown."

With a shriek Bitsy scooted up the ladder and disappeared.

"But if her weddin's such a solemn occasion," Josh began, then shook his head. "Whoever invented weddings got a bit confused. A solemn occasion to be happy? I'd better see where Barry is. He's probably sulking in the barn, seeing he isn't welcome in the house." With that, he thumped outdoors.

"Aggie," Barbara began, laying the flowers on the clean, linen-covered table, "do you think this bouquet is all right? I ran out of bluebells and had to finish up with red prairie lilies. If I were in Atlanta, I could bring in loads of magnolias. But here —" She flung out her hands.

"Here we make do with what we have,"

Aggie said sharply. Then she softened. "I'm sorry, Barbara, but this wedding's worn me to a rag."

"Does it mean so much to Vange?"

"Oh, I don't know. But she's marrying a Keaton. They're *class*. It mustn't be a dowdy affair. Too bad we don't have a church for the occasion. That would be proper."

"With a dirt floor? But Barry and Vange will be just as legally married in Aunt Prudy's kitchen, won't they?" Barbara asked, arranging the flowers in pewter pots and pitchers.

"Of course they will. We're lucky Elder Buck was willing to ride out all the way from Emporia," Aggie said, stoking the fire in the grate with a rattle of lids. "He'll spend the night with the Shreves and conduct a service in the morning. Since the war is over, one doesn't have to be touchy."

"And the North and South will start talking again," Barbara mused.

Bitsy had shepherded Vange down the loft in a flurry of chatter and giggles and into the downstairs bedroom. Aunt Prudy emerged wearing her stiff, rusty-black silk, her hair stretched taut as fiddle strings into its wispy bun. She jerked on her black bonnet that rattled starchily, and scudded to the door.

"Where is Pa? We've got Vange squeezed into the dress, and had all we could do to persuade her to get laced up in a corset. Aggie, you'd better help do her hair. And Barbara, you'd better get dressed," she added, adjusting the shiny black sateen ties of her bonnet. "The guests will be here in less than an hour!"

Barbara scrambled up the loft and took the plaid from its hook on the rafters. Dressing hurriedly, she brushed her thick hair and let the rich curls loose on her back, then scooted down to the bedroom to offer her help.

"I declare, she lost five pounds so she could get into her finery," Bitsy said when Barbara came in. "She vows she won't need the corset."

Vange laughed. "I've been so excited I haven't been eating as much as usual."

Aggie eyed the bride and sniffed. "But you'll gain it all back during the wedding lunch. Keep holding your breath in. At least, we cinched in your waist. Here, let me fix your hair. I declare those auburn curls need more brushing."

"Oh, Aggie," Vange's eyes grew soft and dreamy, "What will I ever do without you?"

"Well, I won't travel with you as your personal maid!" Aggie snapped. Then she grinned feebly. "But I wouldn't trust anyone else to fix you up for your wedding."

The girls, breathless, and showing strains of the solemn moments, shrieked with laughter.

Barbara surveyed the bride shrewdly. "Oh, Vange, you look lovely! Aggie's done a good job, even to fixing that wreath of early primroses for your hair. It's better than the dried morning glory vine you tried the other day."

"Good thing Willie showed you where the primroses grow," Aggie said, taking the pins from her own frowsy hair and running a quick comb through it. She was about to scoop it all up into a bun when Barbara snatched the comb from her.

"Here. Let me do it." She began to shape the straight drab brown hair into soft coils at the nape of her neck.

"Aggie, you're going to be the prettiest girl at the wedding, next to the bride, if I can help it," she mumbled, her mouth full of hairpins.

"You don't look so bad yourself," Bitsy said. "What would we have done without you, Barbie? All the flowers you picked —"

"I haven't done nearly enough," Barbara cut in sharply. "It's just that —"

"We know. You've lost everyone near and dear, except us. And don't you forget that you have *us!*" Aggie opened the door a crack and peered into the kitchen. "The guests are arriving. I'd better make sure everything's in order." She gave herself one final glance in the mirror and flounced into the kitchen.

Vange pirouetted around in her wedding finery. "Aggie does look nice. It was sweet of you to fix her hair and give her the dress of your mother's, Barb."

"Aggie deserves it. She's done so much for everybody."

"Yes. She'll never admit that I could've had a wedding without her."

Just then there was a slight rap at the door, and Aggie peered through the crack. "Come on out, girls," she whispered. "Time to start."

Bitsy took Barbara's arm and pushed her toward the door. "We must go first so the bride can make a grand entrance."

John and Rosie stood near the door beside Aunt Prudy and Uncle Daniel, with Josh beside them, greeting the guests as they came in. The kitchen seemed to bulge with Billingses and Shreves and Griffiths. They sat stiffly on split logs which Uncle Daniel and Josh had set up to form benches. In one corner sat Charlie, dressed in buckskins and a clean white linen shirt, with Willie, face scrubbed and tawny hair slicked, squirming beside him.

Elder Buck waited beside the table, his open Bible in one hand. Barry came in from the lean-to, and paused before the minister, just as the bedroom door opened and Vange stepped out to meet her groom.

Barbara, standing near the lean-to door, caught her hand at her throat. She thought she would choke with pain and joy — the pain because she knew Vange would soon be gone, and joy for the lovely bride who was standing beside her handsome groom with the glow of love in their eyes for each other.

"Dearly beloved," Elder Buck began speaking in a deep voice as he shuffled and minced before the crowd, "We are gathered here in the sight of God and man to join this man and this woman in holy matrimony . . . ."

After the vows, spoken softly, the words were sealed with a kiss of commitment. Vange and Barry held hands and bowed to receive the benediction and blessing.

A bustle of congratulations followed. Aggie flew about the room, plying the guests with cookies and mugs of real coffee.

I should help, Barbara mused, standing near the back door, *but somehow I can't.* She couldn't bear to see her cousin leave; more than that, she felt so empty, so devoid of anything. Perhaps it was because she and Matthew could never share in the joy that shone on the faces of the newly married couple.

Or was that it?

Bitsy moved beside Barbara, her curls already mussed from the light spring breeze that wafted through the open door.

"I guess after those millions of stitches we put into Vange's dowry, all this was worth it. I'd cry for Vange if I didn't feel so much like laughing."

"Laughing?" Barbara echoed. "How can you think of laughing at such a solemn time?"

"It looked so funny to see Elder Buck's mincing footsteps in front of the crowd, as though his shoes pinched his feet."

Barbara smiled in spite of herself. Trust the Moore sense of humor to always lurk near the surface.

But when Vange and Barry drove away in the midafternoon stillness and the guests stood by the split rail fence to see them off, Barbara's tears were starting and she knew she couldn't stop them. It was a mixture of seeing Vange leave and Matthew's death, and she couldn't sort out the two right now. If it wasn't for the Lord, she couldn't stand it.

Suddenly she looked up to see Charlie Warren standing beside her. His buckskin jacket strained against his brawny shoulder, and he stood tall and stalwart, cool and undisturbed as he grinned at her. She wanted to wipe the grin from his face, to hurt him, to make him feel the pain she felt.

"Well, they're off. How does this make you feel?"

"Feel? Oh, what do you know about feelings?" she cried through her tears. "You've never lost the one you loved!"

He put his firm hand over her clenched little fist. "Maybe, Barbara," he said quietly, his voice edged with pain, "I know better than you think."

She flung off his hand and whirled on him. "I doubt that! What you need is a wife like Bitsy. Why don't you get wise? But who else wants a flock of sheep for a rival?" she retorted.

He reached out his hands and cupped her face gently in his palms. "Why don't you speak for yourself, Barbara?" he inquired softly.

Her dark, luminous eyes widened. Then

with a flash of scathing anger, she flung off his hands, spun around and rushed away. *Charlie Warren . . . How dare he? . . . How dare he!*

CHAPTER 24

The cabin seemed strangely empty without Vange's bubbly laughter and bright chatter in the days that followed. Aggie and Bitsy had spent all afternoon planting a new vegetable garden, while Barbara restlessly roamed the spring prairies like a lonely chick. She noticed Josh working on the rail fence as she came slowly around the bend. Pulling down her straw bonnet, she drew her dark blue cape over her shoulders against the chill of deepening afternoon shadows and stopped to watch him.

Josh looked up. "Well, what's so tragic that you've lost your smile, Cousin?"

Barbara leaned against the fence with its wild violets growing in thick bunches beside the trail.

"I feel," she said with a quick shake of her head, "as though the chinks have fallen out of my life."

"Do you miss Vange as much as that?"

"Oh, it's Vange, and Matthew, and feeling as though I'm just a burr on a dog and not much good to anyone."

He laid down his tools and folded his arms on the top rail. "Feeling sorry for yourself isn't going to make things easier, is it?" he said with a boyish grin.

"Feeling sorry," she gasped. "Is that what you think I'm doing? If anyone has a right to feel sorry for anyone, it's you, Joshua Moore!"

He nodded. "I suppose so. But the Lord was good. He let me live. When I think about all those weeks I spent in the hospital with nothing but pain and a horrible stench and the sound of moaning and dying, I still shudder. It was always the thought of my family back here in Kansas that kept me going — that, and my faith in my Savior. He loves you, too, Barbara. 'Who shall separate us from the love of Christ? Shall tribulation, or distress, or persecution, or famine, or sword?' "

Barbara's voice was low. "It was after I learned how much God loved me that I could accept Matthew's death and face life. But when I look ahead and see only emptiness looming —"

"Life will be full again one of these days, Barbara. You'll find someone else you can love. Any girl as pretty as you will never lack for admirers."

"I won't think about that for a long time," she said testily. "But I'm grateful the war is finally over and the world can spin merrily on its way. But there's so much to get done now."

"President Lincoln's goal has been reached," Josh said. "His big dream was to stop the war and unite the nation. But wounds are still raw and healing will take time."

"There's so much to heal! For so long all I could see was the anger of the North toward the South and the hatred between the two. Maybe Lincoln was right in freeing the slaves."

"Of course, he was. God created men equal, and in His own image, didn't He?"

Barbara turned and looked across the prairies that shimmered and dipped in the spring sunshine. She thought of Louisy and Crissie, Pansy and old Isaac and the rest, wondering where they were and how they'd cope with their new freedom. It had never occurred to her that they were created in God's image. They were made for work. But if this were so, surely God would show them how to make a way for themselves.

"Josh," she said, her voice rising, "the world is going to be different from now on, something that will take getting used to. Even these prairies may change." She swept her hand over the scene before her. "But if

President Lincoln can create order out of all the mess —"

"Not only Abe Lincoln. It takes all of us pulling together. It's hard to believe, I know. But by the grace of God, it can be done. He said that both the North and the South must share the blame for the war. According to the news, a brass band led 3,000 people to the White House as news of Lee's surrender came. Lincoln asked the band to play 'Dixie' — that it was no longer a Southern tune. That it belonged to the Union. What a man!"

He picked up his tools and drove another rail into the ground. Barbara watched him silently. *And to think I felt Josh was wrong when he left to join the Yankees,* she thought. *He saw exactly what Matthew saw, only from the opposite end.* Without another word she moved on, following the faint trail toward the cabin.

"Hey! Wait for me!" Someone yelled behind her. She knew without turning that it was Willie.

"What are you up to, William Warren?" she asked, stopping to wait for him, her mood of loneliness gone.

"I just wanted to tell you," he panted, "that Evin Hoops met Charlie on the Trail early this mornin'. Seems Vange and Barry joined up with the wagon train all right at Cottonwood Crossin' and are on their way to Colorado."

"I s'pose Vange didn't even look back," she said dryly. "She seemed so eager to go."

"Of course, she musta looked back!" Willie said brusquely. "She hated to leave her family. But when you get married, Charlie says, 'You go with the one you love.' "

What does Charlie Warren know about love? Barbara bit back the reply. "Oh, well." She shrugged her shoulders diffidently. "Charlie wouldn't know, would he? All he needs is his sheep. Or Bitsy."

"He doesn't want Bitsy," Willie said tartly. "Not Charlie."

"No. Why should he? He's got his sheep. And what girl wants to compete with sheep?" she retorted. Her face reddened as she remembered Charlie on the day of Vange and Barry's wedding.

Then she placed a gentle arm around Willie's shoulders. "I'm sorry, Willie. I shouldn't have said what I did. I was just . . . sore."

"That's all right, Barbara. I know you're still shook up about Matthew. But if this means you'll stay here —"

"What else can I do?" she cried, flinging

out her hands. "The South is lost to me now. I can't go back there." She turned slowly toward the cabin, then paused by the ridge that led to Charlie's sheep pens.

"And the prairie? You still hate it so much?"

Barbara cocked her head and laughed. "Do I like her foolish whims, her changeable moods? Most certainly not!" Then she drew a deep breath. "But the enchantment's growing, I think. I'm beginning to feel almost like Uncle Daniel did, that maybe the Lord led me here."

"Good. That means you'll stay. Do you s'pose school's out for the year?"

"I'm sure of it. With gardens and field work, who has time for school?" she said flippantly. She noticed the faraway look in his eyes and it disturbed her.

"Is anything wrong, Willie? What are you looking at?"

He pointed to the ridge littered with driftwood and dirt. The dirt looked like a deposit of mud that had dried long ago.

"It's Charlie. He . . . he's talkin' about pullin' up stakes and movin' on."

"Moving on? But why, Willie?"

Willie turned to face the valley. "You saw the ridge. If we have a heavy gully washer, this whole valley could flood. The homestead's too near the river and the bottom land is too low. One of these days it's gonna flood us out. The settlement, too. When the settlers first came to Marion Centre one of the Kaw chiefs had shaken his head and warned, 'Heapie much water some day.' "

"Willie," Barbara's heart lurched crazily, "does this mean you'll move away?"

"I don't know, Barbara. 'You can't fight a river,' Charlie says." He lowered his eyes. "I'd better go now. Charlie needs my help with chores. But I'd sure hate to leave you," he added. He swung around and raced down the trail toward the cabin on the other side of the creek.

Barbara felt numb as she walked into the cabin and took off her cape and straw bonnet. Willie was her best friend. If he went away, what did she have left? It was almost like losing Whatley all over again.

At the sudden rattle of clods on the lane, she paused. A rider on horseback clattered toward the cabin and jerked to a stop by the hitching rail,

"It . . . it's the President," he said hoarsely. "Abraham Lincoln's dead! He was in the theater attendin' a play and was shot by an actor. Word come by telegraph at Emporia this mornin'. I've been ridin' my horse hard, bringin' the news out."

"D-dead, you said?" Barbara gasped.

The man nodded, whirled around and turned toward Uncle Daniel who was plowing the north prairie.

Barbara stared after him in stunned silence. It couldn't be true! She grabbed her straw bonnet, then sped toward the fence where Josh was still pounding rail posts. Moisture from the grass dampened her ankles and cockleburrs caught in her skirts.

"Josh!" she called out, her throat dry. "Lincoln's been . . . shot!"

Josh turned, his face horror-struck, and leaned heavily against the fence. "The President? Dead? Oh, God, no! What will we do now?" He swallowed hard and stood silent for a long minute.

"How'd it happen? And when?"

"Last night in the theater. Shot by an actor. That's all I know."

"Oh, Barbara, just when the war —" he gulped. "How can our country go on now?"

Barbara felt a catch in her throat. "I . . . I'm really sorry, Josh."

Without a word, Josh left his work and started for the cabin. Uncle Daniel was already stabling the horses. Aunt Prudy and the girls plodded slowly toward the lean-to door, dragging their hoes after them, as though the family was called in from their work by the death of their best friend.

It was unbelievable that only a few days earlier they had celebrated the end of the war. There would be no wild ringing of bells now, no blowing of whistles — only a solemn, slow tolling of the anvil gong in the blacksmith shop.

When Barbara came indoors, Aggie and Bitsy were crying.

"What will the country do now?" Aggie said, her voice low.

"If only Vange were here!" Bitsy wailed, as if Vange could have helped.

Aunt Prudy went to the bedroom and put on her black, starched bonnet. Uncle Daniel came through the lean-to door slowly, heavily, took off his hat and hung it on the nail above the door.

"God's will be done," he said huskily, bowing his head. "God rest his soul."

Barbara stood by silently, observing their grief. Abraham Lincoln, the man who had fought hard to save the nation; whose faith in his God and fellowmen had gotten the job done. Abe Lincoln — gangly, honest, smart, homely — who had been a settler, too. He had plowed, harvested, split rails, joked and roared with laughter; he had experienced cold and hunger, faced storms — and felt the sting of a bullet, as had so many men who had given their lives for their country.

Tears streamed down Barbara's face. It began to dawn on her what it would mean to the whole country. The war was over. But the leader who was to unite the North and the South was gone. Both Yankee and Rebel would mourn. Still, maybe the mourning could help pull the divided country together. She honestly hoped it would.

CHAPTER 25

President Andrew Johnson took up the reins of government and worked to bring the small remaining skirmishes to an end as the weeks dragged by. All Confederate troops west of the Mississippi had surrendered. The nation, its time of mourning waning, was ready to follow the new leader.

May, the month of wild roses and blue daisies, slipped into June. The prairies, tipped with pink and mauve and bright green, stretched lazily under the deep blue sky shafted with cumulus clouds.

The end of the war brought efforts to cope with change. Uncle Daniel came home from Marion Centre with plans for organizing the county. He was full of talk at the supper table, even out-talking Aggie and Bitsy, who stopped only when decorum demanded.

"It's time we pull ourselves together," he said. "There's long been talk of separating Marion and Chase counties. We mean to organize our own county government."

"I thought we tried that once before," Josh put in, spearing another square of hot cornbread and buttering it,

"Oh, that!" Uncle Daniel chuckled.

"Once the election was to be held at Lank's ranch. When election day came, there weren't enough qualified candidates in the county to fill the offices — unless Indians were counted. So they threw out the ballot box and spent the rest of the day full of devilment."

Josh and the girls laughed so hard that Aunt Prudy had to shush them. "That's about enough. Such shenanigans! Now, Pa, what's different about this election?"

"For one thing, the population has grown to 160 persons, and for another, we have enough qualified candidates. Election's been scheduled for August 7th."

"I'll vote for Henry Minton for clerk," Bitsy put in.

"Vote? You?" Josh snorted. "Women weren't intended to wear pants or vote. I think it says so somewhere in the Bible. I'll look it up next Sunday."

Aggie and Bitsy laughed themselves sick, and Barbara smiled at the humor of the situation. She found herself interested in what was happening in the community. Transplanted to the Kansas prairie, with the frontier so unlike anything she had known, she had become conscious of a change in herself. The Bible was becoming more relevant to her, too.

Of course, William Billings' self-appointed leadership in the community made him a likely candidate for some office. She smiled again. If I'm going to stay here, I might as well take an interest, she decided.

One balmy June morning she picked up a hoe and followed Aggie and Bitsy into the garden.

"If you two can work to make something grow, maybe I can, too," she said when Bitsy's eyes widened at the sight of a hoe in her hands. "It's time I pulled my weight around here."

"You attack the beans," Aggie ordered, pushing Barbara toward the long rows of snap beans. "The trick is to keep the ground loosed up around each plant. When it rains it can soak up the water and hold in the roots. By the way, you'd better wear a slat bonnet. Your straw thing has seen its best days."

"You know I hate slat bonnets," Barbara grumbled, and the two other girls laughed. The *scritch-scritch* of her hoe made her feel as though she were doing something worthwhile, but she didn't have to wear a bonnet to do it!

Bitsy, scratching dirt around tiny cucumber plants, began to whistle.

"Quit it," Aggie rapped out sharply. "Remember 'a whistling girl and a crowing hen always come to some bad end.' You'll never hook a husband that way, my dear little sister."

"Oh, come now, Aggie," Bitsy snorted. "I'm not that desperate. Sure, I've given up on Charlie Warren. He has set his sights on other . . . er . . . things. Woolly things. But I've decided to set my cap for Henry Minton. He's handsomer than Barry Keaton, and for two cents I'd tell Vange so!"

"Why should Vange care? She's married to Barry, and they'll be living it up in that grand white house in Denver. Trust her to know when she's lucky."

Chatter-chatter, Barbara thought. *Like blackbirds in the cottonwoods.* Across the river she heard Charlie's lambs bleating. She wondered if he still entertained thoughts of leaving his homestead for a claim less rolling and low. Was Willie right? Would this river valley fill with water after a good, hard rain?

She hadn't seen Willie in more than a week, for Charlie and Willie had not come to attend church services at the Moores' in some time.

"We sometimes go to Shreves or Griffiths," Willie told Barbara when she asked. "The same God is there, too, Charlie says. But somethin's makin' Charlie rest-less."

Yes, God was there, too. His love was everywhere, Barbara had discovered, and nothing could separate her from God's love. Yet she couldn't bear to think of Willie's leaving. He had been her first friend in Kansas.

The soft June days slipped into July. Vange wrote that she and Barry had arrived safely in Denver and were living in two rooms of a large white clapboard house with gingerbread trim. Barry was busy with newspaper work, and she was fixing up their rooms with cheery white muslin curtains and potted geraniums. There was no wind, and the night air that blew in from the Rockies was always cool and pleasant.

As the weeks settled into summer, winds began to sweep over the prairies — hot, stinging winds that blew piles of fine, sifting soil against the rail fences.

The vegetable garden struggled to survive, and each evening the girls carried buckets of water from the spring to keep the scrawny plants alive.

"We'll have beans to eat, if I have to turn into a tadpole," Bitsy grumped as she lugged another pail of water to the little plot while Barbara carried water to the rosebush

Aunt Prudy had planted on little Sammie's grave.

All day long the winds moaned and crooned over the baking prairie that shimmered brown in the heat.

Aunt Prudy was listless and tired long before dinnertime. Even Aggie had lost interest in her perpetual quilt blocks and food preparation. Bitsy sat beside the wash basin and sponged her neck and face over and over with a scrap of toweling.

"Bitsy, you'll get wrinkles if you don't stop that," Aggie snapped. "How do you expect Henry Minton to fall in love with a gnarled old prune?"

"Oh, Henry has sense enough not to come out in this heat," she sulked. "Wish we lived in Denver with Vange."

"And leave our prairies?" Aggie retorted. "Not on your life!"

Newspaper fans batted only more hot air as they pushed the folded pages back and forth. Barbara sat by the window, her eyes scanning the pages of her tattered novels or her Bible, as the hot, dry days dragged by.

For three weeks the wind blustered and blew and the sun blazed from a brassy sky. Day after day, Uncle Daniel and Josh worked on the claim, trying to turn the hard sod that yielded little more than shards of dust. Sometimes clouds came — high, cauliflower clouds that seemed to hang overhead without movement. But when dusk leaned down slowly and the incessant winds died for the night, the sky remained clear, with no sign of rain.

One late afternoon in early August, Barbara slammed on her straw bonnet. "I'm going out. Maybe it's cooler along the creek," she said.

"Watch for rattlesnakes," Aggie warned. "Although if they've any sense, they'll stay down in the earth where it's cooler."

Barbara walked slowly, the dust stinging her face. *Maybe I shouldn't have come,* she decided. But anything was better than being cooped up in the hot, smothering cabin. Her shoes scooped up the sifted dirt as she plodded down the path toward the river.

When she reached the stream, she saw the water was scarcely more than a trickle. The air seemed even more oppressive as she looked over the short brown grasses beyond.

A sound behind her startled her, and she turned. Willie was slinging a lariat rope to snag a small stump.

"Willie!" she called. "What on earth are you doing?"

He coiled his rope and came toward her. "Just practicin'."

"Practicing for what?"

"Ropin' cattle."

"You going into the ranching business? Or are you going to work for Lank Moore?"

He dropped his head. "Charlie says if he can sell his sheep, he'll head for Western Kansas and start a cattle ranch. I don't have nuthin' else to do, so I figured I might as well practice ropin'."

"Show me how you make a lariat, Willie." Barbara moved beside him.

"You make a noose, a big enough loop, like this," he said, flicking the rope into a knot, "Coil the rest of the rope loose around your hand, makin' sure you have hold of the end. Then you swing it 'round and 'round, like so. Then you let go and — wham! See? It's easy."

Barbara smiled. She didn't exactly "see," but just talking to Willie made time pass more quickly.

A quiet stir among the cottonwoods ended in a hissing whisper.

"Wind's turnin'," Willie said, nonchalantly looking up. "Maybe God's gonna answer our prayer for rain."

Barbara glanced at him quickly. "You think so?"

"Oh, sure. He's in everythin' that happens, Charlie says."

"You mean God? Is He in the weather as well as in the affairs of men?"

"Don't you see, Barbara? He 'lowed the war to stop before President Lincoln was shot. He'll send rain, too. The Bible says, 'And the parched ground shall become a pool, and the thirsty land, springs of water.' Sounds neat, huh?"

"I know. But . . . sometimes it's hard to believe that the war was God's will."

Willie toyed with his rope before answering. "Maybe God knew that was one way of keepin' you here."

Barbara shook her head. "Oh, Willie, I don't understand so much of what God has allowed. Like the war, the Indian scares, Rosie and John's little Sammie . . . and . . . and Matthew. There's so much . . . Sometimes my faith's too small."

"God don't expect us to understand. He just wants us to trust Him, no matter what. At least, that's what Charlie says."

Charlie says. Charlie says. She was driven into silence. There was still so much to learn about being a Christian. *Lord, forgive me for being so slow to catch on,* she prayed silently. *But help me to keep learning.*

A dimness seemed to dip over the prairies

and suddenly clouds blotted out the sunshine. Then a low peal of thunder rolled out of the west and a heavy black cloud swept over the sun. Barbara and Willie looked up at the darkening sky in silence.

With a wave of his hand, Willie started for the creek crossing. "We'd better scoot. Looks like it could rain any minute now," he shouted as he scrambled down the bank.

As Barbara hurried up the path toward the cabin, big single drops of rain splattered from the black sky. Then all at once it poured down in sheets. She ran in the streaming rain, her feet slipping and sliding on the wet path.

Reaching the cabin she threw herself against the door and panted into the kitchen just as Uncle Daniel and Josh barreled through the lean-to entrance.

The thunder that accompanied the streaks of lightning seemed like a continuous bellow. Thunder crashed and rolled over the prairie like gunfire from Bull Run. The wind that blew twisted and lashed through the cottonwoods.

The Moore family huddled by the windows and watched the violent rain fling itself over the prairies. Darkness was gathering now, and great folds of gray were lapping against darker gray. All evening and all night the rain pounded against the cabin. Barbara slept fitfully, for she could hear the harsh, steady drumming on the roof whenever she awoke.

In the morning the rain had stopped, with only intermittent polka dots dripping as the skies gradually cleared and widened. Thin, pink sunlight filtered through the clouds, glistening on uneven shafts of fog along the river.

At mid-morning Aunt Prudy, Aggie and Bitsy went out to survey the damage to the vegetable garden while Uncle Daniel and Josh sloshed into the fields to see if the corn and oats were washed out.

Barbara stood at the south window, gazing at the landscape, now soaked with rain. One day the plains were parched; the next, they seemed to drown in pools of water.

At a sudden pounding on the door, she hurried to open it. Willie stood there, his eyes wide and staring.

"Barbara!" he yelled. "The river's flooded the glen and water's everywhere — all except the branch crick. The sheep's gotta be led into the shed on the ridge, but Charlie's off helpin' the Millers bring in a new colt. He don't know about the river. What shall I do? The sheep'll head for the water if we don't do somethin'."

"Beauregard?" she asked.

"He's as dumb as that Confederate cap'n he was named after!"

Barbara snatched up her straw bonnet and grabbed Willie's arm. "Hurry! Maybe we can stop the sheep."

They ran down the path, their feet squishing in the mud. As the trail leveled out and they neared the river, an ominous roar filled the air.

"What's that . . . ?" Barbara asked fearfully.

"It's comin' from the branch crick," Willie shouted, pointing. "I bet it's gettin' the runoff from the fields now. We gotta hurry and head off the sheep!"

They raced to the banks of the Cottonwood, stopping a few yards from the edge.

"Look at that!" Willie cried. "It's a real flash flood!" Red-colored water churned between the banks and pounded against the sides where the river turned. Debris of all sorts went spinning past. A log rushed by and slammed into the curved bank with a dull thud. The frothing hem of the river leaped and surged, foaming as it thundered along — a mad, molten mass of muddy water.

The glen dipped just opposite the branch creek. If they crossed the branch, they might ward off the sheep from the water and direct them toward the pens above, on the ridge. Already Barbara heard the bellwether, bleating lambs and baaing of ewes in fear.

"Come on!" Willie yelled. "We gotta cross this narrow place, if we're gonna chase the sheep!"

Barbara lifted her skirts and followed Willie's quick figure toward the narrow branch. She noticed his rope under his arm.

"I'm right behind you," she shouted over the roar of the water. "Be careful. The water's rising!"

Willie threw down his coil of rope and stepped closer to the edge to get a better look where the branch joined the river. Suddenly the weakened bank gave way to the force of the current and collapsed. He screamed as the ground crumbled beneath him. He struggled to jump to safety, but it was too late. With a splash, he disappeared into the raging torrent.

"Will . . . ee!" Barbara screamed. "Willie!" She ran to the edge of the creek, wondering what to do next. Suddenly he popped to the surface, spitting, arms flailing wildly.

"The r-o-o-o-pe . . ." he yelled.

Barbara suddenly remembered Willie's rope. *I don't know how to make a noose,* she thought. Clutching one end tightly, she heaved the coiled rope as hard as she could. It landed just beyond him. Barbara's heart sank as she jerked it back; then she stepped back to throw it out as far as she could.

The current had swept Willie against the bend of the opposite bank and pinned him there, sending wave after wave of murky water over his head as the water surged against the bank. She saw Willie's arms thrashing like a windmill. She knew he was tiring, and she had to do something quick. Time was running out. *Oh, God, I can't lose Willie!*

I've got to lasso him, she decided. There was no other way. Throwing off her straw bonnet, she tried frantically to form a noose, fervently trying to remember how Willie had done it. "Make a plenty big enough loop," Willie had said. "Coil the remaining rope around your other hand, making sure you have hold of the end."

The current was sweeping Willie around the bend now. She knew she must get Willie *now,* before the current carried him farther down.

Barbara took a deep breath and with a quick prayer for help, she began to swing the rope. *Concentrate.* With a graceful swing, the rope flew out over the torrent and fell around Willie's struggling figure. Then she tied the other end to a stump for leverage and began to pull hard.

Slowly, it seemed inch by inch, Willie struggled against the current toward the shore. He crawled up the bank, a few yards from the edge, and panted like Woodson after a hard run. Thank God, Willie's safe!

Just then Barbara heard a thunderous sound, and looked up in time to see the branch creek flooding, and a wriggling mass that bobbed with white woolly heads. The noise was like a thousand bleating sounds as the flock of sheep swept out into the raging Cottonwood River.

With an anguished cry, she knelt at Willie's side. "Oh, Willie, Charlie's sheep are all gone! We . . . we couldn't save any of them!"

Willie sat back, coughed up dirty river water, and slipped the rope from his body.

"But you saved my life, Barbara," he gasped. "If you hadn't roped me . . ."

She rocked back on her heels. "God helped me. He really did! And — hey, I had a good teacher. Doesn't that count? I'm just so very thankful you're safe."

For a moment Willie grinned. Then he sobered. "Now I know for sure Charlie an' me is gonna leave. We can't stay here anymore."

A chill swept over Barbara. She knew what he said was true. The two Warren brothers would pull up stakes and move elsewhere. And suddenly she didn't want them to go — either of them.

CHAPTER 26

The sun was setting through a ragged fringe of orange-tinted clouds in the west as Barbara stood in the doorway of the cabin. She was still tired from the exhausting ordeal of pulling Willie ashore the day before. She couldn't get over the disappointment that all of Charlie's sheep had been lost, for she knew what it meant. There was no way he and Willie would stay.

Tomorrow was Election Day, and excitement brewed in the settlement. Of course, there was little competition for the county offices, but it promised to be an interesting day. According to Uncle Daniel, only the commissioners would be elected, the rest appointed.

Compared to when she had arrived over two years ago, things were booming in Marion Centre. William Billings had brought in the first sulky rake just two months ago which made haying much easier. The population was growing. A quarry of native limestone south of town was yielding building materials. And next Sunday the first church service would be held.

"As a Christian, I want to be a part of the church," she told herself with an audible sigh. If Bitsy kept on seeing Henry Minton there might soon be another wedding. As for Aggie, Barbara sometimes worried that the little brown wren would never capture a husband — her good cooking and ability to sew a fine seam notwithstanding. Aggie ought to marry. *I'll encourage her to roll up her hair,* she decided. *Maybe it will increase her chances.*

"I guess it is up to me to be a support to Aunt Prudy," she mused aloud. There was so much work in the garden, and with putting up food for winter, not to mention the washing and mending. She tried so hard to learn all she could.

"Barbara?"

Someone called her name softly, and she turned. Bitsy stood beside her, pulling at the dried yellow climbing roses that had crept up the vine-shaded cabin overhang.

"What you did for Willie yesterday was a brave thing," Bitsy said. "You deserve a medal for that."

"For saving his life?" Barbara shook her head. "I couldn't stand letting Whatley, I mean Willie, drown. I'm sorry we couldn't save Charlie's sheep."

"And I guess it means he and Willie will

pack up and leave."

Barbara nodded in the semi-darkness as she murmured, "I guess it does."

"Aren't you going to stop him?"

"Why should I? If that's what he wants. The river flooded once. It could happen again, and worse. Maybe the whole settlement." She paused with a sad little sigh. "It's just that I'll miss Willie . . . so much. He was my first real friend here. It was almost like having Whatley back."

"I know. But if you love Charlie, you can't let them go just like that."

"Love Charlie!" Barbara burst out hotly. "Who says I love Charlie? I said it was Willie I'd miss!"

Bitsy took her down the path. The big cowslip prairie moon swung to their backs and paled in the deepening twilight. A coyote howled in the distance, and another answered faintly.

"I think you've cared about Charlie for a long time. You're just scared or maybe too stubborn to admit it," Bitsy went on brashly. "Don't ask me how I know. I'm sure he loves you, too. He never gave any of us girls a tumble after you came."

Barbara stopped abruptly in the middle of the path. "I . . . I don't know, Bitsy. I really don't. Yet somehow the Lord's been showing me that I won't go back to Atlanta. What am I to do?" Her last words were like a prayer.

"Just keep praying and trusting, Barbie. The Lord will show you. That's all you can do."

That night Barbara tossed and turned on the rough straw ticking, thinking hard about what Bitsy had said. Did she care about Charlie? She had hated him for so long, and living on the prairie would mean she'd never be a plantation belle again. She would turn into one of those frowsy frontier women. But was that so important? *Dear Lord, what am I to do?*

The next morning Charlie stopped at the cabin on his way home from the election just as Barbara was clearing away the bread-making pans.

He came straight out with the news. "Willie and I are moving next week," he said, taking off his soft felt hat and twirling it in his hands. His dark curls tumbled over his forehead and he pushed them away absently. "My bottom land is too low, and I know the river will flood again. I've got to make a fresh start, somewhere. Especially since I've lost my sheep."

Uncle Daniel and Josh, who had just returned from town, were seated at the table drinking mid-morning coffee.

"Where will you go?" Josh asked, shoving a cupful of coffee toward Charlie. "We'll miss you. We've been neighbors for more than three years now."

"Western Kansas, close to Fort Larned. Some day I'll own a cattle ranch there. I hope to stake a claim where it's flat. I'm tired of the sound of rushing water!"

He avoided Barbara's eyes as she paused with her utensils by the table. "Some day maybe someone can tame the Cottonwood, but it won't be me. At least, the water's gone down today," he added.

"Does Willie want to leave?" Barbara broke in. "Have you asked him if he wants to go?"

Charlie didn't answer. He didn't even look at her. Instead, he got to his feet and turned to Uncle Daniel.

"I wonder what the election results will be."

"That's easy," Uncle Daniel said with a grin. "For commissioners who else but William Billings, Levi Billings and T. J. Wise? They're our most prominent citizens."

Charlie spun around and walked out of the cabin without saying another word.

Barbara pressed her lips together. Why should Charlie ignore her? Hadn't they been neighbors? Hadn't she helped care for Willie during his siege with diphtheria? And Charlie hadn't as much as mentioned that she had pulled Willie from the river. Perhaps he was angry because they hadn't saved the sheep.

I can't let him go away like this, she determined with a stubborn jut to her jaw. I've got to talk to him. She waited until late afternoon, after she had helped Aunt Prudy put up the last jars of dill pickles. Taking off her checkered apron she hung it on the nail behind the door. She had to see for herself if he really planned to leave, or if he was considering Willie's feelings at all.

As she marched down the muddy path still soggy from the heavy rain, she noticed the crossing on the branch creek had returned to a mere trickle over the stones.

Holding up her skirts, she hopped across and made her way cautiously up the slippery banks. As she headed for the little cabin in the glen, she heard the sound of hammering and sawing. Pausing on the path, she saw it. Charlie was forming the bows over the large farm wagon, and the roll of canvas that would be fastened over the ribbing laid on the ground. Yes, it would become a regular prairie schooner. Apparently Charlie's mind was made up.

Talking wouldn't be any use.

The sight filled her with uneasy fear, and she whirled around and sped back to the Moore cabin. *Oh, Charlie . . . Charlie, I know now that I love you! Dear Lord, help me to do the right thing.* Had this been in God's plan all along?

"Josh," she called out as she came toward her cousin who was by the fence pounding in split rails. "May I borrow Petunia for an hour?"

Josh eyed her shrewdly. "Sure. Go right ahead."

She hurried toward the barn. Saddling the horse, she swung herself astride and headed toward town. The ride in the late August afternoon was brisk, and she slowed Petunia to a canter as she neared the Shreve house in its stone-walled enclosure. Charity was outside, clipping the last red rose from the bush she had nurtured so carefully during the summer. As Barbara reined in her horse, Charity looked up.

"Oh, Barbara," she said, dropping her shears. "Do come in and visit awhile."

"I don't have time, Mrs. Shreve. I want to know when Elder Buck will be back for a service."

"He'll be here Sunday for the first church service. Does thee have a message?"

"Tell him . . . tell him to prepare for another wedding," Barbara said breathlessly. Touching Petunia's flanks with her foot, she wheeled around and raced back toward the Moore cabin.

Stabling the horse, Barbara hurried into the cabin, and clambered up the loft. She opened the trunk and rummaged feverishly through its contents. The worn green bombazine she had brought from Atlanta would have to be her wedding gown, instead of the soft, white, watered silk she had dreamed of for years. Somehow, the memory of Matthew had faded into the past. What she had felt for him wasn't love — she knew it now. It had been a romantic illusion. With a sudden catch in her throat, she slipped Matthew's locket into the bottom of the trunk. Some day perhaps her grandchildren would find it.

She took off the straw bonnet and noticed its shabbiness. Aggie was right. It was coming apart at the back. Scrambling back down the ladder, she tossed it on the table, then saw Aunt Prudy's new pink slat bonnet Aggie had just finished. Snatching it from the nail, she jammed it over her dark hair. It's the first time I've worn a slat bonnet, she mused dryly. I vowed I never would.

Aunt Prudy and the girls were nowhere in

sight. They were probably choring or plucking geese.

Slamming out the door, Barbara headed for the little cabin in the glen. The summer evening was sweet and fresh with green shoots stirring in the cottonwoods.

She marched boldly toward the covered wagon where Charlie was tucking the last bit of canvas around the bows. He looked up when she approached.

"Charlie!"

"What's up, Barbara? I know you're fond of Willie, but if you've come to talk me out of leaving . . ."

She stood awkwardly, words forming silently in her mind. He went on.

"I meant to thank you for saving Willie," he continued. "That was a brave thing you did. Seems you've sort of made a habit of saving Willie's life. I . . . I'll never forget it."

"That's all right. I'm just sorry we couldn't save your sheep." The words she wanted to say seemed stuck in her throat.

"But as I said, if you're going to talk me out of going, Barbara —"

"No, Charlie. I . . . I won't do that. I'm asking if I can go with you . . . as your wife."

"Wife?" His deep blue eyes glinted like chips of ice, and he took a long, deep breath, as though he couldn't believe his ears.

"Do you realize what you're saying, Barbara? That you'd be a frontier woman working hard to keep a dugout tidy, battling prairie fires and blizzards, and the infernally hot Kansas winds?"

"Yes, I know."

"It won't be easy."

"I know that, too."

"I can't ask you to do that. Not for Willie. We'll drive along the Santa Fe Trail, then angle off toward the west. It's a long, lonely road. The hot prairie wind will scorch your pretty skin, and there are still Indians on the prowl.

"It can never mean a plantation or a houseful of servants. Barbara," he paused, then went on softly, "all I can promise is my love, a wide open prairie, and faith in the living God who goes with us."

Barbara set her face ahead, and thought of riding in the crude covered wagon, the hot sun blistering her cheeks and roughing her white arms. She must always remember to wear the despicable slat bonnet. Aggie wouldn't have time to stitch up mounds of quilts and comforts for her.

Yes, there would be Indians. But since meeting White Turkey, she had lost some of her fear of them. She knew this was God's way for her — to carve out a new life on the frontier together with the man she knew she loved.

The verse from Genesis nagged at her just like it had with Uncle Daniel: "Leave your country, your people, and your father's household and go to the land I will show you." This was it. God had spoken. All this flashed through her mind in those few moments.

Charlie was watching her, waiting for her answer. She nodded. "Yes, I know all that, Charlie. I've come to trust Jesus Christ as my Lord and Savior. His love is so real! And as long as we're together, you and Willie and I, with the Lord . . ."

Her eyes locked with his for a moment as she noticed how carefully he was listening to every word she said. A smile lit up her whole face as she continued, "By the way, Elder Buck will be in town Sunday to help organize the new church. We could invite the whole settlement to the wedding. I don't have a dowry . . . There isn't time . . ."

"And I don't have a single sheep to offer, much less 12 ponies!" Charlie's blue eyes twinkled.

Reaching the ground in one long jump from the wagon, he came toward her. He touched her lips with his fingers, pushed back the slat bonnet and caressed her cheek

338

softly. Then he bent down and she felt his lips move on hers, gentle and sweet. Looking into his summer-blue eyes, she saw tears brimming the edges, and a lump rose in her throat.

"I love you, Barbara," he whispered hoarsely. "I've loved you ever since I first saw you at the Fourth of July picnic."

"And I love you, Charlie. I know that now."

"Thank God! Then you're not doing this just because of Willie?"

"Oh, no, Charlie. It's . . . you. I think it's always been you. Only I fought it. I didn't want it to be so! But it is."

He kissed her again. Barbara thought she heard Willie's chuckle behind them.

The sun was now below the horizon, and the red glow at the rim of the world faded into pink, then purple. The unearthly stillness of prairie twilight stole over them, soft and enchanting. But Barbara and Charlie didn't notice. The cowslip moon came out, then hid its face behind a cloud rack . . . but for them the world stood still.

(I have plotted a sequel of when Barbara, Charlie and Willie move to Western Kansas . . . and Barbara faces more loneliness . . . but by God's grace and His strength she continues, in spite of nosy neighbors, Charlie's grave illness, her chance to return to Georgia and inherit land — if she moves there. But —)

ELV

The employees of Thorndike Press hope you have enjoyed this Large Print book. All our Thorndike and Wheeler Large Print titles are designed for easy reading, and all our books are made to last. Other Thorndike Press Large Print books are available at your library, through selected bookstores, or directly from us.

For information about titles, please call:

(800) 223-1244

or visit our Web site at:

www.gale.com/thorndike
www.gale.com/wheeler

To share your comments, please write:

Publisher
Thorndike Press
295 Kennedy Memorial Drive
Waterville, ME 04901